A Perfect Day

ALSO BY RICHARD PAUL EVANS

The Christmas Box
Timepiece
The Letter
The Locket
The Looking Glass
The Carousel
The Christmas Box Miracle
The Last Promise

For Children

The Christmas Candle
The Dance
The Spyglass
The Tower
The Light of Christmas

A PERFECT DAY

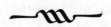

RICHARD PAUL
EVANS

DOUBLEDAY LARGE PRINT HOME LIBRARY EDITION

DUTTON

This Large Print Edition, prepared especially for Doubleday Large Print Home Library, contains the complete, unabridged text of the original Publisher's Edition.

DUTTON
Published by Penguin Group (USA) Inc.
375 Hudson Street, New York, New York 10014, U.S.A.
Penguin Books Ltd, Registered Offices: 80 Strand, London WC2R 0RL, England
Penguin Books Australia Ltd, 250 Camberwell Road, Camberwell, Victoria 3124, Australia
Penguin Books Canada Ltd, 10 Alcorn Avenue, Toronto, Ontario, Canada M4V 3B2
Penguin Books (N.Z.) Ltd, Cnr Rosedale and Airborne Roads, Albany, Auckland 1310, New Zealand

Published by Dutton, a member of Penguin Group (USA) Inc.

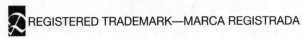

To Keri

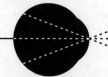

This Large Print Book carries the
Seal of Approval of N.A.V.H.

Acknowledgments

I would like to thank Laurie, Laurie, and Carole, who have walked with me through this book. Thank you for your faith and patience. I love you all. Also my buddy Lisa Johnson. I enjoy working with you and your staff, Lisa. Thanks to the RPE and *Christmas Box* staff. Sorry I left your name out last time, Beck. And Bob Gay. Thank you for your insight as well as generosity. In the final page of this book you will see your influence.

My love to Keri, who lived more of this book than she should have. (She wanted me to tell you that it's not all true.)

A special grazie to all my readers who stood with me through *The Last Promise.* Your support means more to me than you'll ever know.

Most of all I am grateful to God for the inspiration He sends me. This book would not be possible without His mercy and tutelage.

A PERFECT DAY

"All life belongs to you, [young novelist] and do not listen either to those who would shut you up into corners of it and tell you that it is only here and there that art inhabits, or to those who would persuade you that this heavenly messenger wings her way outside of life altogether, breathing a superfine air, and turning her head from the truth of things. There is no impression of life, no manner of seeing it and feeling it, to which the plan of the novelist may not offer a place."

—Henry James
The Art of Fiction

Prologue

It's Christmas night.

Outside my hotel window the world is snow. All is still and white or on the way to becoming so. Only the street lamps show signs of life, changing colors above barren streets that look more like tundra than asphalt. Even the rumbling, yellow snowplows that wake me from my thoughts cannot keep up with the storm.

This snowstorm seems as relentless as any I've seen in Salt Lake City. Salt Lakers are particularly proud of their blizzards, and every native has a story of winter—stories that usually begin, *You call this a storm?* and grow in the telling like battle tales shared by graying war veterans. It's a peculiar character flaw to those of us from cold climates that we feel superior to those who have the sense to live elsewhere.

I remember a Christmas night, when I was a boy, when there was a great blizzard. My father was always through with Christmas weeks before it arrived, and by Christmas night he had already undressed our tree and dragged it out to the curb for the municipal pickup. A storm came that same night, chased by the plows, and the next morning the tree was buried beneath a five-foot snowbank. We forgot about the tree until April, when a thaw revealed an evergreen branch poking free from the melting snow. It was the same Christmas that my mother left us.

Tonight, from my seventh-story window I see a man in a parka and a bellman's cap shoveling the walk in front of the hotel's entrance. The snow returns nearly as fast as he clears it. Salt Lake's own Sisyphus.

It's a night to be home. A night to be gathered with loved ones around brick hearths and hot drinks warming the day's memory. It is a night to bathe in the pleasant aftermath of the season's joy. So why am I alone in a hotel when my wife, Allyson, and my daughter, Carson, are just minutes away?

I see a car below. It moves slowly up Main Street, its headlights cutting through the darkness. The car slides helplessly from side to side, its wipers blurring, its wheels spinning, correcting, grasping, connecting then slipping again. I imagine the driver of that car; blinded, afraid to stop, just as fearful to proceed. I empathize. Behind the wheel of my life I feel like that driver.

I couldn't tell you my first wrong step. I'm not sure that I could tell you what I'd do differently. My mind is a queue of questions. Most of them are about the stranger. Why did the stranger come to me? Why did he speak of hope when my future, *or what's left of it,* looks as barren as the winter landscape? Some might think that my story began with the stranger. But in truth it began long before I met him, back on a balmy June day eight years ago when Allyson, not yet my wife, went home to Oregon to see her father. This is strangely ironic to me, because it all began on a perfect day. And here it ends on the worst of days.

I should say *begins to end*. Because if the stranger is right—and I've learned that he's always right—I have just six more days to live. Six days that I will live out alone, not because I want to, but because it's the right thing to do. Perhaps my loneliness is my penance. I hope God will see it that way, because there is not enough time to heal two hearts. There is not enough time to make right one broken promise. There is only time to remember what once was and should still be.

My thoughts wander, first to the stranger then further back—back eight years to when Allyson went home to her father. Back to the beginning of my story. Back to a perfect day.

Chapter 1

EIGHT YEARS EARLIER. JUNE 10, 1992.
MEDFORD, OREGON.

Allyson Phelps closed her eyes as she rocked in the saddle to the swing of her Morgan's gait. She rode with her father, Carson, who had grown quiet in the last hour, and the only sound they contributed to the mountain was the steady clop of hooves, the sharp metallic click of horseshoe against rock and the creaking of leather.

The trail they climbed was beaten and as familiar to the horses as to the riders. Without coaxing, they plodded along, scaling the top of a ridge that broke along a line of aspen and cedar. It was the hour before twilight, and the setting sun tinged the edges of the ragged peaks in pink and sage. The "pinking hour" Allyson always called it. Allyson shouted back to her father. "It's been too long since we've gone riding together. When was the last time?"

"Been two summers," her father said without hesitation. "Let's stop up ahead and let the horses rest."

She rode thirty more yards, to a small clearing, then pulled back the reins. "Whoa, Dolly." She leaned forward and rubbed Dolly's neck above the shoulder. The bay was damp with sweat from their ride.

Her father tapped his horse's flanks with his stirrups and moved up alongside Allyson.

"Is this okay?" she asked.

He glanced around. "It's perfect."

They had stopped on a ridge overlooking the lush, velvet lap of the Rogue Valley. *God's backyard,* her father called this country, and as a child and full of faith she had fully expected to run into God someday out wandering His back forty.

To some of Allyson's friends at college this expanse of wilderness would have been a frightening place, but to her it was safe and nurturing—a place she could run to when the world outside became too complex. It was a place that had opened its arms to her when her mother, who had no business dying, died out of turn. In such country it was possible to believe that no one ever really died, they just came here.

They dismounted and Carson took the horses' reins and led them over to a blue spruce, where he tethered the straps to one of its limbs. He took from his saddlebag a small knapsack then found a flat-topped granite boulder half-buried in the mountainside and brushed the dirt from it with his hands. "Come sit with me, girlie."

Allyson smiled. She was twenty-four-years old and would forever be "girlie." She walked over and sat down next to him. She pulled her knees up against her chest, wrapping her arms around her legs.

From where they sat the only sign of man's trespass was four hundred yards below them, only visible through the thick foliage to someone who knew what they were looking for—the weathered obelisks and crosses of an overgrown pioneer cemetery, choked and dying itself.

Allyson, like her father, had been raised in

this country and while she had left it behind for school, he belonged to it still and always would. He owned more than a thousand acres of the raw land, but she knew that the opposite was true—that the land owned him.

"It's good to be home again," she said. "Sometimes I forget how gorgeous it is up here."

"Almost as pretty as you," he said then added, "Pretty lonely too, sometimes."

His loneliness always made her feel guilty. "I wish you'd find someone."

"Too late for that," he said. She felt traitorous to suggest such a thing to a man who still loved the only woman he had ever loved—almost twenty years after she had been buried.

"I don't need nobody. I have you."

She leaned into him. "Thanks for bringing me home for the weekend. It's been a good day. It's been a perfect day."

He nodded in agreement, though his eyes, sometimes as deep and dark as a well of ink, held sadness. The steady rush of the Rogue River rose from the valley below them.

"About Robert . . ."

She looked up. "Yes?"

"Is he good to you?"

"He's really good to me. Didn't you think he was sweet to me when he was here last Christmas?"

"He seemed nice enough. But with your old man an arm's length away, he'd be a fool not to be."

"He treats me just as good—whether you're there to scare him or not." She could tell that he wasn't satisfied. "Really, Dad."

"You're sure you want to marry him?"

"I do." She turned to look at him. "You've always said I could marry anyone I chose as long as he loves me as much as you do."

"Does he?"

"It's a pretty high benchmark. But I think he comes close." With one hand Allyson brushed her hair back from her face. "Do you think I'm making a mistake?"

"Would it change your mind if I thought you were?"

"It would bother me." She looked at him anxiously. "Does that mean you do?"

His expression lightened. "No, honey. Robert seems to be a good kid. You know me. No one's ever going to be good enough for my Al."

"I know." Allyson suddenly smiled. "Did I ever tell you why Nancy didn't get married?"

"Who's Nancy?"

"You know, my roommate. You met her at Christmas. She came with Robert."

"Oh, yeah. No, you didn't tell me."

"Every summer Nancy's family rents a beach house in Baja. This last summer she took her fiancé, Spencer, along. They were out swimming in the ocean when she spotted a shark's dorsal fin. She screamed and they both started swimming for shore, but when she got to where she could touch the sand, a wave hit her and knocked her over. She yelled for Spencer to help her and he stopped and looked at her but then he got scared and ran back to the beach house without her."

"He left her in the water?"

"Yep, he did. She was so mad when she got back to the house she didn't speak to him for the rest of the week. He tried to apologize, but really, what could he say? It was kind of a defining moment. Her dad told her that if she didn't have the brains to give him the boot, she deserved what she got."

Carson shook his head. "Maybe we need to plan a beach trip with Robert."

Allyson laughed. "Robert wouldn't run."

"You're sure of that?"

"You've seen me mad. I can be scarier than any shark."

"Can't deny that, girlie."

A whistling twilight breeze fluttered the trees around them. One of the horses whinnied and Carson glanced back at them. Then he said, "When I asked Robert about his family, he didn't say much. Just that he was the youngest of four boys."

"I know. I thought it was odd that we had dated for almost six months and he had never mentioned his parents. But now I understand why. His mother left them when Rob was in middle school. Rob doesn't like to talk about her. His father raised him but he's not close to him either."

"Not much of a family life."

"No, it's not." Allyson leaned her head back onto her father's shoulder. Her voice softened. "But I'm sure about *him*. At least as sure as I can be. I mean, it's a throw of the dice anyway, right? No one marries expecting it to fail. And even when it's good, who knows how long it's going to last? Like

Robert's mother. Or Mom . . ." She stopped. She never spoke of her mother without wondering how it would affect her father.

"No, you don't know," Carson said, though more to himself. "Maybe it is just a roll of the dice." He looked suddenly uncomfortable. "Those were hard days. For all of us."

"I remember the night you came into my room with Aunt Denise and Pastor Claire. It was the worst moment of my life."

"One of mine too," Carson said softly. He seemed especially troubled by the recollection, the memory rubbing across his heart like sandpaper. For a moment they were both silent. Then he cleared his throat. "So the date is still the eleventh of December?"

"Yes. We're threading the needle. Two days after graduation, two weeks before Christmas."

"Then what are your plans?"

"Rob starts his new job in Salt Lake on the fifth. We fly out on the second."

He shook his head. "Wrong state, sweetheart. "

"I know."

"Tell Bob there's a radio station in Medford."

"Dad, he hates to be called 'Bob.' And Medford isn't exactly a hotbed of opportunity. This is a great opportunity for him. KBOX is the number one station in the Salt Lake market."

"That's what he wants to do? Sell radio commercials?"

"No. What he really wants to do is write books. Romance novels."

He frowned. "You mean the kind they sell at Kmart, with the long-haired men with their shirts all open . . ."

Allyson laughed. "No."

"What does selling radio have to do with being a writer?"

"Not much. It's just something to pay the bills until he's able to get published. A friend of his older brother is the sales manager there. And they're going to let him write radio commercials for some of their advertisers." While Carson digested the information, she added, "We're getting a house."

He turned to look at her. "A house? So soon?"

"Rob's dad is helping us. It's one of his rental properties. He's selling it to us without interest, so it's the same price as renting an apartment. It's a Tudor in a beautiful little community south of Salt Lake with horse property. It has a fence around it. It reminds me a little of Ashland. And we'll have a guest room for you to stay with us. You can fly out whenever you want."

"I don't fly."

"Well, it's a long drive, so you better start." She hit his knee playfully. "You amaze me, you know that? You used to ride bulls and yet you're afraid to get on an airplane."

"Bulls don't crash into mountains."

"No, they crash into you."

"Wrong state," he repeated.

They were quiet again. Then Allyson said, "I'm going to miss you, Dad."

He looked forward. "Me too." After a moment he said, "You know things weren't always that great between me and your mom. Sometimes we'd get into it like cats and dogs. When we lived in that little apartment in Medford the neighbors would call the manager to complain about the ruckus."

"Why are you telling me this?"

"I don't want you to take unrealistic expectations into your marriage. Just because the boat rocks, doesn't mean it's time to jump overboard. The relationship will change. All relationships change through time. But that's not always a bad thing. In fact some of the best things to happen to our marriage were the changes. It's part of the growing process." He looked forward again and he sighed.

"You look tired, Dad. Are you feeling all right?"

"I haven't been sleeping well lately. Maybe it's time to head on back. What time is our dinner?"

"I made our reservation for nine. That's not too late, is it?"

"You mean for an old guy like me?"

"That's not what I meant."

He reached over the side of the rock and lifted the knapsack he had brought from the horse. "Before we go I want to show you something."

He took from the pack a thick leather-bound binder overflowing with pages. Its cover was burnished with a flourish and its leather was aged with time and wear. Allyson looked at the book curiously. Though she did not remember seeing it, something about it seemed familiar to her.

"What have you got there?"

"Something I've been working on for

about twenty years." He pulled back the cover. Inside the binder were pages of different sizes and gauges, uneven and dog-eared. The first page was parchment marked with her father's wild scrawl.

"It's your life book. It has your genealogy, letters from Mom and me, your birth announcement, your high school graduation program, thoughts about things—and my thoughts about you. It's time for you to take it."

Allyson took the book in her lap. She gently turned through its leaves, as if it were a sacred relic. Each page contained a piece of the puzzle of who she had become. Without looking up she said, "Dad, this is wonderful. I didn't know you were doing this . . ." She suddenly paused at an aged page with a small note written on lined paper and a photograph taped to its bottom. "Oh, my . . ."

"That's the first love note I ever wrote to your mother."

Allyson read it softly aloud.

To my heart, Alise,
  Wherever you are, wherever you go, I love you and always will.
                                        —Carson

"You have a poetic heart." She ran her finger across the black-and-white photograph of a young woman that was taped to the bottom of the letter. "Is this Mom?"

"She was about your age when that was taken."

"We look alike, don't we? Doris Day hairdo aside."

"You always wondered where you got your good looks."

"I've never wondered." She began turning pages again until she stopped at a leaf with her mother's funeral program. Next to it there was a picture of herself as a small girl dressed for her mother's wake. Her father looked young in the picture, she thought. It made him seem only that much more remarkable to her.

"How did you go on after losing the love of your life?"

"I had you. Failure wasn't an option."

"You've always been there for me. I don't know how I'd live without you."

He smiled, but his eyes revealed deep sadness. Then he said, "Well, girlie, we need to talk about that."

Allyson's heart skipped at his words, and

she moved back from him to look into his face.

"What?"

He didn't answer for what seemed a long time to her. "I don't think I'm going to be able to make your wedding."

She looked at him as if anticipating the punch line of a joke. "What are you saying?"

His lips tightened and his brow furrowed in deep creases. "I guess there's no good way to put this." He scratched his head the way he did when he was troubled. "I have cancer, Al. Pretty bad cancer."

Allyson's mouth opened, but no sound escaped.

"It's pancreatic cancer. The doctors say that there's nothing they can do. I'd even try some of that chemo hocus-pocus if it could get me to your wedding, but the doctors don't think I have that long."

"How long?" she asked. Panic rose in her voice.

"With treatment they say I only have three to four months."

"Three months . . ." Numbness spread throughout her entire body, making it difficult to continue. ". . . And without?"

"They give me two."

She began to cry. "No." Then she erupted angrily. "You don't even look sick. We've just spent the whole afternoon riding . . ."

Carson put his arm around her. "It hasn't gotten me yet, girlie. But it will. They tell me pancreatic cancer is that way. It sneaks up on you. The truth is I didn't feel a thing. I only found out about it because my eyes were turning yellow. They say it's the most fatal of all the cancers." He looked back at her. "Truth is I kind of expected it to be coming along."

Allyson stopped crying briefly and looked at him, confused by what he had just said. "Why would you expect something like this?"

"On account of something that happened a while back. About six weeks after Mom died I was diagnosed with cancer. Had a big tumor growing inside my neck." He pointed to a small scar. "That's where they tested it. I was already in a world of hurt with her loss and wondering how I was going to raise you alone when whammo, the rest of the wave hits. I about lost my faith over it. I couldn't believe that God would do this." Carson looked out over the land around them then continued in a softer voice. "When I was done being angry with God, I made Him a promise. I told Him that if He would let me live to see you grown and married off that I would do everything I could to fill the gap left by your mother—and that I would never touch alcohol again."

Allyson was stunned. "You used to drink?"

Carson chuckled. "Oh yes, girlie, I used to drink," he said, the tone of his voice implying the understatement. ". . . Like a sailor on a weekend pass. That's one of the reasons your mother and I fought so much. A week after my promise, I went back to the doctors. There was no sign of cancer. I remember my doctor looking at one X-ray and then the other as if it were a prank. Some of the doctors tried to explain it away as a misdiagnosis. Doctors don't like to be wrong— think they could wrap up the universe in a handkerchief. But I knew better. God had accepted my deal. I started AA that night. Haven't touched a drop in almost twenty years. Believe me it wasn't easy. There were nights I went outside and howled at the moon. But then I'd look at you and I'd remember why." He rubbed her knee. "I don't think it's a coincidence that the symptoms came just a few days after you told me you were engaged. The way I see it, the Lord fulfilled His part of the bargain."

"How can you be so calm about this?"

"Truth is I'm scared. 'Course I'm scared. Any man who says he's not afraid of dying is a liar or an idiot. Or both."

Allyson lowered her head and began to sob. Carson ran his hand over the back of her head, through her hair, bringing her head against his chest. "Honey, we can see this two ways. We can be upset that I'm being taken out of the game or we can be grateful that I got to play the extra innings." He took her face in his hands and lifted it until she was looking into his eyes. "You have no idea how much I've loved watching you grow up. Or how proud I am of the woman you've become. Frankly, I'm grateful for the extra innings." He turned away so she wouldn't see the tears welling in his eyes.

Tears streamed down her cheeks. "That's why you wanted me to come home this weekend?"

He nodded slowly, his gaze lost in the valley before them. "It's the last chapter of our story, girlie. I wanted one last perfect day."

Chapter 2

Allyson didn't return to finish the summer semester. She spent the next two months at her father's side, at first busying herself with cooking and caring for the house and yard, then, as the cancer became more debilitating, caring just for him. Within three weeks he was having trouble walking and became bedridden. Allyson rarely left him. She even slept on a cot in the same bedroom. I called her every day during this time. I could feel her father's deterioration through her voice, as if life was draining from her as well, and I suppose it was.

I pled with her to let me come and be with her, but she wouldn't allow it. She couldn't explain why she didn't want me there, but she didn't have to. I think I understood. She couldn't mix the two men in her life any more than she could simultaneously entertain thoughts of the wedding and funeral. It would be too much for anyone. She finally asked me to stop asking and promised that she would let me know when it was the right time for me to fly out.

Carson knew that his death would be difficult for Allyson, too difficult perhaps, so he did what he could to protect her. He made all the funeral arrangements himself, choosing a casket, writing his funeral program and his own obituary (which turned out to be as understated as he was) and paying for services in advance. As much as he hated lawyers, for Allyson's sake he hired an attorney who brought to the house the papers to complete Carson's will, and they crossed the t's and dotted the i's, with Allyson physically in attendance and emotionally a universe away.

As the cancer progressed, her father was given new drugs, one of which caused hallucinations. Every few nights Allyson would wake to find him sitting up in bed talking to people who weren't there; usually to her mother.

I can't imagine how difficult it must have been for her, and I have never felt so helpless in my entire life.

On September 9, almost three months to the day since she had learned of her father's cancer, Allyson called. It was time, she said. Her father was dying.

I had met Allyson at the University of Utah in an English literature class. I was working on my masters and was employed as an aide in the class. The first time I saw her I knew that I was in the right place.

Allyson came to Utah on an academic scholarship. I had come to the U because of the help with tuition I received since my father was a professor at the school—which was almost reason enough for me to go elsewhere. I don't know how best to describe my father. The simplest noun seems adequate. Flint. Old and hard and sharp. I don't ever remember calling him Father or Pa or Dad like my friends called their fathers. It's always been sir or, as I grew older, Chuck.

Charles (Chuck) Harlan had run away from home at the age of seventeen and joined the military during the last years of

World War II. He had seen combat in the Navy. But I didn't hear it from him. He saw the kind of action a man doesn't talk about lest he unearth something he'd spent years burying. I blame those years for who he was. I have to blame something.

He married late in life to Irene Mason, a woman fifteen years younger than him. She was also from a military family. She was a staunchly religious woman who bore four sons in five years. She died at the age of thirty-four in childbirth with her last son. Me.

Chuck remarried four years later to a woman he met in the administration building at the university. Colleen Dunn. I've always considered Colleen my mother. Colleen was also younger than Chuck, ten years or so, but the gap in age was the subtlest of their differences. When I was old enough to understand the contrast in their personalities I was astonished that the two of them had ever come together. Truly, love is blind. Or maybe just stupid. They couldn't have been more mismatched.

In the words of her friends, Colleen was a party waiting to happen. She was a large woman with an extra chin or two and a lap that could hold four boys and often did.

What I remember most about her is that she liked to laugh. She sometimes drank too much, nothing hard, dessert wine or sherry and she never drank alone. Unlike Chuck's first wife, she went to church only for us children. I knew her feelings about church but still considered her closer to God than Chuck. Though Chuck never missed a church service, he lacked the graces of faith my mother held in abundance: love, gentleness and mercy. It was as if religion was simply an extension of the military world he had left: a world of rules. Chuck was big on rules. He ruled the home with an iron Bible.

Every now and then it would come down on one of us. One afternoon he caught Stan, my oldest brother, looking at pictures in the women's undergarment section of a department store catalogue. Even though Stan was only eleven at the time, Chuck whipped him with his belt so severely that Stan couldn't walk. He crawled to his bedroom, where he remained until the next morning.

In the end, Colleen stayed with us for nine years: probably eight and a half years longer than she would have had there not been us boys. She stayed as long as she could to protect us from Chuck.

The day she told me she was leaving I suppose that I wasn't all that surprised. Even at the age of thirteen I realized that if there ever had ever been a connection between Chuck and Colleen, it had long been severed. Her laughter was gone. I suppose she went to find it. Right or wrong it didn't lessen the pain any. I told her that I hated her. I might have even told her that I was glad she was leaving. I've always regretted those words and hoped she knew them for the bald-faced lie they were. In my heart I wished that she would take me with her. But she didn't. And Chuck never left.

Looking back I realize that I spent much of my life seeking Chuck's approval. But I learned not to expect it. It would be like waiting for a train after its route had been cancelled. I was both amazed by and envious of Allyson's relationship with her father. What a difference a father can make. Allyson was confident and independent. I was insecure and fearful. To this day I don't know what drew her to me.

*   *   *

I flew in to Portland, where I waited nearly three hours for a commuter flight into the small Medford airport. My thoughts were bent on Allyson and what I was walking into. I had called from the Portland airport and spoken briefly to her, but she wasn't herself. It was like talking to a stranger, and from her voice I knew that Carson's death was very close.

The taxi left me in the dirt-and-rock driveway that led to the Phelps residence. The hills of Ashland were a quilt of color, unlike my first trip to her home, last Christmas, when all was snow. Though the land was even more spectacular than Allyson had described it, her home was nothing like what I'd expected. It looked as if a trailer had taken root in the fertile Rogue Valley soil and grown rooms and steps and a porch with a mosquito screen.

Carson was a handyman and he liked to fiddle with things, his residence being his most frequent victim. Allyson told me that the house had changed form every year for as long as she could remember. She grew up thinking that people just lived that way. She'd come home from school to find her father, hammer in hand, knocking out a wall or building an addition. He had been that way up until the last few months, when his sickness had sapped his strength as well as his ambition. But still he talked about the guest room he was going to build when he felt good enough to get out of bed. They both knew it would never happen, but it was a pleasant fiction all the same.

The taxi's meter read nine seventy-five. Through the open car window I handed the driver a folded ten-dollar bill. "Keep the change."

"Gee, thanks," the driver said sarcastically, stashing the bill in his front pocket.

The taxi's back tires spun as the driver reversed out of the drive. I slung my duffel over my shoulder, climbed the wooden stairs of the front porch and knocked on the door.

An elderly woman opened the door and welcomed me in. She was short and broad-hipped, with silver hair. She wore a pink hand-knit sweater. Her smile and her eyes were pleasant but appropriate for the circumstances. I could see the family resemblance.

"You must be Robert."

"Yes, ma'am."

She reached out and touched my arm affectionately. "I'm Allyson's Aunt Denise."

Allyson had spoken of her many times. Allyson was very close to her. She had become Allyson's surrogate mother after her own mother had passed away. I had not met her last December only because she had gone on an east coast trip with a few of her friends.

"I've heard much about you," I said. "Allyson thinks the world of you."

She smiled. "Allyson is my sweetheart. Please come in."

I stepped into the house, onto the umber shag carpet. I looked around for Allyson. There were a dozen or so people congregated inside, strangers, standing or sitting, speaking in somber tones like people in a hospital waiting room. In the center of the room was a coffee table with a plate of sugar cookies and a pot of coffee. The only person I recognized was Nancy, Allyson's roommate. I turned back to Aunt Denise.

"Is he still . . . ?"

In the land of the dying sentences go unfinished.

She nodded. "He's still with us."

"Do you know where Allyson is?"

"She's with her father. Down the hallway."

At that time Nancy crossed the room. I set down my bag, and without a word she put her arms around me in the way people do when words are not enough. Nancy had been here last Christmas when I flew out to meet Allyson's father. Nothing was the same now.

"How is he?" I asked.

"He's still hanging in there. The nurse told us that he was going to die yesterday. But he's a tough old bird. He's holding on."

"Is Ally alone with him?"

She nodded. "She's been in there for nearly six hours. I checked on her about an hour ago."

"How is she?"

She frowned. "Not well. She asked if I had heard from you."

"Which room is it?"

She pointed. "The room at the end."

I anxiously walked down the shadowy hallway, my footsteps falling softly in the corridor. I opened the door just enough to look in. The room was dark, illuminated only by the light stealing in from the partially opened blinds above the bed. When my eyes had adjusted, I saw Allyson curled up on the bed next to her father. It wasn't hard to imagine that this had happened a million times before, on dark nights when a thunderstorm shook the mountain; a little girl crawling into the safety and warmth of her papa's bed.

She looked up at me. Her eyes were dark but not dull, as there was a peculiar energy in them. I tried to read in her face an invitation or dismissal but saw neither, for she looked at me not as if I were a stranger to the home, but as if she were.

I stepped inside, gently closing the door behind me. Allyson stood up and walked over to me. I put my arms around her and held her in the shadows, her soft face nuzzling against my neck. It seemed, for a while, that only the two of us were in the room; then Carson suddenly groaned and Allyson immediately returned to her father's side. I sat down on a chair at the side of the bed to wait.

The last time I had seen her father he was a mountain of a man, rugged and large as the land he lived on. He was a man who could be thrown by a bull, stepped on and walk away with nothing but a few cuss words. This man in the bed was more desert than mountain. The cancer had left him frail and helpless. I wondered if he even knew that I was there.

For the next hour Allyson and I sat quietly by the bed. Carson was quiet, though he mumbled from time to time and once he looked toward the ceiling and said what sounded like "Not yet," and I followed his gaze, almost expecting to see some personage of another world suspended in the air. But still he showed no sign of dying. It was apparent to me that he was holding on. I knew why. And I realized that I was to play a role in Carson Phelps's passing.

An hour and forty minutes later, when Allyson left to use the bathroom, I took my chance to speak to him. Though I spoke softly, my voice seemed loud and misplaced in the silent room, like a stone thrown into a well.

"Sir, I'm Robert. Allyson's fiancé." He showed no reaction and I had second thoughts about continuing. But I went on. "I know that Allyson loves you very much. She's told me so. I know how you love her. She's told me how you've always been there for her."

My eyes began to water. "I know that's

what you're doing now. You're holding on for her. But with all due respect, you don't have to anymore. You don't know me that well, but I love your daughter too. I love her with all my heart. I think she's the most amazing woman I've ever known. And I promise that whatever life brings, I'll do my best to take care of her. I'll never leave her. You have my word."

When I finished there was only silence. I leaned back in my chair and the room fell again into shadow. For the next few moments Carson was as still as the room. Then his eyes opened and flitted toward me and he said something unintelligible, as much a gasp as speech.

I leaned forward. "What?" I said. "I didn't understand . . ."

Again silence. His eyes closed. I sat back in my chair.

Allyson came back into the room. She sat on the bed and again took her father's hand in hers. And then his eyes opened. For a minute he looked at her and she gazed back at him. A single tear rolled down the side of his face. Then he gasped twice and was gone. For a moment all was still. Then Allyson began to shake, as the reality of his death enveloped her. I quickly went to her, as if to stop her from being swept away with her father. I held her body against mine, my hand around her head pulling it into my shoulder. "He's gone," she said. "My daddy's gone."

Chapter 3

EIGHT YEARS LATER. SALT LAKE CITY, UTAH.

I was a card-carrying regular at the deli across the street from the radio station. My lunch order was as consistent as my attendance: club on wheat, oil and vinegar, extra sweet peppers, no mayo, Sun Chips and a lemonade. The workers at the shop didn't even ask anymore. I ate there every day except for when I was taking a client to lunch at one of the restaurants where my station traded airtime for food. I knew that I frequented the place too much when one of the workers invited me to her wedding.

Though I usually ate alone or brought my lunch back to the station, today I sat across the table from Mark Platt. Platt had joined KBOX three years after me and was my closest friend at the station. He was younger than me, not yet thirty, tall with an athletic build. He had the largest hands I had ever seen.

"I thought you had a lunch appointment today," Mark said, sandwich visible in his mouth.

"So did I. Ellis cancelled. He said he had a crisis."

"What kind of crisis?"

"Of character." I lifted a chip, rubbing the salt off of it between my fingers. "He's lying. He really just didn't want to tell me to my face that they've spent their entire fall budget on KISN."

"You know that?"

"I heard it from one of the KISN reps. I'll bet you lunch that I have an email from him when I get back to the station."

"That's gotta hurt."

"Road rash hurts. This is excruciating. I tell you this isn't my week. First I lost Kinko's, now Kyoto. That last Arbitron was a killer. If our ratings fall any more we're going to have to start paying people to listen."

"We already are."

"I just hope these slicky-boy consultants Stu's bringing in have some magic up their sleeves."

Mark frowned. "I don't know why he wasted the money on them—I can tell you what they're going to say. First they're going to tell us to ax the PD and buy canned, market-tested music. Then dump the morning show and bring in some syndicated program like *Imus*. It's the way of the beast. In ten years there will be only one big radio station in America."

"If that's what it takes."

"You mercenary. These consultants are turning the industry to pabulum. Radio used to be interesting. Now it's the McDonald's of media."

"McDonald's is profitable."

"But how many Big Macs can you eat before you swear off hamburgers?"

My mouth rose in a half smile. "Is that a Zen question: like how many angels can fit on the head of a pin?"

"Something like that." He leaned forward. "So level with me, Rob. Did you get it?"

"It?"

"You know."

I raised one eyebrow. "What are you talking about?"

"C'mon. Doug's job. Word around the station is that Stuart's called a meeting with you."

"He did. But who knows what he wants?"

"Everyone assumes you're taking his place. Why do you think I've been so nice to you lately?"

I laughed. "I'm hoping. I've been working my tail off for the last six months—staying late, working promotions on the weekend, everything."

"I've noticed."

"I just hope Stu has." I took a bite of my sandwich. "The weird thing is, I never thought that I would be at the station this long. This has been the longest temporary job in history."

"Welcome to life, pal. I was only going to hang out with Becca for kicks. I'm still trying to figure out how I ended up married."

"I'm sure she's wondering the same thing."

"I'm sure she is. Speaking of the devil, Becca wanted to know if Carson could come over some time and play with Madison."

"Of course. I'll have my people call your people." I finished my sandwich then found a napkin to wipe my mouth. "So ten years ago where did you think you'd be now?"

"Ten years ago? I thought I'd be a millionaire football player with a bad back and a Ferrari."

"You played football?"

"Did I play football?" he repeated as if the question ranked high in the stratosphere of stupidity. "Don't you ever read the sports page? I was an all-American. I started as a receiver for BYU my sophomore year. I can't believe you've known me for so long and didn't know this."

"Sorry, I don't follow college football. Never have. So what happened to derail your career?"

"I tore a tendon the second game my junior year. Against Airforce. I never got my speed back."

"Bummer," I said, though it sounded ridiculous.

"Yeah, all I got from that gig was a good-looking wife and chronic back pain."

"Funny how you combined those two in the same sentence."

He smiled. "Freudian. Now I'd be happy with just the millionaire part."

"You mean you're not a millionaire?"

"I guess I'm the only one not getting rich at *the box*," Mark said. He broke an oatmeal cookie in two and put the larger of the pieces in his mouth. "Where did you think you'd be?"

"I thought I'd be churning out novels in a remote cabin somewhere."

"Like that Jack Nicholson movie where he types the same sentence over and over."

"Yeah. Just like that." I bent my straw like a pretzel.

"So have you actually written something?"

"I'm halfway through my first novel. But it's taken me almost four years. Seems whenever I get started on my book, life caves in."

"What's it about?"

"You wouldn't be interested. It's a love story."

He popped the second half of the cookie in his mouth. "You're right. Give me something with assault rifles and stun grenades. How long until you finish it?"

"If I did nothing else, maybe three

months. At my current rate, another three years. There's never enough time." I glanced down at my watch. "Speaking of which, I've got to go. You headed back to the station?"

"No, I've got some clients to visit. I'll see you tomorrow."

We carried our trays to the trash bin. Mark said, "Hey, after you're promoted to sales manager, don't forget your friends."

"What's your name again?"

Chapter 4

"This is Mick and Angel of The Breakfast Bunch, *where we play the best mix of today's hits and yesterday's favorites. Join us at noon for the KBOX lunch box and see what we're serving up."*

I reached over and turned off the radio alarm, silencing the morning banter. I kissed Allyson on the forehead then went into the bathroom to shower. A half hour later I was knotting my tie in the mirror when Allyson walked up behind me. She wrapped her arms around me and kissed my neck. "Hmm, Calvin Klein. I love that smell. Dressing up for the meeting?"

"Yep. How do I look?"

She released me and stepped back. "Handsome. Like always. Would you like waffles for breakfast? I just opened a new bottle of that apricot jam I put up last fall."

"Maybe just toast. My stomach's queasy."

When I walked into the kitchen, Allyson buttered my toast and brought it to the table with a cup of coffee. "So what time is your meeting?"

"First thing." I poured milk into my coffee and stirred it with a spoon from Carson's bowl. "Where's Carse?"

Allyson looked at the vacated cereal bowl at the table and rolled her eyes. "She was at the table." She shouted, "Carson, come back in here and finish your cereal. No cartoons before school."

Carson walked into the room holding a miniature violin in one hand and its bow in the other. "I was practicing my violin."

"With the television on?"

"Yes."

"You need to eat breakfast."

"I'm not hungry."

"You will be. Now finish your cereal."

"Hey, sister," I said, "come sit by me."

She scurried over and climbed up on the stool next to me, her blond hair falling over her face.

"So how's school?"

She pulled her hair back from her eyes. "Good."

"What are you learning about these days?"

"Nothing."

"Nothing?"

She shook her head again, tossing her bangs into her face.

"You must have the same kindergarten teacher I had," I said. I turned back to Allyson. "So yesterday I talked to Doug about the job. He says that the sales manager makes an additional fifteen percent, plus retirement benefits and profit sharing. And, the best part is—the sales manager goes on all the media incentive trips. Next year's trip is to Italy: Rome, Florence and Venice."

Allyson's face lit. "Oh, don't tease me."

"It could happen. Assuming I'm not completely crazy and Stu actually plans on making me the sales manager."

"Of course he does. You're his best salesman and you've been at the station longer than anyone else. Who else would they choose?"

"They could always hire from outside."

"Why would they do that?"

"Last week Stu brought in some out-of-state consultants to check out the operation and make recommendations. They've been nosing through everything. Who knows what they'll have to say?" I downed the coffee. "I better go. I'll see you tonight." I kissed Carson on the forehead. "See you, sister."

"Bye, Daddy."

I kissed Allyson at the door. "What's your day like?"

"Vacuuming. Lunch with Nancy." She kissed me again. "Good luck. Call after your meeting so I can plan our celebration."

Chapter 5

I arrived early at work. With the exception of Stuart Parks, the general manager, and the morning on-air talent, the rest of the staff had yet to arrive, leaving the main suite quiet except for the banter of the KBOX *Breakfast Bunch* that played over the office sound system.

Occasionally, during a long stretch of music, one of the DJ's would emerge from the studio for coffee, food or a bathroom break. When I arrived, Mick, the top morning DJ, was rooting through the refrigerator in the employee lounge. On the way back to the studio, he passed my cubicle. He was wearing an Aerosmith cap and Ray-Ban sunglasses and belting out a song by the Cars as if he really could sing. When he saw me, he stopped and held up a square Tupperware container. He lifted its lid to expose a grotesque mass of green and white fuzz. "Hey, man, check this out."

I grimaced. "What's that, your breakfast?"

"This is our new morning feature: I call it *What's in the Tupperware?* A. A tuna sandwich cloning experiment gone bad. B. The national penicillin reserve. C. A poor man's Chia Pet or D. Life in a jar.

"Save it for your listeners."

"Haven't you seen our latest numbers? You are my listeners man," Mick said as he walked back to the studio. "You and my mom."

The day I heard Doug was retiring I had begun compiling a notebook of ideas to increase our sales. At five minutes to nine I picked up my notebook then knocked on Stuart's door.

I remembered the first time I came to this door—the day Stuart hired me. I was actually his second choice for the job. He had originally approached my brother Marshall, a friend of his from college, about coming to work for the station. Marshall had already committed himself to his computer training and turned him down, but knowing that I was about to graduate from college and was still wrestling with a career choice, he recommended me. Back then I was the new kid at KBOX. Now, at the age of thirty-two, I was one of the veterans.

The last three years had been particularly difficult ones for the station. Deregulation had come into the radio industry and massive media conglomerates were forcing the independents to compete or sell out. Stations who for decades had posed no serious threat to KBOX were now reformatted and infused with promotional capital. As an independently owned station, we had dropped from first to seventh in the market and were losing money almost as fast as Stuart was losing his hair.

After a half minute I knocked again and Stuart answered gruffly, "It's not locked."

I opened the door. To my surprise, Stuart wasn't alone. Stacey, one of the newer sales reps—a tall, svelte bottle blonde with cropped hair—was standing to the side of his desk. They simultaneously looked up at me. There was something peculiar about the scene. Stuart had that deer-in-the-headlights look about him while Stacey looked at me with a pert, confident smile. There had been a lot of office gossip about the two of them, and though, out of loyalty to Stuart, I kept myself from it, their appearance this morning did nothing to dissuade me from believing it.

"Good morning, Rob."

"Morning, Stacey."

She gently touched Stuart's shoulder. "We'll talk more later, Stu."

She walked from the office and I stepped aside to let her pass. A trace of perfume followed her.

When she was gone, Stuart said, "Shut the door, Rob."

I closed the door behind me.

"How's it going, Stu?"

Stu's manner was uncharacteristically brusque. "I've had better weeks. Have a seat."

I settled into one of the vinyl chairs in front of his desk.

Stuart looked at me with a pained expression. "I've been meaning to talk with you for some time now. You know Doug's leaving."

"Of course."

"Frankly, between us girls, I don't know if that's good or bad."

"What do you mean?"

"Well, look at things. Our profits have done nothing but fall over the last three years."

"I know," I said, lifting my notebook. "I have some ideas about that."

Stuart acted as if he hadn't heard me. "We've got to plug up the leaks before this ship sinks. As you know, I brought in some consultants to see what we're doing wrong and what we need to do differently." His brow fell. "Among other things, the consultants think that we're carrying dead weight on the sales force."

I nodded. "They're right about that. I have that in my notes."

Stuart leaned back in his chair. "They meant you, Rob."

It took a moment for me to comprehend his meaning. "What?"

"These guys have all the numbers. According to industry standards, you're not selling nearly at the level someone with your tenure should be. You've been here almost seven years and your sales are barely higher than what they were when you first started."

"Things aren't where they were seven years ago. The economy is in the toilet. Every client of mine has cut their advertising budget. And then there are our ratings. We have half the market share we had back then. Not even that." Desperation rose in my chest. "I've more than doubled my accounts since I came here, what more could I do?"

Stuart's gaze was direct. "A lot. Stacey has doubled her billings in the five months she's been with us."

"Stacey," I said angrily. "Well, there's a good reason for that. She inherited the strongest sales list here. Not to mention that every time a rep leaves, you give her the first pick of their sales list. She doesn't have to look for new clients, you drop them in her lap."

"That's not true."

"Name one account that she's brought in on her own."

Stuart couldn't answer me. He blinked slowly. "This isn't about her, Rob. What about Kinko's? We had their account for fifteen years and you lost it—lock, stock and barrel."

I slid forward to the edge of the chair. "I did everything I could to save that account. Kinko's was bought out by the national corporation and they moved all their advertising to their regional buyer and you can't schmooze this gal. She only buys numbers."

"What about Kyoto? What gives with that?"

"The last Arbitron is what gives." I ran my hand back through my hair. I had expected a pat on the back not a kick in the behind. "You think I'm slacking?"

"No, Rob. I know you put in the hours."

I slumped back in my chair. "You're not giving me the position, are you?"

Stuart looked at me bewilderedly. "What position?"

"Doug's job."

Deeper furrows. "No. It's already been given to somebody else."

I suddenly understood that I had never even been a consideration. "To who?"

"Stacey," he said.

"Stacey?"

"You have a problem with that?"

"She's the last one I would have suspected."

"She's right for the job. She's young, en-
ergetic, motivated . . ."

". . . and easy on the eyes."

Stuart frowned at my accusation. I didn't
care.

"So what you're saying is that I'm stuck
where I'm at."

"Not exactly. The consultants say that
having non-progressing salespeople has a
detrimental effect on overall station growth.
They say that in order to revitalize our sales
team, we need to let some people go." His
last words resonated in the quiet of the
office.

"You're firing me?"

"The consultants . . ."

I erupted. "Quit hiding behind your consultants' skirts. They work for you." I shook
my head in frustration. "I know exactly
what's going on here, Stu. I know about you
and Stacey. Everyone talks about you two.
And I know she wants my list. She's hardly
shy about it." I stood. "Congratulations. I'm
sure there will be a nice payoff at your next
little get-together."

Stuart turned red. "Get out of here."

"Just like that. For seven years I've given everything to this crummy job and you throw me out for some airhead blonde you met five months ago. Who's next? Your wife?"

"I said get out."

I walked to the door then turned back. "I just realized why everyone calls you Stu. It's short for stupid."

Chapter 6

There is a place up Little Cottonwood Canyon where the river cuts a steep bank against the mountain and levels into a secluded gorge of stone and tree. It is a place of solitude, and every now and then I go there to think. It was noon when I arrived. My mind reeled. I felt like I had been sucker punched. It wasn't supposed to be this way. Even if radio sales wasn't my first choice of occupation, I had given KBOX my loyalty. Maybe I had been working too hard to notice that the bottom line was blind to such ideals.

I sat in my car for a while, wrestling with whether or not to call Allyson. She would be the hardest to tell. I was certain that she already knew that I hadn't received the pro-motion. She knew me well enough to know that I'm the kind of guy who runs home with an A on his report card and hides it if I get an F. It had always been that way. But she'd never suspect that I'd been fired. She be-lieved in me more than I believed in myself. How could I tell her that her faith had been misplaced?

I should have been better at accepting failure. I had been raised with it. The day I graduated with my bachelor's degree, my father asked me what I planned on doing with my life.

"Go back for my master's," I said.

He thought about it then in his usual tight-lipped manner said, "Might as well. You'll never make it in the real world."

An emotionally secure person would wonder how a father could treat his child like that. But a child raised by such a father isn't likely to be emotionally secure. It was as if Chuck were somehow permanently embedded in my psyche. It was Chuck's echo I heard when Stu fired me. Only now did I realize how much Chuck's curse haunted me.

Chuck would be a happy man today, I thought, because today he had been proven right. I was thirty-two with a family to feed, unemployed and without a prospect in the world—a great big zero. I languished in the darkness of such thoughts. I've heard it said that the most humble of days is when a man compares what he might have been to who he really is. It is the day when life hands you a looking glass and all you can do is stare at your own reflection and scream. Or at least weep. This was my day. Everything was in question.

Chapter 7

There is a pewter-framed picture on our bedroom nightstand that pretty much sums up our family's relationship with Nancy Fox. I don't know who took the picture, but it was snapped on our wedding day. I am standing next to Allyson, my arm around my bride's waist, our bodies as tight together as the stones in those Incan walls that you can't fit a knife blade between. Nancy's body is invisible, but her smiling head is between us, cheek to cheek, happily floating upon our shoulders. She has been there ever since. In my marriage contract, Nancy was somewhere in the fine print.

Nancy had never married, although she had been engaged three times. She gave *catch and release* a whole new meaning. Again and again she would reel in Mr. Right then proceed to bash him over the head, scale him, gut him and throw him back into the lake for not measuring up.

Whenever she'd bring her latest boyfriend over to our house for dinner, Allyson and I would smile at him and ask the usual questions, while a part of me, the part loyal to my gender, would want to hold Nancy down and shout to the chump, "Run, you fool. Run while you still can."

Still, she was obsessed with men and was always looking, bemoaning the fact that all the good ones were taken.

For the last five years Nancy had worked in South Salt Lake at the credit office of R. C. Willey, a large chain of furniture appliance stores, and she and Allyson had lunch together at least once a week at a small café south of Liberty Park. While I struggled alone in the canyons, Allyson was at lunch with Nancy, oblivious to my morning.

"I can't believe the food still hasn't come," Nancy said. "If that waiter wasn't so gorgeous, I'd say something."

"It's a pretty day," Allyson said. "Enjoy it."

"Did you see those men behind you? The good-looking one in the Armani jacket keeps looking over here."

"Why don't you go introduce yourself?"

"What if he's really just looking at you?"

"Tell him I'm married."

Just then the waiter brought out their lunch. "Sorry, ladies. The kitchen's a little backed up."

"No problem," Nancy said coquettishly.

He set a bread bowl in front of each of them. "Two bowls of butternut squash soup. Can I get you anything else?"

"The mind reels," Nancy said.

Allyson shook her head. "No, we're fine, thank you."

"Enjoy." The waiter hurried back inside.

Nancy said, "You know, why do I even bother with men? It always ends up the same anyway. Besides what do I need marriage for when I can live through yours vicariously?" She waved her spoon as she spoke. "You have a handsome husband who is gainfully employed, a nice home and a beautiful daughter. What more could I ask for?"

Allyson sipped her ice tea then replied,

"How about *your own* husband, house and child?"

Nancy laughed. She dipped her spoon into a bowl of soup and paused to taste. "Mm. This is really good. So what is my family doing tonight?"

"We're celebrating."

"Celebrating? Did I miss something?"

"Rob's being promoted to sales manager at the radio station."

"It's about time. He's been there forever."

"Actually, I should say we think he's going to be promoted. But I'm sure he will be. I'm just waiting for his call."

"You have a good life," Nancy said.

"I do," Allyson said. "I'm a lucky girl."

"What are you doing to celebrate?"

"I thought I'd make a roast. Want to come over?"

"I can't. David wants to have a talk."

"You mean *the* talk?"

"Probably. I just hope he didn't buy a ring. It always makes me feel bad when they have to take it back."

"Call me after it's over."

"I always do."

Chapter 8

It was nearly midnight when I got home. I entered the house through the kitchen. There were dirty dishes in the sink and one place setting still on the table. There was a note on the counter that I did not read but guessed it pertained to some Tupperware container in the refrigerator. I went immediately downstairs to my den to write in my diary.

I had started my first diary as a teenager in middle school as an assignment in an English class and I never stopped. For nearly two decades I had recorded every one of the major, and a good share of the minor, events of my life. The practice was now more than habit, it was a form of self-therapy, as my writing had changed from recording events to feelings. I'm sure it saved me thousands of dollars in counseling sessions. There was something about putting my feelings on paper that made them manageable, as if I could just crumple them up and throw them away at will. But tonight, as I sat facing the computer screen, I hadn't the stomach for it. I turned off my computer then sat back in my La-Z-Boy with my eyes closed, my stocking feet up on its footrest.

After a few minutes I heard Allyson's soft footsteps on the floor above me. I could hear her cross the kitchen floor then descend the stairs. Embarrassment welled in my chest. I had no doubt that she had already concluded it had been a bad day. I didn't look forward to telling her how bad it really was.

The lights were off in my den, and the room was only illuminated from a lamp in the hallway. Allyson walked up behind me. She rested her hands on my shoulders and gently massaged me, working up to my neck. I leaned my head back, and she kissed my forehead then drew her long fingers up the sides of my neck and jaw, then up to my temples and massaged again. After a couple of minutes she said softly, "So what happened?"

I took her hands from my head and just held them. I looked up at her. "I got fired."

"Fired?"

"Stuart said that I wasn't performing."

"But you're their best salesman . . ." Allyson looked at me anxiously. "What does this mean?"

"It means what it means."

She took her hands from me then came around the chair and sat in my lap, draping her arms around my neck. "Here, sweetie, let me hold you." She pulled my head into her breast, cradling it in her arms. Suddenly my wall of stoicism cracked. I began to cry. She pressed her cheek against the top of my head.

"It's okay, honey."

She ran her hand down to my chin and lifted it until my gaze met hers. For a moment she just looked into my eyes.

"What am I doing, Al? I've spent the last seven years selling air. Most of my friends are moving into the peak of their careers and I have nothing to show for my time. I'm such a failure."

"That's not true. You're the most wonderful husband and father on this planet. No one could take such good care of us."

"That's a joke. We live hand to mouth. Mark's taking Becca on a Tahitian cruise for her thirtieth. You got a mixer."

"I asked for a mixer. And you're all I need, Robert. You're my life."

I shook my head. "Well, this isn't what I thought my life was going to be. Working at the radio station was supposed to be temporary until I got my writing off the ground. How much more of a loser could I be, getting fired from a career I never really wanted to begin with?"

Allyson stroked my hair then pressed her forehead against mine. "Maybe this is really a blessing, Rob. Maybe it's a sign that it's time for you to chase your dream of becoming a writer."

"And how do we live in the meantime?"

"Ever since Carson started school full day, I've been thinking about getting my old job back at Nordstrom's."

"We can't live on that."

"Not like we are, but we can get by. And we have savings." She knit her fingers with mine. "Rob, you've wanted to do this since you were a boy. You've got to at least give it a try."

I looked down at our hands. They were laced together in a tangle of flesh.

"Rob, I don't want you to hate yourself for what you might have been. But I especially don't want you to resent Carson and me for keeping you from your dreams. So take some time and finish your book. Maybe you could get a job selling on the side, maybe not. But you have to do this. Without dreams life is a desert."

After a moment a slim smile broke on my lips. "I don't deserve you."

"Yes, you do." She pushed her lips onto mine and I lost myself in her softness. "Now come to bed. I want my man next to me."

Chapter 9

New hopes are a fountain of energy. I found myself filled with an exhilaration I hadn't known since I was fresh out of college and the world looked like the up escalator. I made a trip to a nearby office store and outfitted my den with everything I thought I needed for writing: a dictionary, thesaurus, describer's dictionary, notepads, mechanical pencils, Post-it notes, printer ink and reams of printer paper. I purchased several books on writing and the mechanics of getting published and lost myself not only in the craft, but also in the fantasy of being an author. Allyson had done more than throw me a safety line. She had fashioned me wings.

Allyson and I devised a new routine: each morning we would get up together, and I would wake and dress Carson while Ally would make breakfast; then she'd do Carson's hair. Then I would walk Carson to the bus stop while Allyson left for work. Around nine, with my girls and the commotion gone, I would go down to my den, where I would write in solitude for three to four hours straight—until the words began to back up onto themselves. Then I would emerge from my sanctum to walk for an hour to clear my mind and untangle the knots in my story. Then I would shower and dress, make myself a sandwich, then write some more, until it was time to meet Carson at the bus stop.

Then I would take care of Carson until Allyson came home, either writing while Carson played upstairs or commencing my portion of the domestic duties. My job list included washing, vacuuming and cleaning the bathrooms. On weekdays I would get dinner on. Not surprisingly our meals had become noticeably simpler, and sloppy joes and macaroni and cheese became our mainstays.

Allyson was welcomed back to her old job. She enjoyed the interaction with adults and the chance to dress up. The greatest disadvantage was Allyson's loss of time with Carson; that and our diminished income. Allyson made little more than half of what I had made at the station. We knew that this deficit would eventually catch up to us, but that was tomorrow's bridge and I was making better progress on my book than I'd imagined. A hundred and three days into our new life I finished my book. It was a Friday afternoon and I met Allyson at the door holding a stack of paper three inches thick. "Da, da, da daaaah."

She looked at me. "What?" Then a wide smile broke across her face. "You finished it? Already?"

"Already? I've been working on it for four years." I handed her the bound manuscript and she read its cover.

"*A Perfect Day.* By Robert Mason Harlan." She looked up. "I've never heard you use your middle name. It makes you sound like an author."

"Or a serial killer," I said.

She folded back the cover page. "To

Allyson, my soul mate." She smiled. "I love the title."

"You should. You named it."

"How did I name it?"

"That day up on the mountain, when your father told you that he had brought you back home for one last perfect day."

"What does that have to do with your story?"

"My book's about a young woman and the last few months she spends with her dying father."

From her expression I couldn't tell whether she was pleased or upset.

"You wrote about us?"

I suddenly felt as if I'd been caught stealing. "It's based on you and your father. That's where I drew my inspiration. That time I saw you curled up next to your father was the most powerful expression of love I've ever seen. I wanted to write about that."

She again looked at the manuscript, her expression still enigmatic. "Can I read it now?"

"I was planning to take Carson to the zoo tomorrow so that you could just read."

She fingered through the manuscript then looked back up. "This will be hard for me."

"I know. I just hope you think it's worthy of your father."

She set the manuscript down and gently hugged me. "I'm so proud of you. My husband the author."

Chapter 10

Saturday morning came blue and promising as a child's birthday. Carson was excited for our daddy-daughter outing and chattered incessantly as Allyson dressed her and I packed our lunches. For a six-year-old there are few things cooler than the zoo. I was equally excited for the day but for different reasons. Today was my own private Kitty Hawk: my first attempt at literary flight. Then again it could also be the maiden voyage of the *Titanic*.

I realized that asking Allyson's opinion on a book I had worked on for four years put her in a difficult position: because either I had to be a good writer or she had to be a good liar. I hoped the former was true. As we left the house, Allyson, still in her robe and furry, pink slippers, had my manuscript in one hand and a cup of herbal tea in the other and was walking into the living room to start my book.

Carson and I were gone for the whole day, much more time than Allyson needed to read the book. I told myself that it was because I didn't want her to feel rushed. But it's also possible that I was really just afraid of Allyson's verdict.

It was dark when we returned. Carson was asleep, worn out from a day of running and laughing and excess cotton candy. I carried her in to her bed then went to our room. Allyson was in bed with her glasses on, watching the news. My manuscript lay at the end of the dresser.

"Carson's in bed," I said.

She looked up at me without a trace of emotion and my heart stopped. "Come here," she said. I climbed onto the bed, my heart in my throat. She took off her glasses then her mouth drew out into a broad smile as if she could no longer contain her excitement. "It was fabulous!"

"Really?"

"It was so good. I haven't cried that hard for the longest time."

"Crying is good?"

"Oh yes. Crying is good," she said happily. "I couldn't put it down. I read it from cover to cover and didn't even stop for lunch. It would make the best movie."

I laughed and plopped myself backward onto the bed. "I'm so relieved."

Allyson said happily, "You think you're relieved? I've been dreading this day for months. I was terrified that I wouldn't know what to say if I didn't like your book. But I loved it. It's easily the best book I've read this year."

That was saying a lot, because Allyson read a lot. She read everything from soft romances to hard thrillers. "You think so?"

"I know so. I've already told Nancy about it and now she's dying to read it."

I was grinning like a fool. "Oh, yeah!"

"So what now? Do you send it to a publisher?"

"I've been reading up on this. I need to find an agent."

"How do you do that?"

"There's a book called the *Writer's Market*. It has lists of agents. There's a copy at the library. I plan to go there on Monday and choose a few agents then send them my manuscript."

"How long does it take to hear back?"

"Maybe a few months. If I'm lucky. Sometimes people wait years to be discovered."

This jolted her back to reality. "Years? So what are we going to do in the meantime?"

"I need to find a job and hope that lightning strikes."

I slipped off my clothes and got ready for bed. I turned off the lights and Allyson rolled into my arms, but I was far too excited to sleep. Anything seemed possible again. After a half hour I climbed out of bed, picked up my manuscript and went down to my den to read.

Chapter 11

Monday morning I was waiting at the public library as its doors were unlocked. I found the *Writer's Market*, a thick book listing hundreds of publishers and literary agents, and began combing through it. There were more agents than I'd expected. I guessed there to be close to a thousand. The book was classified as reference material and couldn't be checked out, so I skimmed through it, writing down the names and addresses of the first twenty-five agencies that seemed most appropriate for a book like mine.

I went from the library to a copy shop, where I made twenty-five copies of my manuscript. Then I drove to the post office and mailed them all out. I felt a remarkable sense of optimism. I had set the bait and cast my line. Now all there was to do was wait. That and find a job.

I drove around Salt Lake City requesting employment applications from radio stations. Of course every application required work references. This didn't bode well. I had held the same job at the same station for seven years and Stuart had been my only boss. I regretted calling him stupid.

It was two weeks after I sent my book out that I received my first response from an agent. I had been grocery shopping with Allyson, and as I brought the groceries in from the car, Allyson went through the day's mail, fanning the bills back like a deck of cards. Suddenly she stopped and lifted one from the pile. "Robert. You got a letter from an agent."

I laid the sacks I carried down on the counter and took the letter. It had come from a Minnesota literary agency. I looked up at Allyson then I extracted the letter and unfolded it.

Dear Mr. Harlan,
    Thank you for sending your manu-

script, A Perfect Day. *While I found your writing interesting, I'm sorry to say that I don't think I am the right person to represent this material, especially in today's crowded market.*

I'm sure another agent will feel differently. I'm sorry to disappoint you, and I wish you the best of luck.

All Best Wishes,
Howard Guttery

My heart fell. "It's a rejection letter," I said. I dropped it on the counter.

Allyson looked at me, frowning. "Now what?"

"It's nothing," I said. "No one gets accepted the first time. *The Great Gatsby* was turned down a dozen times before it was published."

I'm sure Allyson saw my response for what it was—a coping mechanism—but what I said was also true.

"Don't worry," I said, more for myself than Allyson. "There are twenty-four more agents to go."

Chapter 12

The next weeks passed like torture. The rejections from the agencies continued to arrive. The letters all pretty much said the same thing, kindly worded form letters written by people with vast experience in rejecting. A few of the letters were identical in content.

With each letter my dream seemed farther from my grasp. I stopped picking up the mail. My job hunt was equally fruitless. I had contacted every radio station in the Salt Lake and Provo market, including a few I felt beneath me. I was turned down by every one of them. Between the literary agencies and the radio stations I faced rejection at every turn, and what my father had planted in me was now being reinforced on a daily basis: that I was, in fact, a failure.

Depression set in, accompanied by its myriad symptoms. I put on weight and didn't shave for days at a time. I spent hours in my den either on the Internet or playing mindless computer games. I began sleeping in. Even though it required more effort from Allyson, she never said a word. I believe that she was waiting for it to pass like a bout of the flu or something. But it didn't. One night, after she had put Carson to bed, Allyson came down to my den. I was playing solitaire on my computer.

"Can we talk?"

"Sure," I said, moving a card across the screen.

She sat down next to me. "I'm worried, Rob."

"About what?" My eyes were still locked on the screen.

"Would you please look at me?"

I released the mouse and turned around. "About what?"

"I'm worried about you." She ran her hand across my cheek. "Don't you shave anymore?"

"Since when do you have a problem with facial hair?"

"Rob, look at you. You haven't even showered yet. What have you done today?"

I saw where this was going and turned back to my computer. "I made a few calls."

"Have you paid the bills?"

"No. I'll do it tomorrow."

She took a deep breath. I knew that I wasn't making this easy for her. "Rob. You're taking this so personally."

"Taking what personally?"

"The rejection letters."

"How else should I take them?"

"You've written a great book. It's enough."

I turned back around. "It's not enough. If a tree falls in a forest and no one hears it, did it make a sound?"

She looked at me as if I were crazy. "What?"

"If a tree falls in a forest and no one hears it, did it make a sound?"

"I think you're losing your mind."

"I am. But my point is, it's not a book until it's published."

"A book is a book. Apparently it takes more than a great book to get published.

But you can't stop living because the breaks aren't there."

I shook my head. "You don't understand."

"No, I don't. Who cares what they think about your book?"

"I do. That book was my last hope that I could do something with my life. That I could be somebody."

This was the first time that I had openly acknowledged my fears. Only now, with the words still ringing in our ears, had either of us realized the extent of my desperation. For a moment Allyson seemed unable to respond. When she did her voice was heartfelt. "But you *are* somebody. You're my husband. You're Carson's father. Why can't that be enough?"

"Because that's not how men are judged in this world. I was raised thinking that all that matters is what you accomplish in life. I had one hope. And now it's gone."

Her brown eyes darkened with concern. "Rob, if you don't start doing something besides sitting around playing computer solitaire or whatever it is you do, you're just going to get more depressed. Besides I'm not making enough to keep up with expenses. We're burning through our savings."

I reacted defensively. "What do you want me to do? I've been to every radio and television station in Salt Lake City. No one wants to hire me. Stuart is seeing to that. One call to him and they won't even return my calls."

"But you've never liked radio sales anyway. Why don't you go into a different profession? Like teaching?"

"Teaching? Where?"

"Maybe there's an opening at the university. Your father would know."

Her suggestion came as a slap. I replied angrily, "Like I'm going to ask Chuck for help. I haven't spoken to him for two years."

"He helped us with the house."

"Don't you get it? That was Chuck's way of proving to me that I'm nothing without him. That's not a roof above us, it's a thumb."

Allyson exhaled. "Robert, I don't care what you do—as long as you do something. You can't just sit around the house feeling sorry for yourself."

Her words stung. "So that's what I'm doing? Just feeling sorry for myself?" I turned around and shut down the computer. Then I walked out of the room. Allyson followed me, first with her eyes then physically up the stairs to the back door.

"Rob, where are you going?"

"To get a job."

I slammed the door behind me. As I pulled my car out of the driveway, she stood at the window watching. It had been a dramatic exit, but at this hour I really had no idea where I was going.

Chapter 13

I returned home past one in the morning. I stepped into our dark bedroom and undressed, letting my clothes fall in a clump at my feet. Then I climbed into bed. Allyson immediately rolled over. Her voice came soft from the darkness. "I'm sorry that I hurt your feelings."

"It's okay. You were right."

"Where have you been?"

"Looking for work."

"At one in the morning?"

"I've been talking with Stan. I start working with him tomorrow."

"Installing sprinklers?" Her voice was tainted with incredulity.

"You have a problem with that?"

"No . . ."

"No, but . . . ?"

"No, but I'm afraid that you will." She put her hand on my chest. "Robert, you have a master's degree. You graduated summa cum laude."

"Then I'll be the most educated sprinkler installer in Salt Lake."

Allyson was quiet for a long time. I imagine she was garnering courage for what she wanted to say. "Can't you at least talk to your dad? Maybe it will make things better between you."

I bit back my anger. "What makes you think I want to make things better?"

"But, Rob—"

I cut her off. "End of discussion, Al. I'm going to sleep." I rolled to my side away from her. Allyson turned the opposite direction. Nothing more was said.

Chapter 14

I've always been close to my brothers. The *sons of Chuck* are like war veterans, I suppose, bonded as survivors of the same calamity. I have three brothers, all of them older than me: Stan, Marshall and Phil. Stan is the oldest. He's thirty-six and runs a successful sprinkler and irrigation company. Marshall is one year younger than Stan. He's a software designer for a Provo-based software firm. He is my only married brother. Phil is in the Air Force and stationed in Dunkirk. We rarely see each other, but we email each other weekly. Of all of us, Phil is the most like Chuck. I don't say that to be disparaging, he just fits into the military regimen more naturally than the rest of us. To him Chuck is just a former officer.

I am closest to Stan. More than anyone else, Stan understands my feelings about Chuck. Stan hasn't spoken to him for even more time than I, five years and counting, the likelihood of a reunion growing fainter with each passing year.

Stan had started the Harlan Sprinkler Company as a summer enterprise to earn money for college. The company grew faster than he had expected and he never went back to school. Even though Stan's abandoning his quest for a degree made Chuck mad, Stan didn't care. In fact he seemed to relish disappointing him. And in proving him wrong. Stan's success was indisputable. He had a nice home on the east side, a sports car, a boat, season tickets for the Utah Jazz basketball team and he spent most of his winter skiing when work was scarce. He had a secretary and ran a crew of twelve men. I was the thirteenth.

By this time I had pretty much given up on my book. Of the manuscripts I had sent out, nearly twenty rejections had come back. The remaining five agents didn't even bother to respond. Still my book was being read. Nancy had read it and raved about it. She called Allyson the night she finished it, full of tears and praise. She had shared it with a few other friends at work and they shared it until it had been passed around the entire credit department at R. C. Willey. I wondered how they could love the book so much while the agents rejected it. I figured that the agents knew better than I. And that I better just get used to a life doing something else besides writing.

I spent the first weeks at my new job digging troughs for sprinkling systems and laying sod. I still had the soft hands of a radio salesman and I came home each evening with fresh cuts and blisters. Manual labor gives one time to think. In my case, too much time. When I signed on with Stan, it was under the guise of temporary employment, but I wondered if I, like Stan, would spend my life there.

One night during my second week of work I arrived home with my clothes and body caked with mud as black as tar. I suppose that I looked pretty pathetic, and I could tell that Allyson wasn't sure if she should laugh or cry. Her nose wrinkled as I entered the house. "What have you been doing?"

"You don't want to know."

I had already kicked my shoes off outside, and I pulled off my shirt and dropped it to the ground by my feet. "Just burn it."

"You look like you fell into a swamp."

"Worse. We had to dig out a septic tank. I'm going downstairs to shower then to hang myself."

Allyson walked over and put her arms around me.

"Careful," I said. "This stink is contagious."

"I don't care. Thank you for working so hard for us." We kissed then she stepped back. "Dinner's almost ready so don't be too long."

As Allyson was setting the table, the phone rang. The caller I.D. showed an out-of-area call. The woman on the phone asked for Mr. Robert Harlan, and Allyson cloaked her voice with the formality she reserved for phone solicitors. "He's busy right now. May I take a message?"

"Yes, my name is Camille Bailey. I'm a literary agent for Argent Literistic. Mr. Harlan sent us a manuscript to review and I'd like to speak with him about it. May I leave my phone number?"

"I'll get him."

She called for me. "Robert, telephone."

I was still dressing and I shouted back, "Take a message."

Her voice lowered. "Rob, It's a *book agent*."

I came to the bottom of the stairway with a towel wrapped around my waist. "On the phone?"

She nodded. "Yes."

I answered the phone in my den. Allyson hung up the phone upstairs then came down next to me.

"Mr. Harlan, my name is Camille Bailey, I'm a literary agent with Argent Literistic in New York. You sent our firm a copy of your manuscript *A Perfect Day*. May I call you Robert?"

"Of course."

"Thank you. Is *A Perfect Day* your first work, Robert?"

"Yes," I replied. "Does it seem like it?"

She laughed. "Your book is lovely. I read it last night and I was crying so hard near the end that my roommate thought I had

had a death in the family. Your story was so connecting that I felt like I had."

"Thank you."

"No—thank you. I think you have a real winner here and I think I can sell this. I would like to represent your book, assuming of course that you haven't signed with someone else."

My heart raced. "No, I haven't."

"Have you sent it to anyone else?"

"I sent it to a few other agents." I hesitated with the truth. "Well, actually twenty-five, but they've all sent me rejection letters."

She was undaunted. "Well, they obviously didn't read it."

Allyson looked at me, wanting to know what was being said. I smiled and gave her a thumbs-up.

"I have friends at a few of the movie studios. I'd like to take this to them before we approach the publishers. A film deal drives the price up considerably."

"You mean a movie?"

Allyson's eyebrows rose.

"Possibly. I think *A Perfect Day* would make a terrific feature. At the least it will drive a strong deal with one of the networks for a Sunday-night special."

"I feel like I'm dreaming. What do you think my book could go for?"

"It's best not to speculate. There's such a broad range of possibility. First novels usually don't sell for that much, but I think this is a special book. We'll just have to see how excited the publishers get. But I don't think we'll be disappointed."

Her casual optimism filled me as well. For the first time in a long time I felt bright with hope. "You really think it will sell?"

"I've been doing this for a long time. I know a winner when I see it. But before I send the book out I'd like to meet with you in person. Coincidentally I was already planning a trip to Utah next week. Do you have a free day?"

"For you, any day is free."

She laughed. "Good. How about Tuesday?"

"Tuesday works. What are you doing in Utah?"

"I have an author in Park City I'm meeting with on Wednesday. So I'll just come out a day earlier. I'll have my assistant call and let you know what time I'll be in."

"I look forward to meeting you."

"Likewise. Again, Robert, congratulations on a beautiful novel."

"Thanks for calling."

As she hung up, I erupted, punching the air. "Yeah, baby!"

"What did she say?" Allyson asked excitedly.

"She loved the book. She's sure it will sell."

"This is so exciting. I'm so proud of you!"

I felt like I had just won the lottery. "Did I sound like a real idiot?"

Allyson laughed. "No. Just real."

Chapter 15

By the age of thirty-seven, Camille Bailey had lived two professional lives, both of them in the book industry. The first was in her hometown of Chicago, where for six years she worked as a book editor for Northwestern University Press. At the age of thirty she decided to make a career leap and left the second city for America's first, landing in New York as an assistant agent at a small uptown literary agency. She was employed at the firm for only six months when she was offered a job as an agent at Argent Literistic. I would learn that she had all the qualities that make for a good agent—or poker player, as they are the same. She could be intense and immutable but in the same hour warm and seemingly vulnerable, as if the agent persona was one she wore like a flak jacket to take off when she wasn't doing battle.

She was not married—except to her work. She had a full-grown chocolate Labrador named Barkley that she treated like a child and a condo in TriBeCa not far from where John Kennedy Jr. once lived.

Camille arrived in Salt Lake City the following Tuesday afternoon. I met her at the airport, standing outside the jetway holding a piece of paper with her name written on it in black magic marker. She looked at the paper then up at me and smiled. "Hi, Robert."

"You're Camille?"

"I am. It's so nice to meet you."

I had anticipated a brusque, curt, big-city Manhattanite attired in black. Camille was anything but. She had a warm, homey look to her, more fitted to Des Moines than New York City.

She had booked a room in downtown Salt Lake City at the Hotel Monaco, about twenty minutes from our home. I drove her to her hotel. She checked in then we sat in the hotel's café and got acquainted, discussing the book and the book industry over glasses of Coke.

I asked, "Do I sign a contract with you or just the publisher?"

"Most agents have contracts, but I don't. I decided early on in my career that if someone doesn't want to work with me I really don't want to work with them either."

"Has it ever been a problem?"

"Not so far. Of course once we sell the book you'll have to sign a contract with the publisher."

Her casual confidence in my book was incredibly delicious. I had been starved for respect, and this woman had brought me an entire buffet. After about an hour we left the café and I took Camille home to meet Allyson. Even though Allyson was a small town girl with a dislike for big cities, her feelings did not extend to their people. She liked Camille immediately, and vice versa was evident as well.

Allyson introduced Camille to Carson, who felt suddenly bashful and sat on the opposite side of the room eyeing Camille suspiciously. For twenty minutes she said nothing, until there was a sudden lull in the conversation and Carson blurted out, "I can play the violin."

Camille smiled. "I would like to hear that," she said.

A smile broke across Carson's face and she ran to her room to fetch her instrument.

"You don't know what you're in for," Allyson said.

"How long has she been playing?"

"About a year. She's in the Suzuki program."

"That takes a lot of parental involvement, doesn't it?" Camille asked.

"It sure does," Allyson replied.

Carson returned holding a miniature violin and bow. She curtsied to Camille then ran the bow over the strings in an excited version of "Twinkle, Twinkle, Little Star." Camille applauded when she finished.

"I can play on my head," Carson announced, and immediately set to rearranging her body until her feet were almost where her head had been. She played "Twinkle" again, and there was little difference in the quality.

Camille laughed for a full minute.

Nancy had volunteered to watch Carson while we went out, which was not altogether altruistic as Nancy was just as excited to meet a real book agent as I was. After introductions and Nancy's gushings, we left Nancy and Carson behind and drove to a quaint Italian restaurant near our home for dinner.

Camille perused the menu. "I can't decide. Everything looks good."

"This restaurant is owned by a cute little Italian couple," Allyson said. "We've been coming here for years."

"I love Italian food. In fact I love everything Italian. The food, the clothes, the men. Not to mention the shoes. I visit Italy every year."

"I've always wanted to go to Italy," Allyson said.

"We'll have to go together sometime. You haven't lived until you've celebrated New Year's Eve at Piazza del Popolo in Rome. What a circus." She winked at me. "We'll leave Robert home to baby-sit."

"Thanks a lot."

Only after we had begun to eat did the conversation turn to the book.

"So when do you plan to send the book to publishers?" I asked.

Camille set down her fork. "The truth is, I

already have. After our last conversation I had a change of heart and sent it to an editor friend over at Arcadia Publishing."

"Did they like it?"

She smiled. "You're ruining my surprise. She loved the story."

"Is she serious about it?"

"As a heart attack. She was going back to her boss to discuss an offer. I expect to have something when I get back on Thursday."

"This is exciting," I said.

Allyson beamed. "So you'll be in Utah for two days?"

"Yes. I have a meeting tomorrow in Park City."

"That's what you said," I interjected. "Another author. Would we know his name?"

"You might. It's Stanford Hillenbrand. The funny thing is he's actually a mortician. He's written a handful of books, but none of them have been very big sellers. But he's a great writer. He won the Mountains and Plains Book Award two years ago and was also nominated for the National Book Award. He's a bit eccentric, but I think you'd

like him. I'll get you two together sometime."

"I'd like that," I said. I liked the idea of
camaraderie with another author. I felt like I
had just been welcomed into an exclusive
club.

After dinner, dessert and coffee, we
dropped Allyson off at home then I took
Camille to her hotel. As we neared the hotel
she said to me, "Allyson's very sweet. I'd
like to get to know her better."

"She's definitely my better half. She made
my book possible, you know. Besides the
fact that it's really her story, she took a job
so that I could finish the book."

"That's remarkable. Where did you
meet?"

"At the University of Utah. I met her in an
English class."

"How did she end up in Salt Lake?"

"Initially she came out on a scholarship.
But she really just wanted to ski. She's from
a very small town in southern Oregon."

"I know."

"She told you?"

She looked at me. "I read the book."

I laughed. "Of course." I pulled my car up

to the hotel's front doors and shifted into park. Camille leaned against the door but did not move to open it. "How close were you to Allyson's father?"

"Not very. I've only met him twice. The second time was when he was dying."

"It's amazing that you were able to capture him so vividly in your writing. I feel like I know him. He sounds like a saint."

"A saint with a shotgun. He was a gruff old guy. But boy did he have a soft spot for Allyson. Even when his body was wracked with cancer, he wouldn't leave her. He hung on for days after he should have been gone. The man just wouldn't die." I felt sad as I thought of it. "You know, I've never told anyone this before—not even Ally. But when we were sitting next to his bed waiting for him to die, I realized that he wouldn't go because he didn't have anyone to take care of his girl. When Allyson left the room, I told him that I loved his daughter and I promised him that I would never leave her. He waited until Allyson came back into the room; he looked up at her and he died."

"That's really moving."

"It's something I'll never forget. Allyson's the way she is because of his love for her.

She's the only person I've ever known who loves without an agenda. I'm probably the luckiest man on the planet to have found someone like her."

Camille smiled thoughtfully. "You're a lucky man to realize it. I'll let you go." She unlatched her door then turned back and extended her hand. "It's been a pleasure, Robert. You are just as genuine as your book."

"We've had a good time. I know it probably seems dumb to you, but it's a big deal for us having you here. A real book agent."

"It's a big deal for me too. I'll talk to you Thursday."

Chapter 16

I took Thursday afternoon off to wait for Camille's call. It was nearly five—seven New York time—when it came. "Is Allyson with you?" Camille asked.

"I can get her."

"You'll want to hear this together."

Allyson was upstairs starting dinner when I called for her to get on the phone. She came downstairs and I put the phone on speaker. "We're both here."

"Hi, Camille," Allyson said.

"Hi, Ally. I've got some good news for the Harlan family. Arcadia Publishing has just agreed to publish *A Perfect Day*."

We erupted in celebration. I yelled; Allyson clapped. Even Carson was screaming, though she didn't know why. I couldn't imagine being happier if I had just won the Super Bowl. In fact all that was missing was someone pouring an ice cooler of Gatorade over my head.

All the pain and self-doubt of the last few months were swept away in this moment. I had read about successful authors boasting about their rejection letters, even framing them. Now I understood why. I was now glad for all the rejections, as they made this moment of triumph that much sweeter—like one of those lemon candies that are bitter on the outside and sweet in the middle.

After we had settled down some, Camille continued. "Arcadia would also like to purchase the rights to Robert's next book. Seems someone over there thinks Robert has talent."

"This just keeps getting better," I said. Though the truth is I would have given my book away just to see it on a bookstore shelf, I wondered how much they had offered for it and if it would be enough to quit my day job.

"So let's talk money," I said crassly. "How much?"

"A hundred and twenty-five thousand. Not bad for a first novel."

I was breathless. "Not bad? Do you have any idea how many sprinklers that is?"

"I'm so proud of you, Rob," Allyson said. "Thank you, Camille."

"Thank yourselves. You deserve it. Now go out to dinner and celebrate."

"We will," I said.

"I started making a casserole," Allyson said.

"It will keep," I said. "Let's go out."

"Then I better get upstairs. Bye, Camille."

"Bye, honey." As Allyson started upstairs, Camille asked, "Are you still there, Rob?"

"Still here."

"Take me off the speaker. I need to talk with you in private."

"Carson, would you go up with Mommy?"

"Okay."

I lifted the headset. "Go ahead."

"I talked with Sandra this afternoon. She's your new publisher. They want to release your book the second week of October. They're planning on a fairly extensive book tour. Are you okay with that?"

"What do you mean by extensive?"

"You could be on the road for as long as four weeks."

I was so giddy they could have asked me to sell the book door to door and I would have agreed. "Whatever it takes."

"In the next week or so you'll be hearing from a woman named Heather Welch. She's in charge of publicity over at Arcadia. She'll be planning your book tour."

"Okay. Anything else?"

"Actually there's something I want to get off my chest."

"What's that?"

"I've been thinking a lot about you and Allyson. I'm a little worried."

"About us?"

"I know this might sound a little dramatic, but if your book becomes as big as I think it will, you're going to find yourself in a new world."

"I can imagine."

"Maybe more than you can imagine," Camille said. "What you and Allyson have— your relationship—is a rare thing. It's like a private garden. It's delicate and balanced and you're about to let a million people trample through it."

"You're making this sound awful."

Camille's voice lightened slightly. "Believe me, I'm not trying to ruin the moment, I'm just trying to prepare you for what's ahead. I have a lot of married friends, but none of them have what I think you and Allyson have. I couldn't live with myself if I thought I had in some way been a party to its destruction."

After some thought I said, "We'll be okay, Camille. Allyson is everything to me. If it came right down to it, I'd give it all up for her."

"That's what I want to hear," she said, sounding slightly relieved. "Now that's off my chest, we can get back to celebrating."

"I am very, very excited," I said. "Thank you so much for making this possible."

"You're welcome. I'm glad you're excited. But we've just begun. The next few months are going to be quite a ride."

Chapter 17

Camille was right. The next months brought a whole new world into our little home, from a trip to New York City to meet with my publisher to publicity photo shoots to flight arrangements for my book tour—a hundred details all leading up to the main event. I felt like a kid again, anxiously counting down the days to Christmas.

I think it was Bette Midler who said, "The worst part of success is finding someone to be happy for you." I didn't have that problem. In my small world everyone was happy. Allyson was ecstatic, as were all three of my brothers. I don't know how Chuck felt about it. I never told him. I was sure that he would have found some way to deflate me, perhaps reminding me that I wasn't really a success yet. Like the time I was nominated as Sterling scholar in high school. I came home excited about the nomination, foolishly thinking Chuck would be excited as well. He wasn't. He asked when I would know if I had *really* won.

I continued to work with Stan until the first week of August, in part because I didn't want to leave him short a man, but mostly just to keep myself from going crazy watching the calendar.

Allyson gave notice that she would be quitting her job as well. Though she had some mixed feelings about this, ultimately she was glad to be home. On the Saturday morning following her last day of work, a delivery man came to our door carrying a box.

"I have a package for Robert Mason Harlan."

"That's me."

"Sign here, please."

The outside of the box read: *A Perfect Day. Do not open until October 7.*

I signed for the package, then as he left I shouted, "They came, Al. They're here."

Allyson ran in, followed by Nancy and Carson. "What's here?" Allyson asked.

"My book."

Her face brightened. Everyone gathered around me while I bent over the box, drawing my pocketknife across its lid. I folded back the flap and lifted out a single book. It was beautiful. It was a medium-sized book with a bright cover, a picture of a beautiful landscape of horse country washed by a morning haze. *A Perfect Day* was embossed in gold foil, as was my name—all three of them—Robert Mason Harlan. I extended the book at arm's length. "It's real," I said.

"What a beautiful book," Nancy said. "I'd buy it just for the cover."

"It is beautiful," Allyson agreed. "Just like the story."

I looked at Allyson. "I've always wondered what this would feel like."

"What does it feel like?" Nancy asked.

"I was going to say a dream. But now I think it feels more like I've just given birth. With a gestation period of four years."

Allyson took a copy and carefully opened it.

"I want one." Carson said.

I handed her a copy. "I'll read it to you in a few years," I said.

"May I have one?" Nancy asked.

"Of course."

"I want my copy signed."

"How many are there?" Allyson asked.

I read the side of the box. "Carton holds twenty."

"Good. I told Carson's teachers that I'd get them signed copies."

"I ought to send a copy to Stuart," I said.

"You should," Allyson said kindly, "And thank him. If he hadn't fired you this never would have happened." Allyson always had a way of putting things in perspective. She turned the book over. "That's a nice picture of you."

"This *is* a good picture," Nancy said. "I'd go after you."

"Thanks, Nance," Allyson said.

"They can look," Nancy said. "Just not touch."

Allyson went back to consigning the books. "You need three for your brothers. I would like one for Aunt Denise and her friend Celeste. One for your father."

"Chuck doesn't need one," I replied.

Allyson frowned but said nothing.

Suddenly Nancy jumped up. "Omigosh, I forgot the pancakes." She ran out of the room, chased by Carson. For a moment Allyson and I sat quietly looking at the books. Then I said, "Do you know what this is?"

"My husband's book."

"Much more than that. It's our passport to our dreams. To a whole new world."

"I hope not," she said.

"Why do you say that?"

"I like our world just the way it is." She draped her arms around me, looking me in the eyes. "I'm so proud of you. I knew this would happen someday because no one deserves it more than you. You're the best man I know."

I smiled and then we kissed. Nancy called us for breakfast.

Chapter 18

This is Mick and Angel of The Breakfast Bunch, *where you get more of yesterday's hits and less interruptions. Up next, a flash from the past, Peter, Paul & Mary, "Leavin' on a Jet Plane."*

ONE MONTH LATER.

The radio alarm went off in the middle of my nightmare. I rolled over and hit the snooze button then lay back on my pillow looking up at the dark ceiling.

In my dream I had come home from the book tour and found my home caged behind thick metal bars. I reached through the bars and rang the doorbell several times, but no one came. A passing neighbor told me that he had seen my family at the church down the street. I ran to it. Inside the church I could see Allyson and Carson praying. I tried to get in, but there were bars on the church's doors and windows as well. I yelled for them, but they couldn't hear me. Somehow my voice was gone.

It had been a remarkably lucid dream and it left me shaken. As I stirred, Allyson rolled over into me, laying her face against my shoulder.

"Is it time?" she asked in a thick voice.

"Yes."

"Can't you just call in sick?"

"You really want me to do that?"

"I don't want you to go. Who will keep me warm in bed?"

I pulled her in tighter. I'm sure it seems silly to the well traveled, but in seven years of marriage Allyson and I had never been apart for more than five days. Four weeks was unfathomable. I held her until the snooze expired and the radio again jarred me back to the morning. I leaned over and switched it off then kissed Allyson on the forehead.

"Do you want me to get up and make you breakfast?" she asked.

"No. It's too early." I climbed out of bed and went to the shower. After I had finished dressing, I set my luggage inside the foyer. As I finished a piece of toast, the taxi driver knocked on the front door. While he took my luggage—one large soft-shelled Samsonite bag and a carry-on bag with rollers—I went back in to Allyson one last time. The room was still dark.

"Goodbye, honey," I said softly.

"I'm going to miss you so much," she said.

"I'll call you every day. I promise."

"You better. Did you remember your laptop?"

"Yes."

"I'll email you every day. Did you pack your pillow?"

"Yes." I put my arms around her. "I have everything I need in my bag except you," I said.

She moaned happily. "I love you with all my heart. Don't ever forget that. Especially when some beautiful woman is telling you how much she loves your book."

"The only woman I care about is you."

I laid my head against her chest, feeling her warmth and softness and listening to the comforting beat of her heart. Then I sighed and slowly drew back my hand, holding on to hers until I kissed it then let it go.

"Bye, my love," she said sleepily.

I shut her door then went to Carson's room. She was sleeping soundly. For just a moment I lingered over her, watching her peaceful slumber. I touched her soft cheek and she rubbed it then rolled to her side. I quietly bent over her and kissed her. My heart ached. I would miss my family dearly. Then I went out to the cab and climbed into the backseat. "Salt Lake Airport," I said.

The driver shifted his car into reverse. "You got it."

I glanced back at my home as we drove away. The excitement of the last weeks gave way to melancholy. Suddenly home was the only place I wanted to be.

Chapter 19

I spent eight hours in transit, though it didn't seem that long. The first steps of adventures are never tedious. For the first time in my life I sat in the first class section of an airplane. As a guy who had never really left Utah, I suppose I was filled with a sort of gee-whiz-wide-eyed wonderment. The woman I sat next to asked me what I did for employment, and when I told her that I was an author, she seemed impressed. She wrote down the name of my book and had me sign the back of her boarding pass for her to put in it after she purchased it.

I had a three-hour layover in Cincinnati. As I wandered the terminal, I was amazed to see copies of my book in all the airport bookstores. I couldn't believe that my book was actually there with all the others. I stopped at each store to sign them. The woman at the counter of the WHSmith acted honored to meet me, like I was a celebrity or something. She put *autographed book* stickers on my books and moved a stack of them next to the cash register. While I was still in the store, a woman picked up my book, read the jacket then bought it. I watched her furtively from the magazine rack. It was all I could do to not go over and thank her.

My flight landed in Birmingham at ten minutes past one. I gathered my things and fell into the shuffling line of travelers exiting the plane.

A woman stood just outside the jet way holding a copy of my book. She was fifty something, small and attractive with silver hair, ice blue eyes and a sharp nose.

"Mr. Harlan?"

I stepped from the line. "That's me."

She extended her hand. "I'm Anne, your escort," she said with a melodious southern drawl. "Welcome to Alabama."

"Thank you." We stepped away from the

crowd of exiting travelers. "How did you know it was me?"

She lifted her book. "Your handsome picture is on the cover. Do you have luggage?"

"I have one bag. One *large* bag."

"Baggage claim is this way." She led me to the escalators. "How long is your tour?"

"Twenty-five cities."

"My heavens. Where does Birmingham fall on your tour?"

"This is my first stop."

"No wonder you look so fresh. By the end of your tour, you'll look like the laundry in the bottom of your bag. And you'll feel like it." At the bottom of the escalator Anne looked up to check the carousel numbers. "Your suitcase will be over there."

She smiled when she saw my bag. "That is rather large. I better get the car and meet you out front. That way we won't have to drag it out to the parking terrace."

"It's okay. I can follow you."

"Then we're off."

We took an elevator downstairs and crossed traffic to the parking garage. The air outside was warm and moist, a mere remnant of a Southern summer. She stopped at the rear of a black Buick sedan and opened the car's trunk by remote. She went for my bag but I stopped her.

"This thing weighs more than you do," I said. I hoisted my bag inside while she opened the car door for me. Then Anne climbed into the driver's seat.

"There's a cooler on the floor in the back," she said. "I have Coke, bottled water and juice. Help yourself."

I reached back and took a bottle of water. I opened it and she immediately reached over to take the bottle cap from me.

"Are all escorts as accommodating as you?"

"I don't know, but I'll take that as a compliment. Now buckle your seat belt. The publishers get real upset if we kill their author."

We pulled out of the parking terrace and merged in with the traffic leaving the airport. The road from the airport was lined with dogwood trees and flowers. The air was sweet with the fragrance of magnolias. I decided that Allyson would like Birmingham.

The South had always held a certain romantic if not mystical allure for me. As an aspiring author I had been a fan of Faulkner and Harper Lee, and the ground they walked seemed a bit above the rest of the earth. I was happy to be in the South, and I was reminded of where I was every time Anne opened her mouth.

"Mr. Harlan, you can lean the seat back if you want to rest."

"I'm fine. I'm not tired." I looked her way. "You can call me Rob."

"Thank you. I'm sorry to say I haven't read your book yet. I've had so many authors through lately I'm behind on my reading. But it's a beautiful book. And it sounds just wonderful. Do you mind me asking how your reviews have been?"

"They've almost all been good."

"That's just wonderful. Have you been writing for a while?"

"This is my first book."

"So what gave you the idea for your story?"

"My wife. It's her story."

"How special. How long have you been married?"

"Seven years."

"Seven years. Isn't that just wonderful?"

Anne was big on *just wonderful*. A half hour later we arrived at the Tutweiler—a boutique hotel in the heart of Birmingham. "You'll just love this hotel," she said as she put the car in park. "It's very quaint."

Anne climbed out of the car and the bell captain greeted her. "Welcome back, Ms. Stephens."

"Thank you, Emmett. Mr. Harlan has one bag in the trunk." We walked inside. The attendant at the counter smiled when he saw Anne, slightly tipping his head. "Ms. Stephens."

"Hello, Nolan. I have with me a very important author, Mr. Robert Harlan."

"Mr. Harlan, welcome to Alabama." He lost himself to his computer terminal. "Here we are. Mr. Harlan. One single, king-size bed, no smoking. You'll be staying with us for two nights?"

"That's right," I said.

"Nolan, is it possible to upgrade Mr. Harlan to a VIP suite?"

"Just a minute, let me see if it's available." Nolan consulted his screen, touched his keyboard and returned. "Yes, ma'am. Two nights in the suite, no extra charge. I see that the charges have all been taken care of." He handed me a small package. "The small key inside is to the mini-bar. I'll have your luggage sent right up."

I felt like I had suddenly been upgraded to the first class section of life. "Thank you."

Anne smiled at me. "Get a good night's rest. We start early with the morning news. I'll pick you up in the lobby at five-thirty."

"I'll be ready."

"Would you like me to call before I come?"

"No, I'll just get a wake-up call."

"Very well. Good night, Robert."

Anne left. Emmett, the bellman, stepped forward with my suitcase. "May I have your key, sir?" I handed him the envelope.

"This way, please."

My room was spacious, with gold-fringed drapery and a large Jacuzzi tub. It seemed too large for just me, and I wished that Allyson were there. I unpacked my clothes, hung them in the closet, then lay down on top of the bed without pulling down the sheets. I checked my watch. Alabama was one hour ahead of Utah. Allyson would be eating dinner. I ordered room service; then I called home.

"Hello," she answered.

"Hi, baby."

Her voice brightened. "I was wondering when you'd call. So how's my author? What's the road like?"

"Well, it's been nothing but airports today. My room is nice. I could get used to this. I just ordered from room service: ribs rubbed Southern style, with grits and crawfish chowder. Does that sound Southern or what?"

"It sounds fun."

"I have a big soft bed, cable television. Everything but you."

"If you're a good boy, maybe I'll come next time."

"Then life would be perfect. How's Carson?"

"She's good. But every time she saw an airplane today, she asked if you were on it. I think this is going to be hard on her."

"I guess that makes two of us. On the way here I stopped in the airport bookstore in Cincinnati and they had my book. It was kind of awesome seeing it there next to Grisham and Clancy."

"I know what you mean. I saw it today at Wal-Mart. There was a woman looking at it and I had to tell her that it was my husband's book. She bought it of course."

I laughed. "I have my first book signing and my first television interview tomorrow."

"Are you nervous?"

"A little."

We talked for ten more minutes; then Allyson asked, "What time is it in Alabama?"

"We're an hour ahead."

"I better let you go so you can get some rest before your big day."

"I'll call tomorrow."

"I'll be waiting. Check your email. I sent you a goodnight kiss."

Chapter 20

The next morning I was dressed and down-stairs by five-twenty-five. Anne met me in the hotel's lobby. In spite of the hour she was as perky as she had been at the airport. I think some people just naturally have caffeine in their veins. "Good morning, Robert."

"Good morning. How do I look?"

She straightened my collar. "Cute as a button."

Her Buick was parked at the front curb, watched over by the bellman. Anne handed him a couple of dollars and he opened the door for her while I walked around and let myself in.

We made it to the TV station with time to

spare. Anne signed the visitor book for both of us at the front counter, and an intern led us back to the green room to await my segment. As we walked, Anne said to me, "This is going to be a wonderful interview. The woman interviewing you is named Jana Driggs. She is their most popular morning host. Her producer told me that she read your book and loved it."

"All right," I said. "Good start."

"Here we are."

The green room was small and rectangular in shape. There was a vanity mirror surrounded by light bulbs (a good third of them burned out) and two couches, both threadbare in places. In the middle of the room was a coffee table with a box of Krispy Kreme doughnuts and bottles of apple juice. "Would you like a doughnut?" Anne said.

"No, thank you."

She helped herself to one. About a half hour later a heavyset man wearing a coffee-stained T-shirt and a headset came into the room looking for me. "You're Mr. Harlan."

"Yes, sir."

"They're ready for you. Let me mic you up." He clipped a gator-clamp microphone to my lapel, the wire leading down to a small metal box with a glowing red diode. He handed me the box. "If you'll slide this under your shirt then into your back pocket, we'll be in business."

I did as he instructed, and he led me over to a sofa and coffee table off the side of the main news set, while the morning anchors were still on air giving their reports. He whispered, "Ms. Driggs will be interviewing you right after the next commercial break. She's the redhead on camera right now."

I could see her on a monitor built into the wall behind the set. She wore a bright blue business suit and was reading the news from a teleprompter. When they finished the segment, they broke to a commercial and a cameraman shouted, "We're out." The woman stood and unclipped her microphone, and two of the three cameras spun around to face the corner where I sat. She smiled at me as she walked between the cameras. In one hand she carried a newspaper article. "Mr. Harlan, I'm Jana Driggs," she said, reaching out to shake my hand.

I stood and took her hand. "It's nice to meet you."

She sat down in the chair opposite me.

She lifted the microphone from the coffee table and attached it as naturally as if she were buttoning her shirt. "May I call you Robert?"

"Please."

"I don't mean to gush, but I read your book and I just loved it. I was crying like a baby when I finished it. It was refreshing to read something from the heart."

The cameraman said, "Thirty seconds, Jana."

She leaned over and touched me. "I found myself wondering if it really was a man who wrote this. My husband could learn a thing or two from you."

The cameraman counted down, "Five, four, three . . ." He finished the count with hand signals. Jana's face brightened as she looked into the camera. "Welcome back to *Good Morning Birmingham*. We have in our studio today Robert Mason Harlan, author of a new book from Arcadia Publishing, *A Perfect Day*. It is the touching story of a woman who finds out that her father has cancer, and the last few months they spend together. The cover says it's a tender story of love, renewal and the bonds that transcend life." She turned toward me. "Thank you for joining us here today, Robert."

"Thank you. My pleasure."

She suddenly lifted the folded newspaper that had been in her lap. "A review in *The Baltimore Sun* says your book is 'trite, poorly written and an unabashed yank of emotional strings.' " She looked at me. "Ouch. How does that make you feel when you read a review like this?"

I couldn't have been more blindsided by her question. ". . . Actually most of the reviews about my book have been favorable . . ."

"Would you agree that your book is emotionally manipulative?"

"I . . . I just wrote a story that I thought was meaningful."

"This story is based on your wife's last few months with her father. Do you feel a little exploitative writing about an experience that had to be tremendously personal to her?"

"My wife is glad that I wrote it. I don't think that we share nearly enough of these kinds of stories with each other."

She nodded, as if counting time. "Are you working on something else right now?"

"My book just came out, so right now I'm still focused on this novel."

She looked directly at the camera. "The book is *A Perfect Day* from Arcadia Publishing and you can meet Robert Harlan in person tonight at the Books-A-Million bookstore at Fashion Mall at seven P.M. Pick up a copy and a box of hankies. Robert, thanks for joining us."

"And you're off," said the cameraman. She immediately stood, unclipping her microphone as she did. "That was great, Robert. Thanks for being on the show."

I stared at her in disbelief.

"Would you mind signing my book on the way out? Carl . . ."

"Yes, Ms. Driggs?"

"Take this," she said, handing him her microphone. "And would you fetch my book and give it to Mr. Harlan to sign?"

"Yes, ma'am."

Jana walked back to the main news set. The same man took my microphone and I walked to the studio door where Anne was waiting. "I couldn't hear. How did it go?"

"Think Custer."

She frowned. "I'm sorry. I won't make any more predictions."

In the parking lot I asked, "What's next?"

"We have two radio station interviews. One's a country station, the other a Christian station. Then if you want I'll take you to breakfast."

The next two interviews went reasonably well, though neither interviewer had read my book and the host at the country station was more interested in talking about how to get a book published than what my book was about. When we were off the air, she confided in me that she was working on a book.

I was glad to get back to my hotel room. I exercised in the hotel fitness center then took a nap. I had a short call-in interview with a radio station in Tennessee. A few minutes afterward Heather, my publicist, called to check up on me. I told her about my morning show disaster, and she profusely apologized.

After we hung up, I logged on to the Internet and checked my emails then caught up on my diary. I was nearly a week behind on my writing and it took me more than an hour to catch up.

I ate dinner alone in my room then watched television until Anne arrived at a quarter to seven to take me to my book signing.

On the way to the store Anne asked, "Are you ready for your first signing?"

"I guess. How does it work?"

"They'll have a podium set up and you'll speak for a few minutes. Then everyone will line up to get their books signed. You just thank them for coming and sign their books. I called the store this afternoon and they had plenty of books in."

We walked into the store. A woman was standing near the front to greet us. She stepped forward as we entered. "Hi, Anne."

"Good evening, Becky. I've brought Mr. Harlan with me."

She stepped forward. "It's a pleasure having you in our store, Mr. Harlan. My name is Becky. We have the signing set up on the second floor. Can I get you something from the café?"

"Nothing right now," I said. "Thank you."

"Then we'll get started."

We walked up the stairs. There was an open section of floor with maybe fifty chairs facing a table and a podium with a small sound system. There were a couple people seated in the chairs near the back, but they didn't appear especially interested in our entrance. Anne and I sat down behind the table and Becky stood by our side. After a moment I said, "It doesn't look like anyone came."

Becky frowned. "I'll make an announcement on the store's PA system to let people know that you're here."

A few minutes later her voice resonated throughout the store. "Books-A-Million is pleased to welcome author Robert Mason Harlan in our store today signing his new book *A Perfect Day*. Mr. Harlan will be signing on the second floor. His book will be fifteen percent off while he is in the store."

When Becky returned, the seats were still empty. The announcement only increased my embarassment, as people looked over to see me sitting there alone. I wanted to crawl under the table. Not that anyone would have noticed.

Becky cleared her throat. "Under the circumstances I think we'll forgo the talk," she said. I could tell she was embarassed for me. A minute later she said, "Let me know if you need anything." She left us. A half hour later Anne said, "I need to use the powder room. Will you be okay if I leave for a minute?"

"I think I can handle these crowds by myself."

"Can I get you anything? A water or coffee?"

"No. I'm okay."

She walked away. A minute later a man who had hovered near my table suddenly stepped up, his hands firmly thrust into the front pockets of his jeans. "You an arthur?"

"Yes," I said, resisting the urge to correct him.

"This here your book?"

"Yes, sir."

"They free?"

"Only if you steal them."

The man looked at me blankly.

"No. The bookstore is selling them."

The man nodded, as if just grasping the concept. He picked up a copy then turned it around to look at the picture of me on the back. "You famous then?"

If you have to tell someone you're famous, you're not.

"No. Sorry."

The man put the book back down and walked off. A minute later another woman stopped at the table. "Could you tell me where the rest rooms are?"

"I'm sorry. I don't know. I don't work here."

She squinted at the placard behind me. "Oh. Sorry."

I was glad when Anne returned. As the hour ended, Becky returned. She knew better than to ask how it had gone. I hadn't sold a single book.

"There's a basketball game tonight," she said. "I don't know why the publishers don't check these things first." Her excuse was almost ridiculous, but she was being kind and I appreciated it all the same.

"Well, I need some books," Anne said. "One for my mother and sister."

"You don't need to do this," I said.

"Yes, I do," she countered cheerfully, "my mother would kill me if I didn't get a signed copy."

On the way back to the hotel I had a lot to think about.

"So this is what a book signing is like," I said.

"Sometimes," Anne replied. "Welcome to

the trenches. Sometimes it even happens to best-selling authors."

Anne dropped me off at the front of the hotel and we arranged another five-thirty pickup. In my room I undressed and lay back in bed glad that the day was over. Then I called Allyson. She spoke in a tired, hushed voice.

"Did I wake you?"

"Almost. Carson's in bed with me. We had a rough day. Carson fell off the jungle gym at school and cut her lip."

"Is she okay?"

"She had to get three stitches. That wasn't fun. She kept crying for Daddy."

I frowned. "I'm sorry I wasn't there for her."

"It's not your fault. How did your day go?"

"Almost as fun as Carson's. The television anchor bushwhacked me. Then no one came to my book signing. No, one woman came. But she was looking for the rest rooms. It was humiliating."

Allyson groaned. "I'm so sorry. Did you sell any books?"

"My escort bought two. And I thought this

was supposed to be glamorous." I yawned. "I have another early flight tomorrow."

"You sound tired. Where are you tomorrow?"

"Oklahoma. I'll call from there."

"Okay. You'll do better tomorrow. Hang in there. I love you."

"I love you too. Give Carson a kiss for me."

I hung up the phone. Four weeks suddenly seemed like an eternity.

Chapter 21

I began collecting the plastic room keys from the hotels I stayed at, which gives an idea of just how exciting my life was. The next week was more of the same, though the attendance at my signings grew by three or four people each time. By the time I hit Seattle, there were nearly twenty people waiting for me. For a while I actually had a line. Unfortunately the bookstore had ordered the wrong books by mistake. I had just sat down to dinner with my escort when Camille called.

"Where are you?"

"Seattle."

"How did your signing go?"

"About twenty people came."

"That's progress."

"The bad news is that they didn't have any books."

"What do you mean?"

"The bookstore confused me with another author. They had stacks of books from some mystery writer named Robert M. Carlan."

"I'll scream at your publisher in the morning."

"It's not their fault. It was the bookstore manager. He already apologized."

"I'll still call them. They should have followed through." She hesitated and I could tell she had more news.

"So what's up?"

"I spoke this afternoon with United Casting. They don't think the movie deal is going to fly."

"Why is that?"

"Hollywood isn't keen on books for movies right now. Especially with all the special-effect blockbusters dominating the screens. That's the bad news. The good news is that I have an offer for a television movie of the week. So you'll get at least a week of major promotion when it airs."

I considered the proposition.

"I know it's not what you wanted. Believe me I wanted a feature deal as much as you, but this isn't bad. The network will put at least a half million dollars into promotion. And you're guaranteed to have major star power."

"Like who?"

"The last piece I sold them starred Glenn Close."

"That's impressive. Do you think it's the right thing to do right now? Or should we wait?"

"If we wait we might lose it. I think we need to move on this. Arcadia's been track-ing numbers. Your sales have been a little lower than they expected. They're not wor-ried, not yet at least, but booksellers tend to have a short attention span. If it takes longer to get your book off the ground than we planned, then this will give bookstores a reason to not return your book."

"You're the agent. You do what you think is right."

"I always do."

I hung up the phone disappointed. As ridiculous as it now seemed, I realized that somewhere in my mind I had already con-structed a fantasy of myself at the movie premiere, walking up a red carpet flanked by movie stars and accompanied by the sporadic camera pops of the paparazzi. I went back to eating my dinner.

Chapter 22

It was late Saturday morning, and while I was in the air somewhere over South Dakota, Carson turned off the cartoons and wandered through the house looking for her mother. She found Allyson on our bed looking at a large leather book. The morning sun glanced through the window in a beam that divided the bed in half.

"Whatcha lookin' at?" Carson asked.

Allyson looked up and smiled. "My Life Book."

Carson's nose wrinkled. "Can I look?"

Allyson patted the bed next to her. "Sure. Come on up."

Carson climbed up on the white, embroidered bedcover then crawled on her elbows until she was shoulder to shoulder with Allyson. She pointed at the first picture she saw: a photograph of a little girl on a horse. "Who's that?"

"That's me."

Carson started laughing. "No. You're old."

"I used to be a little girl like you."

"When?"

Allyson touched Carson's nose. "When I was a little girl like you."

Carson pointed at the man next to her in the picture. He was standing in front of the horse holding the horse's reins. He was a tall man and was wearing a cowboy hat. "Is that a real cowboy?"

"That's my daddy."

"You have a daddy?"

The questioned surprised Allyson. She realized that she hadn't spoken much of her father since Carson was old enough to comprehend.

"I used to. He was a really great daddy." She rubbed Carson's hair. "Do you know what his name is?"

"Daddy?"

"No. I call him that. But his name is Carson. That's why we named you Carson."

This made her smile. "Where is your daddy?"

"He went to heaven."

"Can he come see us?"

"I don't know. But we can't see him."

"How come?"

"It's just that way."

"Is heaven like book tour?"

Allyson was surprised that Carson knew what a book tour was. Obviously she had been listening in to adult conversations. "I don't think so. How come?"

"Because we can't see Daddy either."

"No. But Daddy will be coming home soon."

"Will he be home in one hundred days?"

Allyson smiled. "He'll be home a lot sooner than that. Do you miss him?"

She nodded. "Sometimes when I think about Daddy I feel sad. Do you miss your daddy too?"

Allyson turned to her and smiled, but her eyes moistened. "Every day, sweetheart. Every day."

Chapter 23

It was the third day of my second week on book tour, and if I had had illusions of the limousine and champagne lifestyle, they were mostly gone by now, replaced by fatigue and loneliness and the reality of the road. It was Wednesday night. It was two hours before my book signing and I was eating dinner with my escort, a pleasant man named Dick Brown, on the plaza in Kansas City, when Camille called me on my cell. "How are you doing?"

"I want to go home."

"I know. How was your book signing yesterday?"

"Good. There were a couple dozen people there. "

"And they had the right book?"

"Oh, yeah. Someone got the message, because it was the first thing they said to me when I arrived."

"Good. My tantrum was efficacious. Well, this should help lift your spirits. We just got news on the *New York Times* best-seller list." She paused. "I feel like there should be a drum roll or something. Here it goes. *A Perfect Day* just hit the list at number fifteen. You are now and forevermore a *New York Times* best-selling author."

"Yeah, baby!" I shouted.

"I'll email the list to you. Where are you headed now?"

"I have a book signing at Rainy Day Books."

"Oh, one of the classic independents. By the way, Allyson says to remind you that you have a wife."

"You talked to her today?"

"I talk to her almost every day."

"About what?"

"Mostly you."

"Great. I'll call her right now and share the good news."

"Talk to you later."

Camille hung up and I dialed home. "Hey, Al."

"Hi, honey."

"I have some good news. We just hit the *New York Times* bestseller list. Number fifteen."

She squealed. "Congratulations. Does that mean you can come home now?"

I laughed. "It doesn't quite work that way."

"I can hope. Here, someone wants to talk to you."

I could hear the phone being fumbled, dropped, then breathed into.

"Daddy?"

"Hi, sister."

"Where are you?"

"I'm in Kansas."

"Where's Kansas?"

"Far away."

"Are you coming home?"

"Soon, honey."

"It's my violin show tomorrow. I wish you were here to take me."

Her words lodged in my chest.

"So do I, honey. With all my heart."

"Do you want to talk to Mommy?"

"Yes." When Allyson was back on the phone, I said, "That hurt."

"I know. She's very sad that you're missing her recital. She's been missing you a lot lately. A few days ago she asked me if book tour was like heaven."

"Not hardly. Why would she ask that?"

"She said because my daddy was in heaven and I never get to see him either."

I groaned. "That *really* hurts."

"I told her that you'd be home soon. At least that's what I keep telling myself. She's not the only girl who's missing you. So by the way, when are you coming home?"

Allyson knew perfectly well, as she had it marked in big letters on our refrigerator. She was just twisting the blade. "You're not making this easier."

"You're on to me."

"I'll talk to you tomorrow. Let me know how the recital goes."

"I will. I'll email you some pictures. And congratulations on the list. I'm proud of you. Have a good night."

"Good night, Al."

Chapter 24

Over the next week I could feel the change in the seasons. I bought a light jacket and wore it every night. Allyson said that the leaves in the Wasatch Mountains had all changed. It made me homesick. Autumn is my favorite time of the year in Salt Lake, when the nights turn chill and there's a bite in the morning air. I never feel so alive as I do in autumn.

I could also feel changes in myself. Already I felt like a veteran of the road. I was no longer nervous doing radio and television interviews, and I was no longer surprised to find people at my book signings; rather I expected them. Air travel had lost its mystique, and the hub terminals had become all too familiar. But the biggest change I experienced was the deepest and most complex. Instead of missing my family more with time, as I'd expected, I found that I missed them less as I grew accustomed to a different world. I realized that going home would require its own adjustment.

Momentum for my book was growing. While the most obvious signs of progress were the increasing numbers of people at my book signings, there were more subtle indications as well. After I hit the best-seller lists, the bookstore managers and employees began asking to have books signed for them. My biggest signing of the week was in Oregon when I signed at Powell's, an enormous independent in downtown Portland.

There were nearly fifty people waiting for me when I arrived. And there was family. Allyson had made a call to her Aunt Denise, and she and a handful of her friends had driven more than four hours from Medford. While Allyson visited her aunt at least once a year, it had been a few years since I had seen her, and I was surprised at how much she had aged. She didn't look like she felt too good, and she was unable to stand in line. Of course she didn't have to. I went to her and we embraced. Her friends, two gray-haired ladies probably a few years younger than her, stood to each side staring at me in awe like I was Cary Grant.

"Thanks for coming, Denise. That's a long drive to make."

Her eyes were still dark and clear, and they sparkled as she spoke. "That's what family does. We're proud of you, Robert."

I took her hand in mine. Her skin was smooth and warm. "How have you been?" I asked.

"Same old. Every day a step closer to the graveyard." A wry smile lit her lips. "Old age ain't for sissies."

"Don't talk that way. You're not old," I said.

"Oh yes, I am, and proud of it. So how are my girls?"

"They're doing all right. Carson had her first violin recital last week."

"Yes. Allyson sent me pictures. She's growing like a weed. How is my darling Allyson doing with you being gone?"

"It's hard on her."

"And you?"

"It's hard on me too. It's lonely."

"How's your health?"

I felt as if I should be asking her. "I'm tired, but holding up."

"Well, don't overdo it." Her warm smile turned suddenly solemn. "We are all just so proud of you. But you be careful out there, Robert. There are a lot of Jezebels in this world. That family of yours is the most precious thing you have."

"That's for sure."

"That Allyson is one in a million. When she called, we talked about her coming out in the next few weeks. You don't mind, do you? You know I can't go too long without seeing my girl."

"Of course I don't mind."

Denise looked around. "Well, I've taken too much of your time. Your fans are getting restless. We better go before we cause a riot."

She introduced me to her friends and I shook their hands, though they also asked for hugs, which I obliged. Then I signed all their books. We took a snapshot with the four of us and hugged again. Then Denise said, "We brought you these." She handed me a paper plate covered in foil. "Believe it or not they're still warm—my chocolate chip and pecan cookies. I know how you love them."

"You're an angel," I said.

"Almost," she replied. "You take care and we'll see you again soon."

"You drive carefully, now."

"We will. Tell my Ally I'll be waiting to see her."

I went back to my table. As Denise hobbled off, I looked at her once more, and I had the sudden thought that I might never see her again. I quickly pushed the thought from my mind and started signing books.

Chapter 25

I found my anticipation of Wednesday afternoon growing, the day I received the first
news from the lists. Camille caught me on
my cell phone just minutes after I had arrived in Boise, Idaho. I was still in the airport
terminal and was following my escort to
baggage claim.

"*A Perfect Day* climbed to number seven.
You are cooking with gas, man."

"I'm working out here."

"It shows. You're in Idaho today?"

"Yep. My own private Idaho. Hold on,
here's my bag."

I pulled my suitcase from the carousel
then put the phone back to my ear.

"Where were we?" I asked.

"Idaho. Eat a potato for me."

"Why would I do that?"

"Idaho is the spud capitol of the America. You didn't know that?"

"Nope. Didn't know that."

"Man, I'm buying you an almanac. Go sign, or whatever it is that you do."

My escort took me directly to my hotel. It wasn't the Ritz Carlton, or even a Marriott, but it was convenient to the bookstore where I would be signing and it had a gym and a hot tub and the bed was good. Before my signing, I ate dinner at a nearby Applebee's with my escort, an elderly woman with hair a peculiar shade of lavender.

"Do you do much of this?" I asked.

"Every few months or so. We don't get that many national authors through Boise. The local ones don't need me."

"How's this bookstore I'm signing at?"

"You'll like it. It's a Borders superstore."

We finished eating, and as we pulled into the bookstore parking lot, my escort said, "The lot's full. That's a good sign."

I put on my jacket and we walked inside. Near the front of the store there was a small table draped with a crimson cloth and a neat stack of *A Perfect Day*. On an easel next to the table was a poster featuring my photograph and a picture of the book, under which were the words *Book Signing Today. 7–9.*

I groaned when I saw the table with no one around. Just when I thought I was establishing myself, another "no show." The store manager, a tall, gaunt man with a shaved head and a goatee, greeted us as we walked in. "Mr. Harlan, it's such a pleasure having you in our store. Your book has been just flying off the shelf."

"Thanks."

"My name is Troy, I'm the store manager. Before we begin, can I get you a drink? Perhaps an Italian soda from the café?"

Begin what? I thought. "Sure. An Italian soda sounds great. Cherry."

"I'll be right back with that."

When he returned, I took the drink then sat down at the table. After about five minutes Troy said, "There's no rush, but let me know when you're ready to start."

I looked at him. "I thought we had started already."

"I'm sorry, I thought you were going to speak."

"If someone comes, I'll be happy to say something."

He suddenly understood. "We've been sending people to the other side of the store."

"There are people waiting for me?"

He laughed. "Of course. People have been waiting for more than an hour."

"Let's go."

I followed him to the back of the store. I'll never forget what I saw. There was a broad, open area for readings, and additional bookshelves had been moved to accommodate more than a hundred chairs, all of which were filled. Just as many people were standing against the walls or between bookshelves. I heard an audible rise of excitement as I entered the area. It was a far cry from just two and a half weeks earlier when the only books I sold were to my escort. As I walked up to the podium, the crowd burst into applause. It was my first real taste of celebrity, and it was truly sweet. I guess I should have seen the danger that posed for a man who had struggled his whole life with self-doubt, but I was just too busy enjoying the moment.

I spoke for just a few minutes then sat down to sign a mountain of books. It took me nearly four hours to sign them all. I loved every minute of it. It was a night to remember. I couldn't wait to write about it in my diary.

At the end of the evening, as I walked out to the car, I suddenly felt a sharp pain rise up my stomach toward my chest. My heart began to flutter. I stopped walking and raised my hand to my chest. My escort took my arm. "What's wrong?"

The pain subsided almost as quickly as it had come. "I don't know what that was."

She looked concerned. "You look pale. We're not far from a hospital. I'll take you to Emergency."

"I'm okay. It's probably just something I ate."

"I insist."

I spent the next hour being poked and prodded by an Asian doctor named Frank. Dr. Frank couldn't find anything other than indigestion. He diagnosed the pain as probable reflux. By midnight I was back at my hotel. As I climbed into bed, I thought about

Chuck. He had suffered a heart attack at the age of forty. I had little desire to imitate any part of his life, but especially in this realm. Especially in matters of the heart.

Chapter 26

During the last week of my book tour I inexplicably found myself growing more anxious about returning home. I thought I could sense it in Allyson as well. Our phone conversations were shorter and there was less longing. I've heard it said that absence makes the heart grow *fungus*. It might be true.

But my feelings of anxiety all vanished the moment the pilot announced our descent into the Salt Lake valley. I was home again. I couldn't wait to see my girls.

Allyson and Carson were waiting for me right outside the jet way. Carson held a hand-drawn poster-board sign that read

Welcome Home, Daddy surrounded by stars and scribbled balloons.

Carson clapped when she saw me, dropped the poster and ran to me. I squatted down and lifted her in my arms, kissing her face a dozen or so times while she laughed. "I missed you, Daddy."

"I've missed you too, sister."

I carried her to Allyson.

"Hail, the conquering hero," she said, opening her arms.

I set Carson down and put both arms around Allyson and we kissed long and passionately. When we finally parted, she said, "You look great."

I smiled wide. "So do you. It feels good to have you in my arms again."

"I can't believe how much I've missed you," she said. "Take me home, cowboy."

Just then Allyson glanced away from me. Her smile changed. A woman stood a few feet away staring. "May I help you?" Allyson asked.

The woman looked directly at me. "Excuse me, I'm sorry to bother you, but could I have your autograph?"

I forced a smile. "Sure." I fished through

my pockets for a pen then signed the woman's airplane ticket.

"Thanks," she said as she ran off down the terminal.

On the drive from the airport Allyson said, "Yesterday I got a call from a writer from *Cosmopolitan* magazine. She was doing a story on the wives of romance writers. It wasn't pleasant. She asked me all sorts of personal questions. Now they want to come out and take pictures of our house."

"When are they coming?"

"They're not. I told them I'd have to think about it."

"What's there to think about? It's great publicity."

"I don't need publicity. It's none of their business what our home looks like. I share enough of you with the world." She exhaled and I realized how put off she felt by the attention. She continued in a weaker voice, looking out the window. "And to top it off, the writer said you're the only author she's contacted who is still married to his first wife. How is that supposed to make me feel?"

"I'm sorry," I said.

"I'm not trying to ruin anything. I just don't see what our house has to do with your book."

"It's publicity, Allyson. It's what drives book sales. There are hundreds of books out there just as good as mine that never get a chance to be seen." She was still frowning, and it bothered me that she didn't seem to care. "Let's talk about something else," I finally said.

"I have the next few days all planned out," Allyson said. "I'll start with tomorrow. We'll take Carson to Jungle Jim's. Then we're going to dinner tomorrow night with Nancy and her new boyfriend."

"Another one, huh?"

"I'm afraid so."

"What time are we having dinner?"

"Our dinner reservations are for seven."

I grimaced. "I have a book signing tomorrow night at seven."

Allyson looked like I had slapped her. "A book signing?"

"I thought you knew."

"How would I know that? I thought that you were *really* home."

"I am really home."

"Not if you're still on the book tour. Rob,

you've been gone a whole month. When do we get you?"

"Honey, I just have a few things. We can go out after the signing. Around nine."

Allyson shook her head. "Whatever."

"Don't be angry, Al. Every profession has its busy seasons. Think of it this way: if I were a farmer, this would be harvest time."

"You're not a farmer."

Carson said, "Can we get ice cream?"

"No," Allyson said. "We haven't had dinner."

"Can we get pizza?"

"No. I already have dinner at home."

Carson frowned. I glanced down at my watch. "I'm in the wrong time zone. What time is it, five?"

"Five after."

"Camille should have the *New York Times* list."

"She called while I was waiting at the airport."

"Camille called? Why didn't you tell me?"

Allyson looked at me. "Because it can wait. I'm demanding a little equal time, okay?"

"Of course. But it's not going to hurt to return Camille's call. She's your friend too." I fished my cell phone from my jacket's front pocket and handed it to Allyson. "Would you call her for me?"

Allyson shook her head as she dialed. "Hi, Camille, it's Ally. Rob's driving." Pause. "Sort of. Here, he needs to talk to you."

I took the phone. "Hey."

"Hey yourself. You're finally home."

"Finally."

"How's Ally? She sounded a little miffed."

"She just found out that I have a signing tomorrow."

Allyson rolled her eyes. She mouthed, *Thanks a lot.*

"Of course she's upset," Camille said. "She's missed you."

"I know. So what do you know?"

"A lot. You're going to like this. Are you sitting down?"

"I'm driving."

"I knew that. Okay, then don't crash. *A Perfect Day* is the number one book in America."

I shouted in triumph. I turned to Allyson. "We're number one."

Allyson's look of displeasure vanished into one of excitement. She squealed. "Congratulations."

Camille said, "Of course Arcadia is over the top. They've contacted all the Salt Lake media. You're going to have press at your signing tomorrow. They want you to show up at your book signing a half hour early."

"This is unbelievable."

"Believe it. Now go home and enjoy your family. While you can."

"What do you mean by that?"

"Don't worry about it now. I'll talk to you later."

As I handed the phone back to Allyson, I wondered what Camille had meant.

Chapter 27

I woke the next morning for a five o'clock interview with a Philadelphia radio station then went back to bed until eight. Allyson cuddled into me when I returned. "Where did you go?"

"Philadelphia."

"I rolled over for you and you were gone. It made me sad."

"I'm here now."

Carson woke an hour or so later. She came into our room carrying a blanket and a stuffed pink monkey. She climbed into our bed and pushed her way between us. "Carson, don't," Allyson said.

"I want to lay by Daddy."

Allyson groaned. "The competition for my husband never ends."

"Mommy said I could stay home from school 'cause you're home."

"Smart lady, your mommy." We tried to sleep, but Carson moved too much. Finally I said, "Come on, sister, you can help me make breakfast." I kissed Allyson on the forehead then climbed out of bed. I carried Carson out to the kitchen.

"What are we making?" she asked.

"My secret recipe French toast. You can be the egg stirrer."

In the kitchen I handed her a wooden spoon then cracked the eggs into the bowl for her. In addition to French toast, I made Allyson her favorite breakfast, a Denver omelet. I left Carson watching TV and brought Allyson's breakfast to the room. Allyson was still cocooned beneath the sheets.

"Are you going to sleep all day?"

"I feel like it."

"Well, my lady, breakfast is served." I turned on the nightstand lamp.

She looked at the food and smiled. "Thanks."

I handed her the plate then lay down next

to her. She sat up and started eating. "So what hours do I have you today?"

"All of them."

"Don't you have more interviews?"

"I have one. Fort Wayne, Indiana. But I can do it from a pay phone at Jungle Jim's."

"What about your book signing?"

"It starts at seven. But channel five is sending a film crew out so I need to be there by six-thirty or a little earlier."

"What time will you be through?"

"Hard to tell."

"Can you guess? We have to change our dinner reservation and let Nancy know when to meet us."

"Tell her nine-thirty. Two and a half hours should be enough time."

"So we'll take Carson to Jungle Jim's around two. Then tomorrow?"

"I am completely free tomorrow."

She looked relieved. "Good. Because I'm in charge of Carson's school book fair and I need all the help I can get. I was hoping that you could come."

"No problem."

"Can we go to the mall this morning? I've wanted to show you some new Christmas stoneware I'm trying to decide on."

"I'm all yours."

She set her plate on the nightstand and lay on her side next to me. "I'll hurry and get ready. Do you mind getting Carson ready?"

"Course not."

She leaned forward and kissed me. "Thank you for breakfast. You're so good to me."

"I thought it had probably been a while since you've had breakfast in bed."

"It's been a while since I've had *anything* in bed," she teased.

"Sorry," I said, "I was so exhausted last night." I pulled her into me and we kissed again.

"Where's Carson?" she asked.

"Watching TV."

Her lips rose in a sweet smile. "Why don't you lock the door?"

As I climbed out of bed, the phone rang. Allyson looked at the caller I.D. She sighed. "It's New York. You better get it."

I picked up the phone. It was Heather. Allyson crawled out of bed and got into the shower.

Chapter 28

"Sorry to call so early," Heather said.

"It's okay. We're already up."

"I have a few things to go over with you. First, what's this about a hospital visit in Boise?"

"She told you, huh?"

"She did. What happened?"

"Nothing. I just had some chest pains. They couldn't find anything. The doctor thought it might be reflux."

"Did you tell Allyson?"

"No. And I'd appreciate it if no one did. She has enough on her plate."

Heather still sounded anxious. "But you had it checked?"

"Yes. By a doctor. He gave me a clean bill of health."

"Just as long as you let me know if something else happens. We're not trying to kill you."

"I've heard otherwise, but I'll take your word for it. So what's up?"

"A lot. Congratulations on the list. As we expected, we're getting a lot of interest in you from the national press. I just got a call from *USA Today*. They want to interview you for tomorrow's best-seller list column. It's usually pretty simple, just two or three hundred words."

"*USA Today,* that's huge."

"It gets better. They want to run a front-page feature-section article on you in next Monday's edition."

I clapped. "Yeah, baby."

Heather laughed. "Yeah, this is every publicist's dream. To make tomorrow's deadline they're going to have to interview you in the next couple of hours."

"Oh."

"Is that bad?"

"Sort of. I just told Allyson that I'd go shopping with her."

"You still can. It won't take that long.

They're also going to have to get a photographer out there. How's your afternoon?"

"Not good, actually."

Now Heather was concerned. "We've got to work it in somehow. They won't give you the front page without the photo."

I grimaced as I thought about telling Allyson. "I'll work it out. Just find out when they can come."

USA Today arranged to send a photographer at one o'clock the following afternoon—during the middle of Allyson's book fair. I tried to talk them into shooting the photograph at the fair, but they were insistent that they wanted a shot in our home. Allyson wasn't pleased. The interviews ran longer than I told her they would and we never made it to the mall. I ended up taking Carson to Jungle Jim's by myself while Allyson stayed home and cleaned. She was in a worse mood by the time we returned. We left Carson with a teenage baby-sitter from our neighborhood and went to the signing. We arrived at the store a half hour early. I shut off the car and looked over to Allyson, who was smoldering.

"Are you coming in?"

"Should I?"

I sighed. "Come on, Ally." I got out and walked to her side of the car, but she got out before I could open her door. We crossed the parking lot together and walked into the store. There was already a long line of people that serpentined between bookshelves from the back of the store, almost reaching the front doors. The bookstore manager greeted us as we entered. "Howdy, I'm Brent. And I know who you are." He looked at Allyson. "And this lovely lady is your wife?"

"Allyson," she said.

"Welcome. Just look at this crowd," he said to me. "You must feel a little like a rock star."

"It's a little bigger than my first signing."

"I bet." Brent clapped his hands together. "You have some people here from channel five. There's also a photographer from the *Deseret News*, but he's just going to take pictures during the signing." Brent waved the television crew over. A man wearing a tweed jacket and accompanied by a cameraman stepped over. "Hi, Mr. Harlan, I'm Dan Smart from KSL television."

"We watch you all the time," I said.

"Thank you. We're running a piece on you for the ten o'clock news. I have just a few questions then we'll let you get to your fans."

"I'm ready when you are."

Allyson stood just a few feet from me but out of the camera shot. Dan looked back at his cameraman. "Ready?"

He nodded. Dan tilted his microphone toward me. "Robert, your story is the stuff dreams are made of. You write a book and watch it rocket to the top of the nation's best-seller lists. Are you surprised by what's happened to you?"

"Absolutely. It's like winning the lottery."

"Why do you think Americans are responding to your book the way they are?"

"*A Perfect Day* is a story about love and family, and I think, as a nation, we're hungry for this. I think we've strayed a little too far from our homes and families and we want to get back to something real."

I glanced over at Allyson. She was expressionless. Dan asked another ten questions or so, until Brent, who looked more anxious with each passing minute, stepped forward, pointing to his watch. "We better wrap this up before the crowd turns ugly."

"Sure. One last question. Now that you've hit the jackpot, do you plan to move from Salt Lake?"

"No, Salt Lake City is our home. We'll probably move to a better neighborhood."

He shook my hand. "Thank you. And congratulations."

"All right, this way," Brent said.

Allyson and I followed Brent along the perimeter of the store to the back, where the table was. Many of the people in line pointed at me as we passed.

"What's this about moving to a better neighborhood?" Allyson asked.

"Nothing. I just said what first came to mind."

"I'm sure our neighbors are going to be real pleased to know how highly you think of our neighborhood."

"Honey, we live in a box."

"I'm the one who spends all the time there. Certainly not you."

"We'll talk about it later." I sat down at the table with Allyson at my side. There was a stack of books on the table. "Are you ready?"

"What do I do?" Allyson asked.

I took a book from the stack to demonstrate. "First you open the book to the front page and tuck it into the flap like this. Then give the person a Post-it note for each book and ask them to write down the name of the person they want the book signed to."

"Simple enough." She looked around. From where we sat we could not see the end of the line. "They're pretty much all women here. Are your signings always like this?"

I sensed her discomfort. "Pretty much. My readers are women."

I realized that the reality of hordes of women waiting in line to meet her husband had eluded her until this moment. Brent sent the first woman in line to our table. One by one they filed by, asking for hugs or pictures and telling Allyson how fortunate she was to be married to such a sensitive man. A few even asked her if she wanted to swap husbands. She acted amused but she wasn't. After an hour she had had enough. One of the bookstore employees took her place while she went to call Nancy and sit in the café to nurse a cappuccino and wait.

Shortly after Allyson left, I looked up to see one of the few men in line. It was Stuart. It took me a moment to recognize him, as I hadn't seen him since I had left the station. He was dressed in Levi's and a sweatshirt and he looked older, though it was the kind of aging that comes from mileage, not time. He had gained weight and lost even more hair. He smiled when I looked at him, though his eyes showed his anxiety.

Although I was surprised that he had come to my signing, I wasn't all that surprised to see him. Salt Lake City may have a million people, but geographically it's still a small town. I knew it was only a matter of time before we bumped into each other. For months I had wondered what I would say at this moment. Now here he was—the personification of the daily desperation and vulnerability of my old life. Things I was all too glad to leave behind. Even though I was now on top, I still wasn't very happy to see him.

"What's up, Stu?"

"Hey, Rob. I saw that you were in town. I just wanted to stop by and say congratulations."

"Thanks," I said coolly.

"I read that article in the paper. You're famous."

"Whatever that means."

He glanced back at the line. "This is what it means. Just look at all these women. I had to wait in line for more than an hour. Hometown boy makes good. It's a good story." He scratched his head. "No one's called us at the station yet to have you on."

"You know how picky publicists can be. So how's Kathy?" I asked.

Stuart's expression fell. He said softly, "She left me."

"I'm sorry to hear that. And Stacey?"

"She's still around," he said in nearly the same tone.

The silence turned awkward.

I said, "You have a book?"

"Yeah. Could you sign it to Kathy? Maybe write—'from the man who loves you.' "

"If I write that she might think that *I'm* the man who loves her."

"Just sign it to Kathy. With a K." I signed the book then handed it back to him. He just stood there, as if there were something else he wanted to say. His anxiety grew even more apparent. "We were thinking that we'd like to play up our connection with you at the station—have you on the morning show. Help push your book a little."

"How ironic. The last thing you said to me was to get out of the station."

His eye twitched.

"You know, no other station in town would hire me after they talked to you. I couldn't get a job in radio to save my life. I ended up installing sprinklers."

Stuart swallowed. "Rob, I'm sorry about all that. I . . ."

I cut him off. "Don't worry about it. I'm just giving you a hard time. It was the best thing that every happened to me. If it hadn't had been for your firing me, I never would have written my book." I tapped my pen on the table then looked directly into his eyes. "So what really brings you here? One morning's ratings couldn't make that much of a difference."

I had touched the nerve.

"Sterling called. He wanted me to get you to come to the annual client Christmas party. You know the one we have at his house every year."

Though Stuart had always run the station as his own, every now and then Sterling Call, the station's owner, would issue a mandate, reminding everyone who really was in charge. Stuart's voice grew softer, more pleading. "I'll be honest. Things are pretty bad right now. We dropped again in the last book. I think Sterling is looking to sell the station or at the least toss me. He pretty much gave me an ultimatum to get you or go."

"So Stacey didn't turn things around for you after all. Or maybe she did, just not for the station."

Stuart's forehead furrowed. "I made a stupid mistake. C'mon, Rob. How about it? For old times' sake."

"Old times' sake," I repeated dryly. "Okay, I'll check with my publicist. For old times' sake. But don't get your hopes too high. She may think that associating with a non-progressing radio station might have a detrimental effect on my image."

Just then the bookstore manager said to Stuart, "I'm sorry, sir, but we have people waiting."

"See you around, Stu."

As he walked away, Brent said loud enough for Stuart to hear, "They come out of the woodwork, don't they?"

It was a quarter past ten when the line finally dwindled. That's when Brent informed me that there were two large stacks of phone-in orders waiting in the back room to be signed. It was nearly eleven when I finished the signing. I found Allyson sitting alone on a couch at the side of the store perusing a stack of cookbooks. She was upset.

"Ready for dinner?"

"I told Nancy and Steve to go ahead without us."

"Maybe we could still join them for dessert." I took her hand. "Come on. Let's get out of here."

In the car I said, "Stuart came tonight."

"To get a book signed?"

"That and help him save his job. Sterling Call wanted him to get me to come to their annual Christmas party."

"Are you going?"

"Are you kidding? After what he did to us?"

Allyson was quiet for a moment. "Maybe you should turn the other cheek."

"Easy for you to say. You're not the one who got slapped. I say let him get what he deserves."

Allyson frowned. "By the way, Camille called while you were signing."

"What did she want?"

"She said to tell you that the *Today* show wants you on next Monday."

I raised a fist in triumph. "Yeah, baby. the *Today* show. This is what we've been waiting for."

Allyson didn't even smile. "Will they film you here?"

"No. It's in New York."

"I thought so. That means not only do I not have you today, but you're leaving again."

I turned angrily. "Enough of this, Al. All you've done since I got home is complain. You're mad because I've been gone. You're mad because I want to buy you and Carson a nicer house. You're mad because I didn't embrace the guy who stabbed us in the back. You're mad because I made us late for the dinner appointment you set up without checking with me. And now you're mad because the best possible thing that could happen to my book just happened. Can you just relax and enjoy some of this? Or at least fake it so that I can?"

She looked down but said nothing.

"Allyson, I'm not in control of my life right now. But good things are happening. Things I've hoped my entire life for. And I'm here in part because you encouraged me to chase this dream. What did you think this dream would look like? Did you think success would just happen without any sacrifice?"

I went back to my driving. She touched the corner of her eye. A mile from the restaurant she said, "I'm sorry, Rob. I guess that I'm just afraid of losing you."

I said in a gentler voice, "I love you, honey. You're not going to lose me. This isn't going to be forever. In fact, why don't you come to New York with me for the show? It will be our second honeymoon. And when it's over we'll come home and have a nice, calm holiday without a care in the world."

She looked pleased by this. "I'm sure Nancy would take Carson for a few days."

"Great. I'll have Heather arrange the flight."

"When we get back, can you stay with Carson while I visit Aunt Denise?"

"I'd love to. Now can we be nice to each other? Please."

"I'll be good," she said.

"I'll be good too."

Nancy and her date were gone by the time we arrived at the restaurant. We stopped at a Wendy's on the way home.

Chapter 29

Allyson had never been to New York, and as the limo crossed the George Washington Bridge, she seemed as full of awe as a child. "Where's the Statue of Liberty?"

"You can't see it from here." I pointed south toward the Battery. "Camille lives down that way."

"Do you think I should call Nancy?"

"Why?"

"Make sure Carson's being good?"

"Carson's always good," I said.

"I miss her."

It was a forty-five-minute drive into the city, and it was nearly six o'clock when the limousine stopped at the front curb of the hotel. The *Today* show had put us up at the Essex House, directly across from Central Park. Our suite was bigger than the upstairs of our home. At least it had more bathrooms.

I put my arm around Allyson as we stood at the registration desk. "You have no idea how nice it is checking into a hotel and not being alone."

"I haven't been in a hotel since our honeymoon," she said.

"You've got to get out more."

The clerk handed me a piece of paper. "You have a message, sir."

I read it.

"Who's that from?" Allyson asked.

"It's from Heather. It just says that a car from NBC will be out front at five-thirty tomorrow."

"Five-thirty. What time are you on?"

"I don't know. Sometime before nine. Then we'll have breakfast and afterward Arcadia is hosting a toast to yours truly." I took the key and then Allyson's hand. "So we have the night to ourselves. What do you want to do?"

She smiled. "Are you serious?"

*　　*　　*

Early the next morning a stretch limousine was waiting for us out front of the hotel. We climbed in back and drove to the NBC studios near Radio City Music Hall. A hostess led us to the green room. There were others in the room waiting for their segments. I was taken to the makeup room and returned to find Allyson engaged in a discussion with Deepak Chopra, whom she had never heard of and afterward felt stupid that she hadn't. My interview took less than five minutes, and when it was done, I returned to makeup to have my face removed. Camille met us outside the studio. "You were great," she said to me. "I was having my hair cut, and everyone in the salon was saying how cute you are."

"Cute, huh?" Allyson said.

Camille put her arm around Allyson. "Cute is good, Ally. Cute sells books." She looked at her watch. "We have four hours before the champagne toast, so I thought you'd probably want to get some breakfast and then you have time to go back to your room and rest or go shopping, whatever you want. There's a great little place up here, the Stardust Diner. The decor is New York subway. They have great oatmeal and breakfast shakes. Or there's Sarabeth's up on Madison Avenue."

"Doesn't matter," I said. "What do you want, Ally?"

Allyson was captivated by it all. "Whichever is more New York-ish."

"Stardust it is," Camille said, grinning.

After breakfast the women elected to go shopping so we walked over to Saks Fifth Avenue. Allyson walked through the store but didn't buy anything, suffering from a sort of sticker shock. We walked farther up Fifth and the women talked and laughed, and Camille and I finally convinced Allyson that it would be all right to spend some money. She bought a Chanel purse, which she confessed she had secretly coveted. At a quarter of noon we took a cab downtown to the Arcadia Publishing building.

In the back of the cab Allyson said, "Tell me about this toast."

"It's a champagne toast to celebrate the success of my book."

"Who will be there?"

"Everyone at Arcadia who has worked on the book."

Camille said, "This will be your first time

meeting Sandra. She's the head of Arcadia."

Allyson asked, "Am I dressed okay?"

"Yes. It's casual," Camille said, "and everyone's really nice."

"Besides, we're the guests of honor," I said. "They have to be. Then afterwards we'll go to the Metropolitan Museum, where you can see the Monets and Van Goghs you've been dying to see."

Allyson looked as happy as a schoolgirl on a field trip. "This is such an amazing town."

"And there's more," I said. "Camille has a surprise."

"I had to pull some strings," Camille said, "but we have dinner reservations at the Four Seasons."

Allyson said, "Sounds wonderful." Then she laid her head on my shoulder. "It's just so good to be with you."

The Arcadia conference room was noisy and crowded: filled with employees from different divisions of the publishing house, some I had met, more that I had not. The chairs had all been pushed under the table, and the tabletop was bare except for four bottles of champagne, plastic champagne glasses and three large stacks of my book. I could tell that Allyson felt a little intimidated by it all. Camille sensed Allyson's anxiety and stayed close to her. I was glad for Camille's presence.

Sandra noticed us as we entered the room and plowed through the crowd to greet us.

"Welcome, welcome, Robert." She kissed my cheek then turned to Allyson. "You must be Allyson. I'm Sandra."

"Sandra is the boss around here," I said.

Allyson smiled. "It's a pleasure to meet you."

"It's my pleasure. I've looked forward to meeting you since I first read the book. I'm an Oregon girl myself. I was born in Lake Oswego, just outside of Portland."

"Really? I have a second cousin who lives in Lake Oswego."

"It's a beautiful part of the world," Sandra said.

"Hi, Sandra," Camille said.

Sandra nodded. "Ms. Bailey, I'd say we've done well with your author."

"Yes we have," Camille said sparingly.

Sandra turned to an employee who was

standing nearby waiting to meet us. "Kim, we need some champagne for the Harlans."

"Of course." Kim took two glasses from the table. As she handed me my glass, Sandra said, "Kim is the graphic designer who designed the cover for *A Perfect Day*."

Kim said to me, "It's good to finally meet you. Congratulations."

"Congratulations to you as well. Everyone loves the cover. Especially Allyson."

"You did a beautiful job," Allyson said.

"Thank you. You're Rob's wife?"

"Yes."

"It's nice to meet you."

Sandra walked to the center of the room. "Your attention please. Your attention please." The room settled at the sound of her voice. "I would like to propose a toast." She waited until the last of the rumblings had died then raised her glass. "First, Robert, you did a magnificent job on the *Today* show this morning. We are all very proud to be associated with you. So here's your toast. To Robert Harlan, our newest number one best-selling author. May it be the first of many. And may there be many, many more perfect days."

"Here, here," Camille said.

Everyone applauded.

"Thank you," I said.

A moment later Sandra took me aside. "I understand that the tour has gone well."

"It gained momentum."

"Amen to that. Your sales are increasing nicely moving into the holidays. Which is good since there are a few big authors about to release. It's a tough fall lineup. But it's always tough. There are some things we want to do to keep you on top of the heap. Heather will get with you before you leave."

I looked around the room. "In the meantime," I said, "we're going to find someplace to sit."

Sandra put her hand on my back. "Don't get too comfortable, you have books to sign."

I rejoined Allyson and Camille, and we sat down near the back of the room. Ten minutes later Heather walked up to me. I stood and gave her a hug. "Welcome back, world traveler. Congratulations."

"Thanks."

"We tried to lose you out there but you just kept coming back."

I laughed. "I thought so. Heather, this is

my wife, Allyson. Heather's the one you can blame for taking me from home."

"Thank you, Rob," Heather said sarcastically. "Now that she hates me." She turned to Allyson. "We've talked on the phone a dozen times, but it's a pleasure to finally meet you in person. Robert has told us so much about you."

"Thank you for taking such good care of him. He says you treat him like a VIP."

"Around here he is a VIP." She said to me, "We need to talk before you leave. I've scheduled some phone interviews for you this afternoon if you don't mind. Both *Time* and *Newsweek* are doing stories. *Time* wants to send a photographer to the lobby of your hotel in an hour."

I looked over at Allyson. "Looks like I have to work."

"I'm sorry," Heather said. "Did you have plans?"

Camille stepped in. "It's okay, Ally. We'll go to the Met without him. Then we'll go shopping for you and Carson and spend all the money Rob just made."

Allyson smiled. "Serves him right."

"If Carson likes Barbies, there's an FAO

Schwarz that has an entire floor of Barbies. We'll go crazy."

"Where will we meet up?" I asked.

"Let's meet back at the hotel at six. Our dinner reservation is for six-thirty."

"He should be done by then," Heather said. "By the way, where would you like us to send your fan mail?"

"I have fan mail?"

A subtle smile lit her lips. "A bit."

"Just send it to my home."

Camille turned to Allyson. "Ready to blow this joint?"

Allyson nodded then kissed my cheek. "I'll see you later, honey."

The women left, leaving me alone to sign books.

Chapter 30

We ate dinner at the Four Seasons, an elegant midtown restaurant and a favorite among publishing's elite. Allyson commented that it was the nicest restaurant that she had ever been in. Certainly the most expensive. "I could buy a week's groceries for the cost of our meals," she said.

When we got back to the hotel, Allyson went to the phone and called home to check on Carson. From what I understood from the conversation Carson was already asleep and Nancy asked for a blow-by-blow account of the day's events.

While they talked on the phone, I undressed and lay back on the bed, surfing through channels on the television. When

Allyson hung up the phone, I turned off the TV. "Finally we're alone. Come here, Al."

"Just a minute," she said, smiling. She went into the bathroom and took out her contacts and undressed. When she emerged, she was wearing one of the hotel's robes. She ran her hands down the sides of it. "These are comfortable."

"Come here, gorgeous." She kneeled over me on the bed, and I slipped the robe down over her shoulders. We began to kiss. Then she lay on her back and sighed.

"Tell me I can do this, Rob."

"Do what?"

"Champagne toasts, *Time* magazine, the *Today* show." She let out a small gasp of exasperation. "Your world is so big."

"We're just us. That will never change."

Suddenly her eyes moistened and she turned away. I didn't understand.

"Honey, what's wrong?"

"Promise me that no matter what happens, no matter how big your world gets, you'll never leave me."

I lifted slightly up from her. "Why did you say that?" I asked gently.

"It's what always happens when someone gets famous. They move on."

"I'm not famous. And nothing's going to happen."

"I already feel like something is happening—like there are forces trying to pull us apart."

"I'll never leave you, Al. I don't think I could."

"Why not?"

I put my hand on her chin and gently turned her face toward me. Her cheeks were streaked with tears. I brushed them back then said, "Because losing you would be like cutting off my air supply."

She smiled at this.

"My world would be nothing without you, Al. You're everything."

She looked into my eyes. "Promise?"

"Yes." I gently caressed her face with my hand. She closed her eyes and I softly drew my finger across her eyelids then down the bridge of her nose to her full lips. I circled her lips with my finger then leaned over and kissed her. We kissed for a long while. Then I said, "I'll get the lights."

I got up and turned off the lights then crawled back into bed. I pulled Allyson to me and she sighed with pleasure.

"When was the last time I told you how much I love you?" I asked.

"About thirty seconds ago," she replied happily.

"Then I—"

She stopped me by putting her finger on my lips. "Enough words," she whispered. "Just love me."

I fell into her embrace, dissolving into her warmth and softness, until nothing else in the world existed or mattered but my beautiful wife and the sweetness of her love.

Chapter 31

The next morning I woke Allyson with a kiss and a rose, holding the flower inches from her nose until she woke. She smiled sleepily. "Where did you get that?"

"From the breakfast tray. I ordered room service."

She looked around. "What time is it?"

"Ten something."

"Oh my goodness. I don't remember the last time I slept in this late."

"It's only eight in Salt Lake."

She sighed. "Last night was wonderful."

I smiled. "Oh yes." I kissed her then took her hand. "Come eat before your breakfast gets cold."

She climbed out of bed. We sat at a linen-covered table that had been wheeled in. I lifted the silver plate warmers from the food.

"One Denver omelet, hash browns and English muffins. Your favorites."

"Everything looks delicious." She lifted a knife and spread orange marmalade across her bread. "Did I hear the phone ring?"

"An hour ago. I got some exciting news," I said.

"You get more exciting news than anyone I know."

"There's a literary club in Orange County called Roundtable West. They've had everyone from Walter Cronkite to Richard Nixon speak to them. They just invited me to come out and speak. And guess who's on the program with me?"

"I can't."

"Senator Dole and Bob Hope."

She shook her head. "I can't believe your life. When is it?"

"The day after tomorrow."

Her smile fell. "Then you won't be coming home with me today?"

"No, I'll fly direct from here."

"And then you'll be home?"

"I have that speaking engagement for the National Society of Readers in Sacramento on Friday, so Arcadia plans to just keep me in California."

Her frown grew. "And then you're home?"

I didn't answer, and Allyson immediately knew that I was hedging. "What's up, Rob?"

"They want me to go back out on the road."

Allyson calmly laid down her utensils. "When did you find this out?"

"Heather told me last night. She says she has a stack of media requests on her desk four inches high."

"You've already toured."

"I know, honey. But now is the time when it will really pay off."

"It did pay off. You hit number one. What more do you want?"

"As much as I can get. Stopping now would be like running a marathon and quitting on the last mile."

"But your book is already number one. There's no place else to go."

"Arcadia thinks I can double my sales."

She stood and walked away from the table. "I can't believe this. You told me that we'd go home and have a nice, calm holiday. You told me that I could go see Aunt Denise this week."

"I also told you that I'm not in control of my life right now."

"Then don't promise things that you can't deliver." She went to the bathroom and locked the door behind her.

I walked to the door. "Come on, Ally. It comes with the territory. It's just our life."

"It's not our life, it's *your* life. This has nothing to do with me or Carson."

"Well, it should. You should be excited about this. Any other wife would be."

She opened the door. "Any other wife? Are you talking about someone in particular?"

"No," I said angrily. "But the women I meet at my signings certainly would."

"Then I guess you'd be better off with one of them, wouldn't you?" She shut the door again.

I groaned. "You're driving me crazy." I grabbed some clothes from my suitcase and headed for the door. "I'm going to the gym."

Chapter 32

The universal weight set was cathartic. I couldn't remember the last time I had lifted so much weight. When I returned, Allyson was lying on the bed staring at the ceiling. She had changed her clothes, and her suitcase was packed and sitting next to the door. She didn't speak to me. I went in and showered and dressed. When I came out, she said, "Camille will be here in twenty minutes. You don't have to go to the airport with me."

I sat down on the bed next to her. "Are we going to make up before you go?"

"I'm too tired to do it again."

I stood. "I'm going with you to the airport." I left the room alone. I took our luggage downstairs and waited in the lobby. It was raining outside and the air felt damp. Camille arrived about the same time Allyson came down. I put Allyson's bag in the trunk then climbed in the back of Camille's car. Camille immediately sensed the tension between us, and on the way there she and Allyson spoke casually to defuse the awkwardness. I sat in the back quietly.

When we arrived at the airport, I checked Allyson's bag at the curb then walked with her into the terminal. We stopped outside of Security. "When will I see you again?" she asked. Her voice had softened.

"I'm afraid to say."

"When can I see Aunt Denise?"

"You can go now."

"Who would watch Carson?"

"How about Nancy?"

"Nancy works during the day. Besides she's been watching her the last two days already."

"Why don't you take Carson with you?"

"She has too much going on at school right now."

"Then we'll just have to wait."

"I hope she can," Allyson said. "She's been really sick this last week."

I frowned. "I'm really sorry, Al. I don't mean to keep letting you down."

She looked down for a moment then up into my eyes. "I know. It's just hard." We kissed. Then I waited until she had passed through Security. She smiled at me from the other side of the screening and blew me a kiss. But there was sadness behind it. There was distance between us that I had never felt before. I walked back to the car and slid into the front seat next to Camille. She pulled away from the curb.

"Want to talk about it?" she asked.

"Not really."

"Don't worry. She'll get used to it."

I looked over at Camille. "That's what I'm afraid of."

Chapter 33

I left New York at eight A.M. the next morning and changed planes at the Delta hub in
Salt Lake City. I only had an hour between
flights, and I didn't really feel like I was
home. Just another airport. My flight landed
at John Wayne International shortly before
noon. I felt dizzy. When I left New York, there
had been freezing rain and turbulence, and
the first half hour of the flight made me airsick. I had my laptop with me and finally
caught up on my diary. I vowed not to get
behind again.

It was warm when I got off the plane. I
was overdressed for Southern California. I
claimed my suitcase and walked out to the
curb, where a gray stretch limousine was

waiting for me. The chauffeur was wearing a uniform. He recognized me and walked out to get my bag. "Are you Mr. Harlan, sir?"

"Yes, I am."

"Pleasure to meet you, sir. I'm Barry, your driver."

As we pulled away from the curb, he asked, "Have you done Roundtable before?"

"No. This is my first time."

"They hold their meeting at the Balboa Beach Yacht Club. You'll enjoy yourself. Nice folks."

I didn't respond. I still felt a little airsick from the ride, and I lay down across the seat and shut my eyes. A half hour later the limousine let me off in front of the yacht club. I had arrived ten minutes after the event was to begin, and while a few guests were still at the registration table, most of the people were already seated for lunch. A woman stopped me at the door.

"Excuse me, sir. Do you have a ticket?"

"No." Just then a woman with striking red hair and Gucci-framed eyeglasses stepped up to me.

"It's okay, Janice, Mr. Harlan is one of our

celebrities." She smiled warmly. "You're so young to be so successful."

"I guess luck can strike at any age."

"And humble too. A rare virtue in these parts. I'm Margaret Burke. I run Roundtable. Thanks for coming at the last minute. I know you were cutting it close with your flight."

"It wasn't too bad. My flight was a little late. New York wasn't quite as balmy as it is here."

"It never is. We've already started serving lunch. We have a seat reserved for you up front with our other celebrities, if you'll follow me."

We walked into the dining room. The room was spacious and crowded. There were several hundred attendees, mostly women, all elegantly dressed. Margaret led me over to my table. I was seated directly across from Bob Hope, his publicist and his wife Dolores. At the table next to us was Senator Bob Dole and several of his aides.

Margaret introduced me to the Hopes. Dolores smiled pleasantly, while Mr. Hope only looked up when Dolores told him to. I wasn't offended. I couldn't help but wonder how many thousands of times this had taken place for them and how old it must

212 RICHARD PAUL EVANS

get. We shook hands. "Pleased to meet you," I said.

Mr. Hope replied, "Do you know whose place you took on the program?"

"No, sir."

"Raquel Welch. So I won't say that I'm pleased you're here."

I chuckled. "My father is a very big fan of yours. You performed for his outfit during World War Two."

"Then your father has my admiration. You give him my best."

"I will, sir."

I wondered what Chuck would think to see me here at the same table as one of his greatest heroes. It was one of his dreams to meet Bob Hope. Chuck hated celebrities—he considered them un-American leftist ingrates—but Bob Hope, Jimmy Stewart and John Wayne were exceptions. I remember at a young age sitting in my room and hearing "Thanks for the Memories" from the Bob Hope television special and Hope's voice followed by Chuck's laughter. These were magical moments in our home. Chuck didn't often laugh. It was as if Mr. Hope had some strange authority to grant Chuck permission to chuckle: I think he felt that laughing at Hope was a patriotic duty of sorts.

Margaret introduced the speakers, pointing out that we were all "Bobs." I was the first on the program, which was fine with me. I had little desire to follow Hope or Dole. I spoke about my book, and to my surprise, the emotion in the room ran strong. It was a generous audience and I noticed a few of the women taking Kleenex from their handbags. Our time was limited to fifteen minutes apiece, but I only took ten. Even though I had the number one book in the country, I was still relatively unknown and I had few delusions that anyone in the audience had come for me, especially since I had been invited only a few days previously.

When we had finished speaking, we stayed at the head table and the members of the club lined up in front of us to have their books signed. At the end of my line was one of the few men in the audience. He was what Allyson would call a *natty dresser*. He wore a dark, pin-striped suit with a bright red power tie. He was tall, maybe six-two with the large shoulders of a linebacker. He exuded confidence, a sort of inevitability that comes to those who become accustomed to getting what they want. He wore a broad, likeable smile as he stepped up to me.

"Mr. Harlan, you handle yourself well with the ladies. You had them all in tears."

"Thank you."

"I have the same effect on women but for different reasons." He extended his massive hand. "Darren Scott, the Summit Agency."

"It's a pleasure."

"I have two copies of your book, one for Vanessa, the other for Julia."

I signed the books then handed them back to him.

"Thank you," he said. "Your book is going to translate well to the big screen. You haven't sold the film rights yet, have you?"

"Actually I have."

He shook his head and frowned. "Scooped again. Who's the lucky studio? Warner? Paramount?"

"Actually we sold it to television."

He looked stricken. "Oh, don't tell me that. Anything but that."

I felt foolish. "Why?"

"You need an agent, my friend."

"I have an agent. Camille Bailey of Argent Literistic."

"And she advised you to settle for television?"

I felt embarrassed to be a party to such apparent incompetence. "None of the studios were interested."

"They're always interested in making money. You just need to know how to play them. With your book the key would be to attach the script to a big name, a Julia Roberts or Sandra Bullock. I could have done that for you with one arm behind my back."

Suddenly I felt sick inside.

"Who did you say your agent is?"

"Camille Bailey."

His brow furrowed. "Camille Bailey. Haven't heard of her. And I know everybody who is anybody." He handed me a card. "How long are you in town?"

"I fly out of LAX Thursday afternoon, but I'm staying in Beverly Hills until then.

"I live in Beverly Hills. Do you have a dinner engagement for tonight?"

"Just room service."

"Why don't we go out to dinner?"

"Sounds nice."

"Good. You're staying where?"

"At the Beverly Wilshire."

"I know the number. I'll call and let you know where and when."

As he walked away, I felt as if I'd just been invited to a whole new world. And Darren Scott knew the way.

Chapter 34

I arrived at the Beverly Wilshire shortly before five. There was a message waiting for
me from Darren Scott. Our reservation was
at seven-thirty at Le Dolce, a haute Italian
restaurant within walking distance from the
Wilshire. Darren assured me that I wouldn't
be disappointed as the restaurant catered
to a celebrity clientele.

I connected my computer to the Internet
and pulled up my email. I answered a few
letters then caught up in my diary. I still had
time, so I began searching the Internet for
homes. I found a Salt Lake real estate service specializing in luxury homes and began
looking through their listings.

I found exactly what I was looking for—a

six-bedroom home on the east bench of the valley. It had a dark brick exterior with a gabled roof and a turret topped with a finial. It had all the creature comforts a human could hope for, including a home theater system with a large-screen television, theater chairs and surround sound audio. It had two kitchens (one for entertaining), a sauna, a steam room, a Jacuzzi tub in the master, hand-carved stair rails and walk-in closets in every bedroom. Closets are a big deal with Allyson. For years I kidded her that our home has walk in closets, you just can't go that far once you're inside.

Judging from the picture on the website, the yard was lushly landscaped, with cobblestone walks and statuary. There was a swimming pool and a tennis court in the backyard, and the front yard overlooked the Salt Lake Valley. The home was situated at the end of a private drive, with an electric gate. The only thing missing was a price. I scrawled the agent's name and number then called.

"This is Chris."

"My name is Robert Harlan. I'm on the Internet right now and looking at a home you represent on Fairfax Court."

"Oh yes, the Stringham mansion. That is a beautiful home. We just listed it yesterday."

"How much are they asking?"

"Frankly not enough. Only seven and a half. They're practically giving it away."

The idea of three-quarters of a million dollars being a "giveaway" seemed ridiculous. But from what I could see it looked like it was worth it.

"Would it be possible to see it?"

"I'm available this afternoon if that's convenient for you."

"Actually it's not. I'm calling from Beverly Hills."

This seemed to please him. "Oh yes, many of our clients are from Beverly Hills. Are you relocating to Utah?"

"No, I'm from Utah. I'm just here today on business."

"Would you mind if I asked what business you're in?"

"I'm an author."

"Of course," he said, his voice slightly animating. "I had wondered if you were *the* Robert Harlan, but I didn't want to say anything. I haven't read your book yet, but my wife has. She loved it. She'll be thrilled to know we spoke. Now, what day would be most convenient for you, Mr. Harlan?"

"I'm flying home next Sunday around four."

"I would be happy to pick you up from the airport."

"Thank you, but my wife will be there. But we could come directly from the airport."

"Excellent. Let me give you the directions."

Chris spelled out the way to the home and we hung up. I looked at the house again. It was much more house than we needed. I suppose that it wasn't really a house I was looking for. Maybe it was vindication. Or, perhaps, proof positive that Chuck Harlan's son was not a failure. With a home like that not even Chuck himself could dispute it. I couldn't wait to see the house. I couldn't wait to see Allyson's face when she saw it.

Chapter 35

The walk from the hotel took longer than I had expected and I arrived at the restaurant five minutes late. The restaurant's lobby was dark and lit by flickering sconces that were mounted on the walls next to oak trellises wrapped with grape vines. There was Italian opera music softly playing. I approached the maître d'. He was an older Italian man, good-looking, bald with a goatee. Next to him stood a young, dramatic-looking blond woman, model slender and wearing a silk periwinkle gown that almost matched her lipstick. The maître d' glanced toward me then went back to his reservation book. After I had stood in front of his table for about a minute, he looked up at me. "May I help you?"

"I have a seven-thirty reservation."

"Your name please?"

"It's Robert Harlan. I'm with Darren Scott."

His expression changed at the mention of Darren's name. "Of course. Mr. Scott is already seated." He turned to the woman. "Jeanette, please escort Mr. Harlan to Mr. Scott's table."

"Certainly." She smiled at me. "Follow me, please."

Darren Scott was seated at what must have been the most desirable table in the restaurant, a secluded corner table overlooking the lake. He stood as I approached.

"Robert. Thanks for making time to join me. I know how tight these book tours are. You practically have to schedule a potty break."

"Pretty much."

"Have you been to Le Dolce before?"

"No. I've never been to Beverly Hills before."

"It's not easy getting reservations here unless you know someone."

"And you know someone?"

He smiled broadly. "I know everyone. But that's my business." He gestured to my chair. "Have a seat."

A waiter immediately appeared at our table. "*Buona sera,* Mr. Scott."

"Good evening, Enrico."

He poured water into our crystal goblets, put my napkin in my lap and presented us menus. He handed the leather wine list to Darren. After he left, Darren said, "Your book is just amazing. I read *A Perfect Day* a week ago on a flight to New York. I'm not exactly the sentimental type, but it's one of those books that you wish you were alone when you read it so you could bawl your eyes out. You really have talent."

I smiled. "Thanks."

Another waiter approached us. "Good evening, Mr. Scott. Have you gentlemen had time to decide on your meals?"

I nodded and Scott gestured for me to order first. "I'll have the Pasta Florentine with white truffle oil."

Darren nodded as if impressed with my selection.

"And for you, Mr. Scott?"

"I'll have the same."

The waiter walked away.

"I'll order anything Florentine," he said. "We filmed the sequel to *Silence of the Lambs* in Florence. I left addicted to Chianti and white truffles and five pounds heavier." He took a drink of wine. "So tell me, how's Arcadia treating you?"

"They've been great."

"The author has the luxury of being friends with the publisher. It's a different world for an agent. Do you know what's the difference between a terrorist and a publisher?"

"No."

"You can negotiate with the terrorist," he said, a grin crossing his face. "So how about your agent. Camille Bagley?"

"Bailey. With Argent Literistic."

He had the same concerned look he had earlier. "How do you think she's doing?"

"I think she's doing all right. She got me a book deal, didn't she?"

"I'll give her that. Of course with a book like yours my grandmother could have gotten a book deal for you."

"She's the only one who did. I received more than twenty rejection letters."

"You never sent me a copy of your book."

"No. I didn't."

Darren took a drink of his wine. "How long is your contract with her?"

"Actually we don't have one. She doesn't believe in them."

He nodded casually, though I could tell this information pleased him.

"Did she consult with you before she threw away the motion picture rights?"

"I wouldn't say she threw them away."

He raised a hand. "Please, don't get me wrong. It's a huge accomplishment for a first-time writer to get anything produced. But to be candid, *A Perfect Day* was written for the big screen not the little one. I don't know how long your agent has been in this field, but it's really a rookie mistake. She should have held out. I would have sold the feature rights. No question. And you would have had A-list stars playing the roles, maybe Newman as the father, Julia Roberts or that hot newcomer Naomi Watts as the young Allyson." He took a drink of wine. You easily lost a million dollars going with television. But more important than that, you might have jeopardized your career."

Just then the waiter returned with our salads. After he left, I asked, "How did I jeopardize my career?"

"By losing the prestige that comes from making the big screen. Think of all the big-name authors. What was it that pushed them to the next level? They signed movie deals. "

"You think she made a mistake?"

"To put it mildly. But it happens. I'm sure this Bagley is a nice lady, but at the end of the day a million bucks is still a million bucks. Eventually it adds up to some real money."

"You don't think she's qualified?"

"I didn't say that. To get you started, I think she was fine. Some people make great bird dogs. But now I think she's out of her league. You're a rocket right now. Rockets have several stages. The first stage gets you out of the atmosphere; then it falls off and the next booster ignites."

"And you're the next booster?"

"I can get you to the stars." His face was filled with confidence. "It would be a shame to see your career fizzle due to someone else's lack of experience. You've worked too hard to get to where you are."

I picked at my salad. "I don't think I could leave her."

"I thought you said you didn't have a contract with her."

"I don't. But she's a friend."

"Since when do friends cost you a million dollars?"

I looked down at my food.

"Listen, change is part of this industry. It's not a matter of friendship; it's a matter of smart business. That's why they call it the publishing *business*. Let me put it this way: if you stopped selling books, do you think this Bagley would still be out there pounding doors for you?"

"I don't know." I looked up. "But you've heard the saying *Dance with who brung you to the dance.*"

Darren chuckled. "Of course. And if you believe that, you're going to waste a lot of time dancing with ugly women." He took a bite of his salad and chewed it slowly. When he'd finished, he said, "I've been in this business a long time, Rob. I've seen hundreds of authors come and go. There are those who flash by like a falling star and are gone. Then there are those who stick. They become the stars that society uses to chart their journey. You're big right now, Rob, huge. I think you're bigger than anyone realizes. Including you. You have the potential to change millions of lives for the better. What a gift. How many people can actually say they changed the world? The difference between the flashes and the stars is that the stars know when to cut ties and they have the courage to do it. Things change. I know. I've the ex-wives to prove it."

"How many times have you been married?"

"Too many." He laughed. "Of course there's an argument that once is too many."

"I'm happily married," I said.

He nodded. "I thought I was happily married."

"What happened?"

"It started with the little resentments: the time away, the lack of attention, the female colleagues. Pretty soon she's treating you like the furniture. Actually, worse. At least the furniture gets polished once a week. Make no mistake, you'll get all the blame for it. But at the heart of it all is her jealousy. It ends in court with a stack of papers marked *mine* and *yours*." He shook his head. "You're a lucky man if it's all smooth sailing."

"Actually things are a little rocky right now."

Darren frowned. "I'm sorry. And people think fame and fortune is the Holy Grail. Listen, Robert, no one can tell you what to do because it's your decision. But what you need to decide is how big you want to be. And how much of an impact you want to have on the world. Because the world is yours if you have the courage to take it." He leaned back in his chair. "Or in this case maybe you need to decide what you don't want to happen. Because you could always end up back in Utah digging ditches for sprinklers." He poured his glass full with wine. "I've seen worse happen."

After a minute I said, "I'll think about it."

Chapter 36

When I got back to the Wilshire, my phone's message light was flashing. Allyson had left a voice message. Her voice was strained and I could tell that she had been crying, but all she said was to call as soon as possible. I frantically dialed home.

"Ally?"

"This is Nancy. Is that you, Rob?"

"Yes. What's the matter?"

"You better speak with Allyson. She's right here."

Allyson took the phone. "Rob?"

"What's wrong, honey?"

"Aunt Denise died last night."

Her words stunned me. "When did you find out?"

"This afternoon." Allyson started to cry. "She was like a mother to me."

I felt sick with guilt. Even though she didn't say it, we both knew that had I not gone straight to California, Allyson would have been at her aunt's side—she would have had one last chance to say everything she needed to. "When is the funeral?" I asked.

"Friday. When can you be there?"

"I don't know." I looked down at my watch. "It's one o'clock in New York. I'll call Heather in the morning and have her check on flights."

We talked a few more minutes but my words were weak. I groaned as I hung up. Guilt continued to cascade over me. *It wasn't my fault,* I told myself. *How could I have known she was going to die?* But my excuses rang hollow. Whether it was deliberate or not, I had stolen another precious part of Allyson's life.

At six the next morning I called Heather to tell her of my plight. Aunt Denise's funeral would be during my largest speaking event to date—a prestigious televised event with nearly four thousand book buyers in attendance. We both knew that it was the wrong event to miss, but Heather said nothing of it. She said she'd check flights to Portland and talk to the people at my speaking event then get back to me. The phone rang a half hour later.

"What did you find out?" I asked.

"Flights are no problem. One leaves from LAX to Portland every three hours and there's availability on all of them. The problem is with your event."

"What did they say?"

"Straight up, they freaked. They say they've spent thousands of dollars promoting you and your book and people are flying in from all over the country to hear you speak. They say if you pull out, you will, and I quote, cause irreparable damage to their conference and their credibility, costing them hundreds of thousands of dollars. They hinted that they will seek financial compensation."

"You mean they'll sue me."

"Precisely. They also threatened to blackball you with their subscribers. Like I said, they freaked."

"This day just keeps getting better."

"They're a pretty influential group, Rob.

Their newsletter reaches more than one hundred thousand book buyers."

"Is there someone else who could take my place?"

"I asked them. They said absolutely not. They said that the people coming to this event overwhelmingly signed up to hear you."

"What am I going to do?"

"I don't know. But the association wants to know within a half hour if you're going to be there. They only have a few days to try to fill your spot."

"I don't have a choice, do I?"

"Not a good one."

I hung up the phone; then I called Allyson. From her voice it was clear that she was deeply hurting. "Are you okay, honey?"

"I'm not doing too well. I fly out at three. What time will you be there?"

My stomach knotted. "I can't come, Ally. I have to be in Sacramento for my speaking event."

She didn't say anything.

"Honey, they say that they'll sue us if I don't show up for their event. They'll also blackball me with their subscribers." I waited for a response, but she said nothing.

It was excruciating. "I know you need me right now. I'm so sorry, honey."

"Me too," she said softly. Then she said, "I've got to go, Carson's late for school."

"Will you call me when you get there?" I asked.

"Sure." She hung up. The distance between us now seemed insurmountable. My life had become a Rubik's cube, and twist it as I might, I had no idea how to make it work.

Chapter 37

While Allyson flew to Oregon, I flew in to Sacramento for my speaking event. In spite of the circumstances, the event went well. The audience gave me a two-minute-long standing ovation. Afterward I signed what felt like a thousand books. It was surreal. The hosts of the event were cordial and acted as if nothing had happened. I guess I did the same. I had returned to my hotel room when Camille called. "How did your speaking event go?"

"It went well."

"Good. I heard about your dilemma. I'm glad it wasn't my choice."

"The whole thing was really awful. Still is."

"Life hands us all kinds of pop quizzes,

doesn't it?" Her voice was oddly estranged. I wondered if she was upset at the choice I had made. "Listen," she said, "I've been meaning to ask you about your dinner with Darren Scott?"

I was stunned. "How did you know about that?"

"The book world is a small, small world, Rob."

I tried to downplay it. "Scott's an interesting man."

"He *is* an interesting man. So was Saddam Hussein. So how does Mr. Scott rate my performance?"

"Truthfully?"

"Of course."

"He thinks that I lost at least a million dollars by selling the television rights."

Camille seemed nonplussed. "He might be right. But anyone can say that after a book has hit the list. The TV deal helped get the bookstores and the press interested in the first place. If we hadn't done the deal, you might not have ever hit the list."

"You don't think the book would have succeeded on its own merits?"

"I don't know. And neither do you. Do you think I lost you a million dollars?"

"Like you said, who knows?" We were both quiet for a long time. Then I said, "Listen, Camille, I've decided to give Darren a try."

There was a long pause. "You're leaving me?"

"Don't make this personal, Camille."

"I made it personal the day I decided to take a chance on you."

"And you've been paid well for taking that chance."

"It's not about the money, Rob."

"Come on, let's be honest here. You're an agent. It's always about the money."

"I can't believe you're talking like this. Tell me, did he wow you with his client list then tell you that he only works with the big names?"

"Yes."

"Did you stop to consider that maybe it's because he drops them at the first sign of trouble?"

"It's the way the business works. Survival of the fittest. If I stopped selling books, how long would you be around?"

"Actually, Rob, I have a dozen authors who don't sell. But I care about their writing so I keep going to bat for them." She exhaled in exasperation. "Why am I having this conversation? I hope you get what you deserve." She dropped the receiver.

I laid the phone back into its cradle. I felt bad for hurting her, but Darren Scott was still right. I mean, how would I feel about her when I was back installing sprinklers?

Chapter 38

The United flight touched down in Salt Lake City on time Sunday afternoon. I walked out into the terminal wondering what kind of reunion Allyson and I would have. I had only spoken with her for a few minutes since the funeral. Just long enough to let her know when I'd be landing. Maybe it was a blessing that I would only be in Utah two days before I left again for New York. Honestly I was surprised that she had even agreed to pick me up.

She was waiting for me in the terminal. Alone. She looked worn and tired, her eyes red as if stained from days of crying. We hugged each other, but it was without feeling.

"How are you?" I asked.

She looked at me dully. "I've had better weeks."

"How was the funeral?"

"Why? Want to write a book about it?"

I felt like I had just been slugged.

"I'm sorry, Ally, I . . ."

"I don't want to talk about it."

We walked out to baggage claim without another word. We had driven several miles when Allyson said, "Camille called to share her condolences."

"I bet you had an interesting talk."

"So you really did fire her?"

"If that's what she wants to call it."

"She's been really good to us."

"We've been good to her."

Allyson looked out the window and said nothing until I pulled off I-15 onto the Twenty-First South off ramp. "Where are we going?"

"We have an appointment."

"With whom?"

"It's a surprise."

Twenty minutes later we snaked up the tree-lined streets of the east bench until we reached the large, wrought-iron gate of the Stringham mansion. Chris, the real estate agent, was parked out front waiting for us. He climbed out of his car. He was very tall, blond, and even though it was late afternoon he wore Ray-Ban Aviator sunglasses, which he removed as he walked over to our car. I rolled down the window. "Mr. Harlan, it's a pleasure, sir." He looked past me. "Mrs. Harlan."

Allyson just looked at me. "What's going on?"

"This is the house I'm thinking of buying."

Allyson looked out at the place. "You want something this big for the three of us?"

"Yeah." I climbed out.

Chris sensed the tension between us and walked away. He pressed a code into a keypad, and the intricate wrought-iron gate opened. As we walked in, Allyson walked up behind me. "Do we really have to do this now?"

"I made an appointment. We'll be here a half hour then we'll go," I said curtly.

The house was even more spectacular than its pictures. The foyer was tiled in rose-streaked marble. A beautiful crystal chandelier hung above. The walls were covered in fabric or stained wood and there was beveled and leaded stain glass in various windows throughout the house.

Chris did his best to point out the features he thought Allyson would be most interested in. She listened and responded politely but remained deep within herself. After we finished the tour, I thanked Chris and told him I'd get back to him in a few days. He handed me his card; then Allyson and I climbed back in our car and headed home.

We drove for a while before I said, "That was *pleasant*."

"You really want to live there?" she asked incredulously.

I didn't answer her. Twenty minutes later I pulled the car into the garage and hopped out, leaving my luggage in the back.

Inside the house there were stacks of books piled high on the counters and kitchen table. "What's with this?" I asked.

"People just bring them over for you to sign them. Every time I leave, there's a new stack of books on the front porch when I get back. I don't even know most of these people."

"Another argument for moving," I said. I walked around them, lifting the morning's paper that lay on the counter.

"Don't forget your mail," Allyson said.

I looked up. "What mail?"

Allyson pointed to six large cardboard boxes lined up against the wall. "Your publisher sent them."

I walked over to the boxes. I crouched down and began lifting envelopes. "I didn't know people really wrote to authors," I said. "Have you ever written to an author?"

"You."

For the next few minutes I rummaged through the letters while Allyson made dinner. The letters I read were mostly letters of gratitude from readers, sharing their own feelings about my book and their own fathers. One woman wrote that my book had changed her life. After she read it she decided to forgive her father and visit him. They were happily together again. She thanked me for the miracle. One woman wrote that her sister had recently died and her last request was to have my book read to her as she lay dying.

Allyson broke my reverie. "Were you going to ask where your daughter is?"

I looked up suddenly, drawn back into the moment. "I'm sorry. Is she home?"

"She's with Nancy. She's spending the

night. Nancy thought we might need some time alone together."

I looked at her. "Do we?"

She didn't answer. She just looked at me with the dark, dull eyes of a complete stranger. I say dull, but the truth is her glare was sharp and it cut deeply. Deeper than I could understand. Suddenly I felt completely displaced. I didn't belong here. The distance that had grown between us was a complicated maze of hurt and bickering. It was more than I could stand. Without another word I walked out to my car and drove away.

Chapter 39

I wasn't driving anywhere but away from a seemingly impossible situation. I ended up downtown. I stopped at Hires Drive-in on Fourth South and ate dinner, then dropped into a Borders bookstore just a few blocks away. My book was centered on the Christmas gift table. It was a *Staff Pick*. I got myself a hot vanilla crème steamer from the café, picked up the latest book by Baldacci, then sat down and read. I knew the workers recognized me—I saw them talking and furtively pointing at me—but they never got the nerve to ask me to sign my books. I was glad. I wanted to be left alone. Only when they closed did I leave.

All the lights were off when I returned

home. I undressed in darkness, brushed my teeth then climbed into our bed. Neither of us spoke to the other. I knew that Allyson wasn't asleep. I could tell by her breathing. About a half hour later she started to cry. It was a soft whimper at first that rose into a sob. I reached over to touch her but she recoiled from me.

"Ally."

When she could speak, she said, "I'm so tired of all this. I'm tired of hurting. I'm tired of fighting. I'm tired of being alone. You've changed, Rob."

"How have I changed?"

"In so many ways. Look at that house you want. You're willing to get rid of our home and memories just like that?"

"This was never our home. It's my father's."

"It's his house, but it's *our* home. It's where all our memories are."

"And they're all painful. You're getting all sentimental with this, but the bottom line is I was living a life of quiet desperation."

"All painful? What a horrible thing to say." She rolled over. "Is it really that much better than us?"

"Is what better?"

"Your new world."

I erupted. "Have you considered that you might be the problem? You're the one turning every good thing bad. This little shell you live in was killing me. Finally I'm happy. Finally Robert's getting a little something his way besides a kick in the teeth. Have you considered that? Or does my happiness even matter to you?"

"Of course your happiness matters to me."

"No, I don't think it does. I think you're jealous of what's happening to me."

Her mouth gaped open. "I don't want what's happening to you. I couldn't give a damn about a best-seller list or what some women's magazine thinks about me. But that's all you think about now. Maybe I am jealous that I have to take a backseat to every reporter or to every woman who loves your book. But you're not the only one whose life has changed, Rob. And whether you believe it or not, it's not for the better."

"So would you go back to how things were? Me out there digging ditches."

"I never wanted you to work for Stan."

"Like I had a choice. Come on, honestly. Would you go back?"

The question hung in the air between us sharp and threatening as a blade. There was no sound but her occasional sniffing and my heavy breathing. Then she answered softly, "In a heartbeat, Rob."

I pulled the covers off and got out of bed. "Then I guess that's the difference between us. Because I'll never go back to that miserable life. And if you don't like who I've become, then this isn't going to work. Because this is who I am and I'm not going back."

I went to the dresser and began taking out clothes. As I dressed, Allyson asked, "What are you doing?"

"I think we need some time to think about where we're going." I turned to look at her. "I think we need a separation."

"A separation? That's the whole problem, Rob. We're already too separated. We're a whole world apart and there are a million of your readers between us." She started crying. "Just come back to bed."

I went to the closet and gathered more clothes. When I turned around, Allyson was standing next to the bed, her cheeks wet. "Where are you going?"

"To a hotel. I feel more at home there."

Her eyes widened with desperation. "I'm sorry, Rob. Please don't leave us. Please don't break up this family."

I stopped at the doorway. "We already left each other, Ally. It just took me a while to see it."

She began to shake, and her hurt turned to anger. "I wish you had never written that damn book."

"I know. And that's the problem."

"I feel sorry for you, Rob, if you think you can replace us with them. They don't love you. They can't love you because they don't really know you. You're as much a figment of their imaginations as the characters in your book."

For a moment I stood silently in the doorway. For a moment neither of us spoke. Allyson had raised a hand to her mouth, and even though the room was dark, I could see that she was trembling. A part of me screamed to repent of my anger—to do whatever it took to hold us together. But another voice, a weary and angry voice, spoke instead. "It's too much, Ally. The current is too strong. I just can't hold on anymore. I've been thinking about this for some time. I'm just going to move out. It will be easier that way. For both of us. I'll come back tomorrow for my things."

I walked out of the room. As I shut the front door, I could hear her sobbing, but still I walked. For the first time I knew there was no turning back.

Chapter 40

ONE WEEK LATER.

A storm rolled into the valley and stalled. The snow fell softly, enveloping our Tudor in a peaceful icing of white. Allyson held a cup of herbal tea up to her chin, a thin wisp of steam rising from it. Across from her Nancy looked out the living room's picture window. It was a quiet moment for both of them, the snow erasing the color from the landscape.

"I love November snow," Nancy said.

"More than February snow?"

"Much more." Nancy glanced around the room. "So when are you getting your Christmas tree?"

"I don't know. I just keep waiting."

"For Robert?"

Allyson nodded.

"I saw him on television the other day," Nancy said. "I think it was C-SPAN."

"Then you've seen as much of him as I have."

"What do you hear from him?"

"Nothing. Nothing at all."

Nancy frowned. "How's Carson handling it?"

"She's confused. Sometimes she's angry and she doesn't know why. When I told her that her daddy wouldn't be home for a while, she curled up in a ball on the couch. I asked her if she wanted to talk about it. She didn't."

"How do you cope?"

"Not very well." She sighed. "I just can't believe he could really have changed that much. His life has always been Carson and me. I keep waiting for the return of the real Robert. But all I get is Robert Mason Harlan. It's like his body has been taken over by this famous author."

"Success does that to people."

"I wouldn't call losing your family success."

Nancy shook her head. "No, it's not."

Allyson exhaled and forced a smile. "He'll be back. I mean, who could walk out on me? I'm a good wife. I keep a good home." Her eyes began to moisten. "I've gained a few pounds, but I'm still pretty, aren't I? I still get looks."

"You're beautiful, Ally."

"Just because there are a million women who want him, why should I worry?" She stared at her cup. Her voice fell. "If I hear one more of them tell me how lucky I am to be married to Mr. Romantic, I'm going to slap someone."

"You're a wonderful wife and mother. Rob's lucky to have you. This isn't your problem. It's his."

"It feels like my problem. It's just so incomprehensible to me. My father stayed true to my mother even after she died. Divorce just was never an option."

"No one's talking about divorce, Al."

"Not yet anyway." She wiped her eyes. "It's the unknowing that's driving me crazy. Not knowing what he's going to do or how long it's going to last. Where's that crystal ball when you need it?"

Nancy looked down at her teacup. "Well, I could read your tea leaves. My mother's aunt taught me how. She used to come over for tea and afterwards she'd read everyone's tea leaves. She was brutal. She'd tell them that their husbands were cheating on them or going to die in some horrible accident. It was always some great evil that was going to befall them. She'd leave all these women freaked out of their gourds. But they'd never miss a tea."

"Was she ever right?"

"You would think in ten years that the odds would make at least one of her predictions true, but no. Nothing ever did. Though one of the ladies kicked her husband out of the house for a week, until he could convince her that he really was going to his Kiwanis meetings."

"I'd be happy just to see the past clearly. I don't even know where we went wrong. Everything made sense at the time. Now nothing does."

"I know that feeling."

Allyson took a long drink of her tea and let it warm her. "Was it really just me? Did I drive him away? Was I too demanding?"

"No, Ally. It's just a bad stretch. He'll be back."

"I'm just afraid that the longer he's gone

the less likely it is that he'll return. He never meant to cut off his father, but it's been more than two years since they spoke."

"He'll be back." Nancy forced a smile. "Who could leave a gorgeous babe like you?"

Allyson looked up sadly. "What do I do in the meantime, Nancy?"

Nancy reached across the table and took Allyson's hand. "I wish I knew what to tell you, honey. I really do."

Chapter 41

THE NEXT DAY

The elevator at Argent Literistic opened directly into the agency. Camille was walking toward the elevator when the receptionist stopped her.

"Camille, there's a call for you. Should I tell her you've already gone for the day?"

Camille looked at her watch. "Who is it?"

"Allyson Harlan."

"I'll take it." She walked back to her office and lifted the phone as she leaned against her desk. "Ally, how are you?"

"Not very good. Do you have a minute?"

"For you I do. Are you all right?"

"No. I wanted to see if you've spoken with Rob lately."

"No. He doesn't call me anymore. We've only talked once since he fired me. What's wrong?"

"He left me."

Camille exhaled in exasperation. "Oh, no." She sat down in her chair. Her voice lowered. "I'm so sorry, Allyson. I'm sorry for what I've brought on your family. You don't deserve this."

"It's not your fault."

"I feel like it is. I feel like I'm responsible for creating this monster."

"No. It's not your doing. I just don't understand how he can leave us."

"Sometimes people lose themselves. It's not the first time I've seen this."

"But this is *my* husband. I have no idea what to tell Carson. I don't even know what's going on."

"What have you told Carson so far?"

"That Daddy's on book tour again."

"That was probably wise for now."

"I don't even know where he is."

"He's in New York. He has a book signing then a meeting with Arcadia tomorrow." Camille was silent for a moment as she explored a thought. Then she said, "Do you want him back?"

"I do."

"Maybe there's hope yet."

Chapter 42

While I had grown used to New York's night-time bedlam and usually slept well, a car alarm had gone off below my hotel window around three in the morning and I was up for nearly an hour. I woke late and lay in bed thinking about Allyson. Six months ago the thought of us being separated was unthinkable. Today just going home seemed impossible. The thought of it left me feeling hollow.

I put my mind on the day ahead. It was busy. My stays in New York always were. I had a book signing, a meeting with Arcadia to discuss my next book, then dinner with Darren. Even though Darren was L.A.-based, he was truly bicoastal. He was in town for a movie premiere, and we had arranged to hook up. He was bringing a contract.

This reminded me that Camille would be at my meeting with Arcadia. The two-book contract I had signed with Arcadia had been through Argent Literistic, so I'd still be working with Camille for at least another year. I wasn't looking forward to seeing her in person.

I rolled over and turned on my cell phone to check for messages, but I'd forgotten to charge it. I plugged it into its charger then went to my computer to check my email. I had an email from Heather and one from Darren. I opened Heather's first.

Robert,

Welcome back to NY. Congrats on the WSJ mention in this morning's paper. I just want to remind you of your signing this morning at ten. B&N, at Union Square. They're expecting a large crowd. Shall I pick you up?

Heather

P.S. I'll bring a copy of the article with me.

I looked over at the clock on the night-stand. It was already a quarter of nine. I typed back,

no, i'll meet you there.—rob

I opened Darren's email.

Rob,
*   Q. How many mystery writers does it take to screw in a light bulb? A. Two. One to turn it most of the way in, the other to give it a surprising twist at the end. Congrats on the new list. Don't know what hotel you're at. I left a message on your cell. I'm still planning on dinner tonight. Want to hook up earlier?*
*   —DGS*

I wrote back.

*   sorry, cell phone was out of juice. dinner's still on at noho star. i have a book signing at ten—union square barnes & noble. meet me at starbucks across the street from the northwest corner of union square park.*

*   rob*

I disconnected, wrote in my diary, then got dressed for the day.

The crowd at my book signing was even larger than anticipated. The manager guessed that nearly five hundred people were crowded into the mezzanine level of the store. While I signed, store personnel walked through the line reminding customers that I would not be personalizing books, and the crowd was moved past the table with the efficiency of an assembly line, with someone on my left opening the books and someone on my right pulling the signed book away from me and returning it to the customer.

After ninety minutes the line didn't seem to have diminished much, and eventually one of the workers closed off the stanchion, sending customers away. When I finished, I went to the back of the store, where there were another two hundred books that had been called in. Heather stayed with me through it all, and after we were done she walked outside with me. We stopped outside the store while I put on my coat. The sidewalk was crowded with holiday traffic.

"That was a good signing. Your readers love you."

"It was big," I said rubbing my wrist. "You wouldn't have any Tylenol in that bag, would you?"

"No. Do you have a headache?"

"A wrist ache."

"All that signing is going to give you carpal tunnel. I can find you some."

"Don't worry about it. There's a drugstore on the corner."

"I've heard some authors say that those magnetic bracelets help. I'll send you one." She reached into her bag. "I picked this up for you." She took out a copy of the day's *Wall Street Journal* and handed it to me. "Your mention is on the front page," she said, pointing it out. "Right there."

I began aloud. " 'Arcadia's surprise blockbuster, *A Perfect Day,* along with the usual showing from their stable of best-selling authors has put Arcadia's quarterly profit percentage back on top of the publishing heap.' "

"I just spoke with my mole over at the *Times*. You're still holding strong at number one. Everyone at Arcadia is happy. I'm sure

Allyson must be thrilled with how things are going."

"I wouldn't count on it."

Heather smiled. "That's hard to believe. I'm sure Allyson's very proud."

"Allyson and I are separated," I said.

Her smile vanished into a look of embarrassment. "I'm sorry. I didn't know."

"It's recent." Just then an elderly woman wrapped in a shawl stopped a few feet from me. "Good book," she said and walked off.

"Thank you," I said after her.

Heather asked, "Have you eaten today?"

"No. But I'm meeting a friend at Starbucks." I glanced down at my watch. "I'm already late."

"Then I'll let you go. I'll see you at three for the sales meeting. Do you need anything?"

"No. I'm fine. I'll see you later."

"Bye-bye."

Heather turned and walked away. I walked to the café.

The Starbucks was crowded, and I glanced around for Darren but didn't see him. I ordered a vanilla crème frappucinno and a cranberry scone then looked around for a place to sit. Fortunately a couple near the register vacated a small table for two. I sat down as soon as they left, and began reading the paper that Heather had given me.

I kept my eye on the door, waiting for Darren. A few minutes later a man walked into the café. He glanced around as if he were looking for someone. He looked directly at me then went up to the counter to order. He was short and slender, almost feminine in form. He was bald in front, and what hair he had was long and gray. He wore no color— black-and-white gingham slacks and a black jacket and black turtleneck. He left the counter carrying a drink in its cardboard sleeve and a rolled-up *Newsweek* magazine in his other hand. He looked around for a place to sit but found nothing. Finally he walked up to my table and stood behind the vacant chair across from me.

"Mind if I sit here?"

I looked up. "Sorry, I'm expecting someone."

The man again glanced around the room then pulled the chair out with his foot and sat down anyway. I looked at him. "I said I'm waiting for someone."

He said coolly, "I'll leave when he comes."

I reminded myself that this was New York and went back to my paper. The man leaned forward slightly. "Are you who I think you are?"

I tilted my newspaper down until I could see him. "That depends a good deal upon who you think I am."

"The author of that new book everyone's talking about."

"I'm Robert Harlan."

"Cool. Hey, congratulations. I read your book just last week. You must be really proud, your first novel and it's a blockbuster best-seller."

I tried to act unaffected but found myself instinctively adopting the tone of voice I used with the press. "I'm one of the lucky ones. Thank you."

"I'm sure you get sick of people asking you this, but is your book really based on your wife's last few months with her father?"

"Yes."

The man looked pleased with the confirmation and sat back in his chair. He took a sip of his drink then looked at me thoughtfully. "I'm a little puzzled why you left a part of that out."

I thought his comment amusing. "Exactly what part would that be?"

His brow furrowed. "Correct me if I'm wrong, but when your wife's father was dying you promised him that you would never leave her. But it's not in the book."

I looked at him. "How did you know that?"

"Not that the book needed it. Look how well it's doing. In fact maybe it's better this way since you have, in fact, left her. It might be kind of embarrassing. Anyway who's to say that deathbed promises count?" His voice lowered. "But then again you haven't done that well on the other side of life either. Like the promise you made to little Carson the day she was born. You told yourself that you'd never leave her. Not the way your mother left you—both your mothers for that matter."

I set down my paper. "Who are you?"

He smiled innocently. "Just another fan, Robert."

I wasn't sure how to respond. There was no way he could have known these things. Allyson didn't even know them. I nervously glanced down at my watch, wondering where Darren was.

"He's not coming."

I looked up. "Excuse me."

"He's not coming."

"Who's not coming?"

"The guy you're waiting for. Your new agent Darren Scott—a man so big he needs two first names. Mr. Big Shot went to the wrong Starbucks. You'll still have plenty of time to hear him name drop over dinner tonight."

This little man was getting to me. It was like watching a magician play a card trick an inch from your nose that you can't figure out. Only he was playing with my life. I reacted angrily. "I don't know what you're up to, but I don't have time for your little game."

The stranger leaned back and raised both hands as if in surrender. "Sorry. I didn't mean to upset you. I'll just go back to my reading." He buried his nose in his magazine. I went back to my paper, though only superficially, as I found myself rereading the same article. After a minute the man said casually, "By the way, you're right. You don't have much time."

"What's that supposed to mean?"

"Just that when it's your time it's your time."

"What are you saying?"

"That pain in your chest you've been complaining about, the one Dr. Frank said was reflux? Well everyone's going to be scratching their heads over that one. Of course you could have another physical but don't bother. They won't find anything. Like I said, when it's your time it's your time."

As I looked at him, my cell phone rang. I glanced down at the caller I.D. then lifted the phone to my ear. "Hello."

Darren's voice boomed. "Where are you?"

"At Starbucks. Where are you?"

"Which Starbucks?"

"The one on Union Square," I said.

"You said to meet you at the Starbucks on Sixth and Twenty-second."

"No, I didn't."

"I have the email in my pocket."

"I didn't even know there was a Starbucks on Twenty-second. I meant this one."

"Well, I'm not a mind reader. Should I come down or do you want to come here?"

I looked down at my watch. "We don't

have time. I've got a meeting with my pub-lisher in a half hour. I'll just catch up with you tonight at dinner."

"Let's make sure we're on the same page," Darren said. "The Noho Star, on Lafayette and Bleecker."

"Right. There's only one. Eight o'clock."

"See you then."

I slid the phone back into my coat pocket. The stranger was again reading his maga-zine but wore a smug grin. I eyed him for a moment. "Who are you really?"

He set down his magazine. "Who I am is unimportant. Who you are or, more signifi-cantly, who you've become, is the real mat-ter at hand." He looked at me intensely. "May I call you Bob?"

Before I could voice my objection, he said, "You're an important guy, Bob, so as you're so fond of saying, I'll just cut to the chase. You seem pretty caught up in this whirlwind of success. You've broken some promises, big promises, and you don't have much time to make up for it."

I blinked slowly. "What you just said. What do you mean by 'not much time'?"

"Don't be obtuse, Bob. The bell has rung, pencils up, please turn your test over. And frankly you better hope they're grading on a curve, because you haven't been doing too well of late. Your father-in-law isn't the only one you broke a promise to. Remember your wedding day, when the preacher said 'until death do you part'? You went one up and said, not until death, but forever. Remember that? Now Mrs. Forever is nursing a broken heart and wondering if she'll ever see you again." His voice slowed. "You have until New Year's to pack your bags."

The stranger abruptly stood, pushing his chair back with the motion. "You know, Bob, humans are funny. They all believe that death is some kind of an accident, something that wasn't really supposed to happen." His eyes took on darkness as he spoke. "Wake up, Bob. Death is everyone's destination. Even best-selling authors."

His expression lightened. "By the way, your three o'clock meeting with your publisher has been postponed until Monday morning."

He dropped his magazine on the table. "You should look at this. There's a great article on Chihuly. Man, I love Chihuly," he said. He walked toward the door, stopped to hold it open for a woman, then walked out, disappearing in the crowds that flooded the sidewalk. My mind spun like a roulette wheel. Just then my cell phone rang. I slowly answered it.

"Hello?"

"Hi, Robert? This is Heather."

"Hi."

"Sandra and some of the salespeople got hung up in another meeting, so the three o'clock meeting has been postponed. Would Monday morning at ten be okay?"

I couldn't believe this. I didn't answer.

"Are you there?"

"Sorry. The phone was just cutting out. Monday's fine."

"I already called Camille. So you don't need to tell her."

"Thanks. Have a good weekend."

"You too."

Things were getting more surreal by the moment. I took out my planner and wrote in the meeting. Then I began counting days to January first. According to the stranger I had exactly forty days left to live.

Chapter 43

I got off the subway at Bleecker and walked up the stairway to the Noho Star restaurant. Darren was already seated near the back of the restaurant, looking at a menu. He was dressed in a black Armani suit with a narrow, gold tie.

"Sorry I'm late," I said, sitting down. "I'm still figuring out the subways."

"I'm glad you came," he said. "After this afternoon I thought you might just be pulling my chain."

"No. Honest mistake."

Darren reached into his jacket pocket and brought out a folded sheet of paper. "Here."

"What's this?"

"It's your email asking me to meet you at the Starbucks on *Twenty-second*."

I looked at the paper. It did say Twenty-second. "I'm losing my mind," I said. "This day has been surreal."

"How so?"

I considered whether or not I should tell him. From what I knew of Darren he wasn't exactly the type who went in for angels or psychics. I was sure he'd think I was crazy. Still this thing was bothering me and I had to tell someone.

"While I was waiting for you at the Starbucks, this guy sat down at my table. He recognized me and started asking the usual questions. But then he started telling me things about myself. Things he couldn't possibly have known."

Darren gazed at me with a look of concern. "What kind of things?"

Just then a waitress walked up to our table. "Are you gentlemen ready to order or do you still need a minute?"

I looked up from Darren's gaze. "I know what I want. How about you?"

"I'll have the salmon and a glass of Chardonnay," Darren said.

"And for you, sir?"

"I'll have the Mexican salad. And a home-made ginger ale."

"Very good. I'll get your drinks." She walked off.

"He knew what kind of things?"

"Personal things. Intimate details about my past. About my marriage."

His countenance turned grave. "That's frightening. This is the dark side of celebrity. There are crazy people out there who get obsessed with celebrities and learn every-thing they can about them. It might seem harmless, but stalkers are a very real dan-ger."

"He didn't seem like a stalker. The thing is, the stuff he knew isn't anything he could have researched. I mean he knew things not even my wife knows."

"Like what?"

"He knew that you were at the other Star-bucks waiting for me."

The waitress returned to our table with our drinks. "Here you are, one Chardonnay, one ginger ale. I'll be back with your meals shortly."

"Take my advice. If you see him again, notify the police."

I pulled the paper off my straw and rolled

it into a ball while I thought. "So what would you do if you found out that you only had forty days to live?"

He laughed. "Now, there's a question. I suppose I'd eat, drink and be merry. And run up a credit card bill to match the national debt." Suddenly his expression turned grave. "Wait, this stalker you met didn't tell you that you had just forty days to live?"

"No. Of course not. It's just . . ." I looked at Darren then stopped myself. "It's just an idea I had for a book."

He nodded. "Good. Glad you're thinking about it. That reminds me of a joke. A writer died, and upon arriving at the pearly gates St. Peter gave him the choice of going to heaven or hell. He decided to check out each place first. They first went to hell. There he saw hundreds of writers chained to their desks in a steaming sweatshop. As they worked, a demon whipped and yelled at them. 'This is horrible,' the writer said. 'I want to see heaven.'

"So St. Peter took him to heaven. There he also saw hundreds of writers chained to their desks in a steaming sweatshop. There an angel whipped them.

" 'Wait a minute,' said the writer. 'This is just as bad as hell.'

" 'No it's not,' replied St. Peter. 'Here, your work gets published.' "

Darren finished the joke with a satisfied grin, and I obligingly chuckled. Then Darren opened the leather portfolio that was on the chair next to him. "I brought my contract." He set a small stack of paper on the table. The contract was nearly as long as the one I had signed with my publisher. I started to look it over but stopped at the beginning of the third page. "This will take me a while."

The waitress returned with our meals. "There you gentlemen are. Can I get you anything else?"

"Just our check," Darren said. She set it on the table. The sound of the subway rumbled below us like an earthquake. Darren looked at me intensely. "It's just a standard agency contract. If you want, you can just sign it now and then read it on your next flight."

I stared at the stack. "I'd rather read it before I sign it."

"It's not a big deal," he said. He changed the subject. "So you said that you and your wife are separated."

"Yeah."

"Are you still talking?"

"Not since I left Utah. I don't know what I'm doing."

"Well, be smart about it. Maybe the best thing to do is to sign the contract after the divorce is final. She's already going to get a chunk of the stuff you have with Bagley. This way she can't claim any ownership of future royalties."

"I didn't say we're getting a divorce."

"No one intends to get a divorce," he said. "At least not at first. I better give you this." He reached into his pocket and brought out one of his own business cards. He wrote a phone number on the back of it then set it in front of me. "Benson is one of the best divorce lawyers in the country. When you're ready, give him a call. Tell him you're a client of mine. He'll take care of you."

Darren went back to eating. I had lost my appetite. I picked at my salad for a while then said, "I'm not feeling too good. I think I'll head on back to my hotel." I reached for our dinner check, but Darren put his hand on it. "I've got it."

"Thanks."

"You fly back to Salt Lake City tomorrow?"

"No, I've decided to stay in New York until next Wednesday."

"I'm shuttling up to D.C. for the weekend, but I'll be back Sunday night. Let's get together for lunch on Monday."

"Sure. I'll see you then." I turned to go.

"Rob."

I turned back. He was holding the card with his attorney's number. "You forgot this."

I took it from him. "I'll give you a call."

"See you Monday."

I took a cab back to my hotel.

Chapter 44

Monday morning I hit the snooze button on my alarm clock but then got up anyway. It had been a restless night. A restless weekend for that matter. Three days after meeting the stranger I was more agitated than ever. My dinner with Darren hadn't helped matters. His contract still sat unread on the desk in my hotel room. I didn't know when I would get to it.

I turned on the shower then went to my computer to check my email. When the screen came up, it suddenly went dark and there appeared a red flashing number 37 that took up my entire screen. I had never seen anything like it. I tried pushing keys but nothing happened. I restarted my computer, but when it booted up the number was still there. Forgetting the time difference, I called my brother Marshall, the software designer. He answered on the fourth ring.

"Marshall, this is Rob."

"What time is it?" he asked groggily.

"Sorry. I forgot it's still early there. Should I call back?"

"No, I'm awake now. Where are you?"

"New York."

"So what's up? Besides us."

"I need your expertise. When I turned on my laptop this morning, there was a flashing number."

"What kind of number? Like an error code?"

"No, it was a large, red, flashing number thirty-seven. It took up my entire screen and froze my computer."

"Just the number thirty-seven?"

"Exactly."

"What else is on your desktop?"

"I'll check." I looked at my computer. The number was gone.

"That's strange. It just disappeared. Now my email is up."

"What kind of computer do you have, a PC or Mac?"

"A PC. Do you know of any viruses that do this?"

"Not that I've heard of. But that doesn't mean anything. There's a new one born every minute. You have virus protection don't you?"

"Yes."

"What's your laptop doing now?"

"As far as I can tell everything's back to normal."

When something vexed my brother, it was difficult for him to let it go. "I'll send an email out over the web and see if anyone else is reporting this. It's not a function of your Windows calendar is it? Some kind of an automatic reminder."

"A reminder of what?"

"That there's thirty-seven days left in the year."

My heart froze. "Could be. Thanks, Marshall. Sorry to wake you."

"No problem. Things going well out there?"

"The book is doing well."

"And you?"

"Ask me in a few months."

He laughed. "Love you, man. We're proud of you. Call if there's anything else I can do."

Chapter 45

I arrived at the Arcadia meeting shortly before ten. I cut my arrival as close to the appointed time as possible, as I was uncomfortable with seeing Camille and I didn't want there to be much time to languish in awkwardness. I was led up to the conference room on the fourth floor. I was the last to arrive. Camille was already seated, as were Sandra, Heather and several others from the Arcadia sales force whom I had yet to meet. Camille looked up at me as I entered. She showed no emotion, positive or negative, but motioned for me to sit by her.

The meeting went well. The purpose of it was to discuss how to parlay my recent success into a chain of best-sellers. Someone suggested that my next book be a sequel to *A Perfect Day*. I didn't feel comfortable with this, but I told them that I'd think about it. In truth the meeting was as much a backslapping session as anything else. The success of my book had far exceeded everyone's expectations.

The meeting ended an hour later. I thanked everyone before leaving and we exchanged holiday wishes. Camille stood next to me until it was just the two of us. On our way out of the room I said to Camille, "I'm sorry about the other day."

She looked at me like a hurt friend. "So am I. But we still have a year to work together so we might as well keep things civil." She looked down at her watch then said, "I've got a lunch meeting to go to. You headed back to Utah tonight?"

"Not until Wednesday. Are you leaving town?"

"I'm headed home to Chicago. Have a good Thanksgiving."

"Thanks. You too."

She walked away. As I watched her go, I tried to hold back the flood of sadness and guilt with Darren's words, reminding myself that *it's just business*. The truth is I felt slimy.

Just then Heather walked up and handed me a folder. "Here's an update of your media. I'm headed out of town, but you can always reach me on my cell. I checked your flight for Wednesday, and I was able to get you upgraded to first class after all."

"That's good news. Thanks."

"You're welcome. Be sure to check in early. The airport's going to be crazy and if you miss your flight you might not make it home. Do you need me to arrange for a car?"

"No, I'll just grab a taxi."

"Then I'll run. Have a safe trip home. Happy Thanksgiving."

"Thanks. Take care."

As I walked from the office, the receptionist stopped me. "Excuse me, Mr. Harlan. I have a message for you." She handed me a slip of paper with nothing on it but an address and time. "A gentleman just called and asked if you'd meet him for coffee."

I looked at the note. *Starbucks on Greenwich. Noon.*

"There's no name here."

"I'm sorry, but he wouldn't leave one. He just said you'd know who it was. I figured since he knew you were here he must know you."

"I already have a lunch engagement."

"Yes, he knew that too. He said that I should say . . ." She lifted a paper. "He was rather particular. He made me write this down. He said, 'Considering your new paradigm, Bob, your lunch today is relatively inconsequential.' "

I glanced at my watch. It was ten to twelve. "All right. Thanks."

On the way out I called Darren and cancelled our lunch.

Chapter 46

I arrived at the Starbucks and found the stranger sitting in the back of the café reading the *New York Times*. Almost immediately he turned to look at me. I got a coffee and scone then sat down across from him. He looked pleased to see me. Almost cheerful. I'm sure I looked otherwise.

"Hey, Bob."

"For the record, I hate being called Bob."

"I know. Sorry. It just has a nice ring to it."

I rubbed my forehead. "So what do I call you?"

"Michael."

"That's pretty unoriginal."

"I guess. I didn't choose it."

"Tell me something. Why is it that we meet at Starbucks?"

"I thought you liked Starbucks."

"It seems like there are more appropriate places."

"Such as?"

"Such as a church or synagogue or something."

Michael nodded as he considered my query. "Two reasons. A, you don't go to a church or synagogue." He leaned back and lifted his drink. "And B, churches don't have vanilla crème Frappuccinos."

I raked my hair back with my hand. "So what's with the number on my computer screen?"

He smiled, "The countdown. Pretty clever, don't you think? I thought it would help keep you focused."

"What would be most helpful would be for you to just leave me alone."

Michael rubbed his chin as if considering this. "No, I don't think that would be helpful."

"You're just wasting your time. I don't believe you."

"Why? Because Darren Scott told you that I was a stalker?"

I wondered how he knew that, but I hid my surprise. "Are you?"

"I suppose in a cosmic sort of way. But I don't believe that you don't believe. You wouldn't be here if you didn't."

"I don't believe I'm going to die. I feel fine."

Michael chuckled. "Famous last words. I know a man who actually put that on his headstone. *I feel fine. Really.*"

I didn't find it amusing.

"Of course you don't believe me," he said. "All belief is a choice. If I were you, I wouldn't want to believe me either." He took a drink of his coffee. "I've seen it a thousand times. Everyone goes into denial at first. Ducks head for water; people head for denial." He just stared at me, tapping his fingers on the table. Finally he said, "What proof would you have?"

"Perform a miracle."

"You want a sign?" He looked around the crowded room. "Right here?"

"Why not?"

"What kind of miracle would make you believe?"

"I don't know. Make something disappear."

"Something disappear," he repeated. "That's a peculiar request." He took a deep breath, closed his eyes then raised his hands to his temples. "Okay, here we go." He reached over, took my scone and shoved half of it into his mouth in one bite. He chewed until he had pushed the rest of it in.

I looked at him dryly. "I'm real impressed."

Michael continued to chew, speaking with his mouth full. "Not bad. Not bad at all. I'll have to get one of those next time."

"Glad you enjoyed it."

He swallowed then wiped the white crumbs from the corners of his mouth with a napkin. "Listen, Bob, I'm a messenger, not a magician. I don't part water, turn sticks to serpents, call fire down from heaven—any of the classic miracles. It's not in my job description. I just know things."

"Things?"

"For instance, I know that your publisher wants you to write a sequel to *A Perfect Day*, which, under the circumstances, you're not real comfortable with. I know that you just got your flight home upgraded to first class and that your daughter is making her acting debut this afternoon in the first grade's Thanksgiving program, which, sad to say, you won't see." He took a drink. "For starters."

I just looked at him in astonishment.

His expression turned more serious. "Don't believe me for my sake, Bob. My being here has nothing to do with me. It's not like I'm here to earn wings. What a stupid notion: as if angels have wings. Actually, angel folklore is the height of nonsense, right up there with the Easter Bunny, but I digress. This is about you. You're the one who's ticking down. If you want to waste what little time you have left, go right ahead." He stood, dropping two dollars on the table. "That's for the scone. I'll see you later."

"When?"

"When you're ready to stop wasting your time."

As he walked away, a new emotion replaced the skepticism I had felt. Fear.

Chapter 47

Allyson sat on the third row of the Meadow Moor Elementary School auditorium, waiting for the Thanksgiving production to begin. The room bustled with parents happily visiting with each other or squatting near the front of the stage, positioning for optimum camera angles. The burgundy stage curtain was still down, and all that was visible on the stage was a lone microphone stand.

Allyson sat alone at the end of a row of chairs near the center of the auditorium. She held a video camera in her lap. Suddenly a rotund woman with silver hair crouched down next to her. She had a wide, animated face, an appropriate canvas for the bright makeup she wore.

"Excuse me, are you Mrs. Robert Mason Harlan?"

Her use of the three names was a dead giveaway to the woman's intent. Allyson turned to look at her. "Yes, I am."

The woman sat down in the row behind Allyson, leaning over the chair next to her. "I am such a fan of your husband."

Allyson forced a smile. "I'm sure he'd like to hear that."

"I cried all last night reading that book of his. And it was my second time reading it." She raised a hand to her breast. "How he can pull a woman's heartstrings like that is beyond me. You are so lucky."

"He can certainly bring out the emotion," Allyson said. She looked forward, suppressing her true feelings. To her relief the school principal walked out to the microphone. Allyson said to the woman, "I think they're about to start."

"Is he here?" she whispered.

"No. He's on the road promoting his book."

Her face fell in disappointment. "Well, you give him my best, dear."

Allyson was glad when she was gone. The principal thanked the usual teachers and staff as well as the parents who helped, and the curtain opened to a large papier-mâché stone painted with the words *Plymouth Rock*. It was a few minutes into the play that Carson came out dressed as a pilgrim girl. She wore a pinafore and a bonnet, which unintentionally became the most memorable part of the production. Her bonnet fell off, and to the delight of the parents, she walked through her lines with one hand holding it to her head. Then it fell to the floor and a little boy dressed as an "Indian" slipped on it. He began crying and a teacher ran out on the stage and carried him off. Then Carson picked the bonnet up again and held it to her head as she delivered her main line, "We have much to be thankful for."

Allyson slipped out of the auditorium before the lights came up and anyone else could stop her. She walked around to the back of the stage and found Carson in the center of a great commotion of children pulling off their costumes. When Carson spotted her mother, she ran to her. "Mommy, Mommy! Did you see me, Mommy?"

"Of course. You were great. I was so proud of you."

"My hat fell off. But I put it back on after Tanner slipped on it."

"Is he okay?"

"He's crying." She looked around. "Where's Daddy?"

Allyson hid her frown. "His airplane broke in New York. But I videotaped everything for him, and when he comes back we can watch it. You know how much he likes to watch you."

"Yeah, he doesn't like to miss me."

"No, honey. He hates to miss you. He loves you so much. Do you know what he'd say if he were here?"

Carson shook her head.

"He'd say 'Let's go get an ice cream cone to celebrate.' "

She smiled. "Let's go, Mommy."

Chapter 48

Arcadia closed early for the holiday, and everyone I knew in New York had left the city. Maybe even Michael, since—with the exception of my daily computer reminders—I hadn't heard from him either. I wondered if he'd find me in Utah. I doubted it. I flew back the day before Thanksgiving.

My flight home was uneventful, as I slept through most of it. I arrived shortly after seven—after dark—feeling as displaced as if I were still on book tour. The thought of going home was there; I missed my family, but the tension of seeing Allyson was just too much. There was no reason to expect anything to be different between us.

I had put a thousand dollars earnest

money down on the new house, but the closing wouldn't be until January 3. In light of Michael's forecast, I actually wondered if I would ever occupy the house.

Shortly before I left New York, I reserved a room over the Internet at the Hotel Monaco in downtown Salt Lake City—the same hotel Camille had stayed in on her visit. I booked the room until January 1. As had become my habit, I reserved the room under an alias. Ernest Hemingway. I did so for privacy. These days I needed privacy about as much as a senior center needs an orthodontist.

It had snowed twice while I was in New York, leaving Salt Lake City as white and cold as a bowl of ice cream. There was an inversion trapping fog in the Salt Lake basin, and the air was gray as slate and had the musty, thick smell of the Great Salt Lake. The *Lake Effect,* they call it.

When I flew out to New York, I had left my car in the airport's long-term parking lot, and I returned to find it covered with nearly six inches of crusted snow. It looked like an igloo with wheels. It took me nearly fifteen minutes to clear it all off. Then I drove into downtown Salt Lake.

I was exhausted from the flight and actually looked forward to a night of nothing but HBO and room service. As I completed checking into the hotel, the clerk handed me my key then said, "Mr. Hemingway, I think you have a message."

"That's odd. No one knows that I'm here."

"Just a second and I'll check." She retrieved the note and handed it to me. "This came in about a half hour ago. It's addressed to Ernest Hemingway a.k.a. Bob."

I took the note from her.

Welcome home, Bob. We need to talk. I know you love the chocolate Cokes at Hires Drive-in on 400 south so I'll meet you there at ten fifteen. Your flight was on time, so that should still give you enough time to clear the snow off your car and check in. See you soon,

Michael

I looked up at the clerk. "I guess someone did know that I was here." I took my luggage to my room and lay down on the bed for a moment. Then I drove about a mile to the drive-in. I felt naked. I wondered if there was anything Michael didn't know about me.

Chapter 49

As I expected, Michael was already there. He was seated at a table in the corner of the room, eating fries and reading the *Tribune*. His eyes followed me until I sat down at the table across from him.

"Welcome to Utah," I said.

"I've been here. How was your flight?"

"I slept through it. How was yours?"

He smiled at the question. "I took the liberty of ordering you a turkey sandwich with cranberry sauce—being that it's Thanksgiving tomorrow. And your favorite drink, a chocolate Diet Coke, which must be an oxymoron. I ordered one for myself to see what it tasted like."

"How did you know I was staying at the Monaco?"

"Same way I know everything, Mr. Hemingway. So have you reached any conclusions?"

"About what?"

"About me, to begin with."

"You tell me. You seem to know everything about me."

"So it would seem. But I don't know everything. There are things that you don't know about yourself. That's what makes this exciting."

"This is exciting to you?"

"Sorry. Wrong word. By the way, Carson was great in her play last Monday. Her bonnet fell off, but it just added to the moment if you know what I mean."

I shifted uncomfortably in my chair. "Listen, I've been thinking about everything and I have reached some conclusions."

Michael laced his fingers together and leaned forward, his chin resting on his hands. "I'm so glad. Tell me."

"I've concluded that this isn't fair."

At first he just looked at me. Then, to my dismay, he started laughing, first to himself then loud enough that even the people on the other side of the restaurant turned to look at us.

"I'm glad you found that amusing," I said sarcastically.

"Bob," he said, his mouth still bent in a grin. "You really don't want to talk about fair. Children starving in Ethiopia isn't fair. A little girl praying every night for her daddy to come home isn't fair. If I were you, I don't think I'd get all hung up on 'fair,' Bob, because that dog don't hunt." He pushed a little back from the table. "Bottom line, when it comes to the scales of justice, you've been found wanting."

I sat back, cowed by his response. "So here we get to it. That's what this is all about. I sinned, so God is going to kill me."

Michael's smile vanished. "It doesn't work that way, Bob. That's a human-drawn caricature—God striking people with lightning bolts like he's a hit man. Think it through. If that's the way it was, then prisons would be empty and good people wouldn't die. Right?"

I half nodded. Just then the waitress, a pretty redhead with a name tag that read *Nancy,* arrived with our order. "Saved by the fries," Michael said. He looked up at the waitress. "Hello, Nancy."

"Hello."

He pointed to me. "Do you happen to know who this man is?"

She looked at me then shook her head. "No."

"This is Robert Mason Harlan, author of the number one book in America. You have a celebrity in your midst."

I wanted to crawl under the table.

"It's very nice to meet you," she said.

"Likewise," I replied, flushed with embarrassment.

"May I get either of you gentlemen anything else?"

"No, we're fine," Michael said. After she left us, Michael grinned. "Now, where were we? Oh yes, death. You have to stop thinking of death as a punishment. It's not. At least no more than birth. They're very similar experiences when you think about it— coming from darkness into light through a long, dark tunnel. They're both portals. You humans just happen to be on *this side* of the portal, so you view birth as beautiful. You don't know what's on the other side of the portal, so you fear it. There's nothing more frightening to humans than the unknown." He stopped to take a drink of his chocolate Coke. "But it's like this chocolate Coke. Sometimes the unknown isn't bad."

I rested my head in my hand. "So how do the *powers that be* decide when it's your time?"

"The powers that be," Michael laughed. "Actually you're not far from the truth. But I can't really answer your question. It's quite a complex process. But I can tell you that it's not like a lottery, where things just happen at random. You have to realize that this earth is just another stopping place on the game board." He paused thoughtfully, looking at his drink. "No, not a game board. It's actually more like basic training." He looked back at me. "Your father was a military man, you understand that. Anyway, these decisions were made a long time ago. In fact, you had a part in deciding when and where you were going to enter and exit. You just don't remember."

"That's hard to believe."

"Most spiritual things are hard for mortals to believe. That's why they act so stupid in the flesh—putting immense value on things that don't last. There are people on this earth who spend their lives chasing gold, but in heaven it's used as asphalt for roads.

"Or take fame for instance. For one brief moment a man finds himself on a throne. And for a while he believes himself special—a little bit better than everyone else. But then he discovers that his throne is just another seat in an ongoing game of musical chairs and eventually he's going to lose his place. Sometimes he spends the rest of his life trying to get back to the chair.

"You know what I'm talking about. Sports stars who retire then find the void too much, so they return, playing way past their prime. The beautiful trying to hold on to the glory of their youth, so they resort to plastic surgery until their faces are tight as snare drums. Rock stars who go on reunion tours, and on it goes.

"But they have it all wrong. The simple truth is that we don't come to earth to make a name for ourselves just so time can erase it. That's not what it's about."

"Then what is it about?"

Michael smiled. "Finally you're asking the right question. But you already know the answer. You've always known." He looked into my eyes and his gaze pierced me. *"It's about learning how to love."*

As if to punctuate the revelation, he abruptly stood, dropping a twenty on the table. "Think about it."

"Wait. How do I get ahold of you?"

He just smiled. "I'm around."

I sat there with my sandwich and fries and no appetite. I just sucked on my Coke and thought. Michael was long gone when the waitress stopped again at the table. "Your friend left you."

"He usually does."

"Is everything okay with your food?"

"It's great. I guess I'm really not that hungry."

"I'll put it in a container for you. Would you mind signing your napkin for me?"

In my state of mind the request seemed ridiculous to me. I wouldn't have wanted my signature if it were attached to a blank check. "I'd be happy to," I said. "May I borrow your pen?"

"Of course." She handed me her pen and I signed the napkin. She folded it in half and tucked it into her apron pocket. "Thank you.

May I get you a refill on your chocolate Coke?"

"Sure. You only live once."

She smiled and walked away with my cup.

Chapter 50

In spite of the hour I wasn't the least bit tired. Even though I had slept on the plane, I knew my wakefulness was more likely due to my meeting with Michael than any sleep I'd stolen. His words stung me. I felt as if I had come to take an exam, only to find that I had been studying for the wrong test.

I drove past my hotel and took the interstate twenty minutes south to South Jordan, where my home was. It was still lightly snowing, and even though the powder did not stick to the streets, the roads of our little neighborhood were void of traffic. The fog was particularly dense at this end of the valley, and visibility was limited. I drove slowly in front of the house then stopped and turned off the car.

Our home's lights were off except for those in our bedroom. I wondered what Allyson was doing. Nancy's car was in the driveway, which was no surprise, as she always spent Thanksgiving with us. To say I felt homesick would be like comparing an aneurism to a sinus headache. As I sat there in silence, my cell phone rang. The prefix was a 310 number—the Beverly Hills area code. I shut off my phone without answering it and stowed it back in my pocket. I just sat there in silence looking at the house. Only twenty yards, yet a world away. What would it take to go back? The sad truth was, more than I had to give. A half hour later I drove back to my hotel alone.

I slept in the next day until noon. I ordered a turkey and mashed potato dinner from room service, which is pretty pathetic when you think about it. I was glad when the day was over.

To my surprise I didn't hear from Michael the rest of that week or the next, though the countdown on my laptop continued.

The week was relatively quiet for media. I averaged three to five call-in radio station interviews a day.

I wished that I were on the road again. Not that I cared anymore about the book, but because anything would beat sitting around in the same hotel room in downtown Salt Lake City. I must have watched every in-room movie there was. Perhaps most telling of my frame of mind was that I didn't even bother to check on the best-seller lists anymore. Instead I found myself checking my cell phone several times a day hoping that Michael had called, only to see Darren's messages piling up. On Friday I received a local call from a number I didn't recognize. I answered, hoping it was Michael.

"This is Robert."

The voice hesitated. "Rob, it's Stuart Parks."

My anger for him was pretty much gone now, though mostly displaced by disinter-est. "Hi, Stu. What's up?"

His voice came tinged with nervousness. "We haven't heard from your people yet. I was wondering if you had a chance to con-sider my request to come to the station's

Christmas party. It's on Monday the twenty-third."

"I don't know, Stu. I really don't know where I'll be. Probably in New York."

He exhaled. "I'm desperate, Rob. Sterling has made it clear that if you're not at the company party, there are going to be changes. You know how compulsive he gets about things. If you could just come for five minutes, stick your head in, shake a few hands, it would mean the world. I'll even pay you for your time. A thousand dollars for twenty minutes. And I'll throw in some backstage passes to the Styx reunion concert. I know you're an old Styx fan. Just tell me how much you want."

"Don't grovel, Stu. I don't need your money."

"I know that. Just please reconsider. Please, Rob."

I exhaled. "I'll let you know, Stu."

"When should I call back?"

"If I can make it, I'll call you." I hung up.

Chapter 51

The next Sunday, December 8, I attended a small nondenominational inner city church. It was during that meeting that I had an epiphany of sorts. The sermon that day was on Abraham's sacrifice and the angel that stayed his knife. Of course I was grasping, but it occurred to me that perhaps there was a way out of my predicament that didn't end with my death. I was a little more than three weeks away from D-day (as I had come to call it), and I desperately needed to talk to Michael. I was suddenly filled with a new fear. What if Michael had no intention of returning? As I left the church, I prayed that he would come back.

The next day my prayer was answered.

There was a note left at my hotel saying that he would gladly meet me next Wednesday at six P.M. at Hires.

I arrived at the drive-in a half hour before our meeting. To my surprise I saw him drive up in a Cooper. It had never occurred to me that he drove. I wondered what kind of address he had on his driver's license.

He walked in, brushing snow off his shoulders. He smiled when he saw me. He crossed the room and sat down next to me.

"You beat me here," he said.

"I'm not always late."

"Not always." He took off his coat.

"I ordered for you. It came up early; I hope it's not cold."

"You got me a Big H?"

"Yeah. And a chocolate Coke."

"Thanks." He looked at me intensely. "So, you prayed me here—what do you want?"

He knew about my prayer. I wondered how that worked, if there was a celestial switchboard operator of sorts and someone slipped him a message—*Robert Harlan prayed, asked if you could get back to him.*

"Where have you been?" I asked.

"I've had a cold."

I looked at him. "A cold? You get sick?"

"Everyone gets sick. So how are you feel-ing?" he asked.

"Okay."

"Any more chest pains?"

"Why do you ask questions to which you already know the answer?"

"Sorry. Bad habit. In a former life I taught school."

"I have a question for you."

"Just a minute," he said. He took out a wadded Kleenex and blew his nose. "Sorry. I know about your question. You want to know if you can get out of this. If maybe this is like a spiritual test or cosmic *Candid Camera,* however you want to describe it. Something designed to see what you would really do under the circumstance—like Abraham."

His insight never ceased to amaze me. "That's exactly what I wanted to ask you."

"What did you plan to do?"

"To start, I could go back to church or make a big donation to a charity or some-thing. Or what if I just swallow my pride and go back to Allyson?" My own desperation caught up to me. "I want to do those things anyway. It's like my whole paradigm has changed."

"Classic," Michael said, shaking his head. "Classic."

"What do you mean?"

"You're following the rituals of death perfectly. You're now in the bargaining phase. But the answer to your question is *no*. In the first place, going to church isn't doing anyone a favor but yourself. Second, you can't take anything with you anyway, so you're not really giving up anything, now are you?"

I lowered my head and rubbed the back of my neck.

Michael continued. "As far as going back to your wife, I'm not so sure she'd take you back. The first rule of a broken heart is to protect it from any more pain. Do you think she'll take you back?"

I lost my patience. "You tell me. You're the one who knows everything."

"No. You have to figure this one out by yourself."

"So no matter what I do I'm going to die?"

"Everyone dies." He nodded slowly. "Remember our first meeting? I said that the test is over. Time's up. It's just the way it is, Bob. I'm sorry it's not to your liking."

"So what's the point of any of this if it's

already over? Am I supposed to go running back home just so that I can leave them?"

"This life is almost over, but you're not."

"What do you mean?"

"Do you think this life is it?"

When I didn't answer, he answered for me.

"No, you don't think that. You just don't think about it."

"So you're saying that there really is a heaven and hell."

"Yes."

I raked a hand back through my hair. ". . . With fire and brimstone."

"Do you have any idea what brimstone is?"

"No."

"It's sulfur. The stuff they make matches out of. Puts out a real stench when it burns. But you need to ask yourself what harm is fire or sulfur if you have no body to be burned?"

I mulled it over in my mind. "I've never thought of that."

"It's a metaphor, Bob. You want to know what hell is? What brimstone and burning *really is*?"

"Yes."

"Hell is the perfect recollection of every evil thing you've done in your life, every thoughtless word, every cruel, evil thought or action. It's knowing that you could have helped your brother and didn't. Hell is *clarity,* Bob. It's nothing more than clarity." He leaned forward as if to confide in me, his gaze intense. "Do you want to know what heaven is?"

I was locked into his gaze. "Yes."

His voice was barely above a whisper, "It's the *same thing.*"

Michael leaned back while I processed the revelation. He spoke softly, as if he were also saddened.

"You know, Bob, the truth is, with the exception of this last run, you've lived an admirable life, which is saying something when you consider the start you had. Your mother dying. Your stepmother leaving. A father seemingly incapable of showing love. For over seven years you worked a job you didn't like because you were committed to taking care of your family. You watched others unfairly promoted around you, and still you held your post. And when you were fired, unfairly, you kept on. You laid sprinklers and dug up septic tanks and came home every day with blistered hands and an ego to match. You thought you were a no-body. But heaven is full of nobodies. Except we call them saints. The sad fact of the matter is that your timing leaves something to be desired. Bad luck, I guess."

"That's me, all right, Mr. Lucky."

"Actually you are lucky, Bob. Most people don't know when it's their time. Between the day that I first came to you and January 1, more than two million people will exit this rock. More than fifty thousand souls a day. Do you know how many of them never get to say goodbye to a loved one? How many leave unfinished business? How many die with unspoken words on their lips? I know you don't feel lucky, but you're one of the privileged."

"So why me? Why didn't I just get hit by a semi and save everyone the trouble?"

"I don't know. Maybe it's because in your heart you're still that saint." He stood to leave. "But your opportunity is nearly gone, Bob. There's about three weeks left in the year. And you're still a long way from home."

Chapter 52

I sat by the phone in my hotel room for nearly a half hour gathering the courage to call Allyson, only to have each attempt met with a busy signal. I felt several chest pangs as I waited, as forceful a prompter about my circumstance as a cattle prod.

In my quest to reach Allyson, I had forgotten that I was supposed to be on a nighttime call-in interview with a Tulsa radio station, and the show's producer panicked and frantic calls were made to Heather. I didn't even think about my mistake until Heather caught up to me on my cell phone. She reached me before my fourth try for Allyson, and even though my heart was elsewhere, I called into the radio station for the final twenty minutes of an hour-long interview. As soon as I had finished, I tried Allyson once again. She must not have checked her caller I.D. because she answered brightly.

"Hello."

"Hi, Ally."

"Who's this?"

"It's Rob."

She went silent. It had been nearly four weeks since we'd spoken. The silence turned painful.

"How are you doing?" I asked, regretting the question almost immediately.

"How am I doing? I'm fine, Robert. Everything's great. My husband shares the most intimate experience of my life with the entire world then leaves me because of it. My six-year-old daughter is traumatized and not only spontaneously breaks out in tears, but now she wets the bed every night. But besides that everything's just great."

I winced. "Yeah. Dumb question."

"So what is it, Robert? I'm busy right now. Being a single parent is a little time-consuming."

"I wanted to see what you and Carson were doing for Christmas."

"You're kidding, right?"

I took a deep breath. "Listen, Allyson, this isn't easy for me."

"Easy? I guess I'm a little hazy on how these things work. I'm supposed to make it easy on the guy who breaks my heart and abandons me and my child?" Her voice cracked. "So if I'm supposed to act happy that you called, frankly, I just don't feel it."

I took another deep breath. "You have every right to be angry, Allyson. And I know this is going to sound really stupid, but I just wanted to ask if I could spend Christmas with you."

I waited for her onslaught. She was silent for a moment then she said calmly, "The other day I asked Carson what she wanted Santa to bring her for Christmas. She said 'my daddy'."

She was silent again, effectively letting the weight of Carson's words sink in.

"Yes, you may come home for Christmas. But you may not stay at the house. Go live in a hotel or in that mansion on the hill. I don't care where you stay just as long as it's not here. And just in case you really don't get it, I am so off limits to you that I might as well be on another planet. There will be no touching—emotionally, spiritually and especially physically. If you so much as brush up against me, you're gone. Do you understand?"

"I understand. When does Carson get out of school for Christmas break?"

"The twentieth is her last day. It's only a half day."

"How about if I pick her up from school?"

"I'll pick her up."

"I'll meet you at home. I was thinking that I'd first take her ice skating."

"She'd like that."

". . . If you want to come along, you're welcome to join us."

"Carson could use a little one-on-one time with her father. I don't."

"If it's okay with you, then I'll take her to dinner too. Then you can have a free evening. I'm sure you haven't had enough of those lately."

My words disarmed her. "That would be nice."

"Thank you, Allyson. I know I don't deserve this."

"This isn't a favor, Robert. It's for Carson. Only for Carson. And you're right, you don't deserve it. By the way, happy anniversary."

She dropped the phone in the cradle.

Of all the years to forget my anniversary, I thought. It had been brutal, but at least my foot was in the door. I looked at the calendar in my day planner. Nine days until the twentieth. That would leave me just twelve days until New Year's. What could I possibly accomplish in just twelve days? There were entire years of my life that I couldn't remember. What I wouldn't give for just an extra week or two.

Chapter 53

Nancy stood at the sink cutting tomatoes for salad while Allyson kneaded bread into hamburger for meat loaf.

"So what do you think it is," Allyson asked, "guilt?"

"Was he drinking?"

"Rob doesn't drink like that."

She gestured with the knife. "You don't know that. The man's changed." She went back to her slicing. "It could be that he's trying to fatten the goose."

"What do you mean?"

"My cousin went through this with her divorce. Her husband hired a hot-shot divorce lawyer who advised him to turn on all the charm he could muster until the divorce papers were signed. The second the papers were signed, he turned back into Frankenstein. He even told her that that's what he was doing, 'fattening the goose to protect the golden egg.' What a loser. She's lucky to be free of him."

"No one's filed for divorce."

"Would it surprise you if Rob did?"

Allyson frowned. "I don't know."

"Have you told Carson that he's coming?"

"Not yet. I want to make sure he's not going to back out. She's been through enough disappointment."

"You did the right thing." Nancy put the knife down, lifted a tomato slice and ate it. "He's up to something. I don't trust him."

"I'm not sure that I do either. But for Carson's sake I'll give him a chance. But I'm keeping him on a very short leash." She held her thumb and forefinger about an inch apart. "Very short."

Chapter 54

Standing at the doorway of my own home waiting for Allyson to answer the door was excruciating. I was left to stand there for several minutes, and I wondered if it was intentional. While there might possibly have been a part of Allyson that wanted to see me badly, I suspected that the larger part of her just wanted to see me badly maimed. Hell hath no fury . . .

Allyson looked out the peephole in the door. Then the door opened. Allyson's expression was stoic, steeled for the encounter. For a moment she just stared at me.

"Hi," I said.

"Hi."

"May I come in?"

"Sure." She stepped aside. Suddenly Carson came running up behind her. "Daddy!"

I stooped down and lifted her in my arms. "Hi, pumpkin."

"Where have you been?"

Allyson looked at me sternly, her arms folded at her chest, awaiting my reply.

"I've just been working too much," I finally said. "Are you ready to go ice skating?"

"I'm wearing a sweater."

"I can see. Is it new?"

"Mommy bought it."

"I still think you better get your coat and mittens. It's really cold."

"They're right here," Allyson said, handing me Carson's small down parka. "The gloves are in the pocket. Where are you going skating?"

"I thought we'd go to the rink at the Gallivan Center."

"When will you be back?"

"Eight or nine."

"She'll need to have a bath when she gets back."

"I'm staying at a hotel near the center. She can have a bath there. Where will you be?"

"Nancy and I are going to see a show. Don't keep her out too late."

"I won't. I'll just put her to bed and wait here for you. I have a book in the car, so be as late as you want."

Allyson looked at me warily. "All right. Just don't give her too much sugar. Do you have a house key?"

"Yes. Unless you changed the locks."

"No, I didn't."

"Then we'll be on our way."

Carson grabbed my leg. "Carry me, Daddy."

I lifted her. I said to Allyson. "I'll see you later."

She didn't say a thing.

The rink was crowded, and we stood in line for nearly forty minutes just to rent our skates, which is more like a week in child minutes. By the time we got on the ice, Carson was already complaining about being too cold.

"How about we go back to my hotel and watch a movie and order pizza."

She smiled. "Yeah."

We went to my room at the Monaco. Carson liked the place but was baffled by it all. "Why do you live here?" she asked. "How come you don't come home?"

I didn't know what Allyson had told her. "Right now I'm staying here because I'm still on book tour."

In Carson's mind my book tour was a great enigma beyond her understanding. As such, she accepted my excuse as plausible. I bathed and dressed her in a T-shirt of mine that fell like a night gown on her; then we ordered pizza and hot chocolate from room service and lay on my bed to watch an in-room movie—an animated feature for children. We ate on the bed, which was a special treat as it wasn't allowed at home, and before the movie was over Carson fell asleep, her warm, little body cuddling into mine. I held her until the end of the movie. Then I put on her coat and carried her down to my car and drove her home. I tucked her into bed then went out to the living room sofa to read.

I decided to wash the dishes in the sink

and ended up cleaning the entire kitchen. I had only been reading for fifteen minutes when Allyson returned. I saw her before she saw me.

"Hi."

She jumped. "I didn't see you there."

"How was the show?"

"It was good." She looked around the kitchen. "Thanks for cleaning up."

"You're welcome."

She hung up her keys and then her coat. "How was skating?"

"We only skated for about ten minutes. She got cold, so we went back to the hotel."

"I didn't think she'd last long. What did she have to eat?"

"Pizza. And hot chocolate."

"I'm sure that made her happy."

"It did." I closed my book. "What are your plans for tomorrow?"

"I haven't finished Carson's Christmas shopping. I was going to try to find a baby-sitter."

"Well, you have me. I can take her all day. Maybe we could have dinner together to-morrow night. The three of us."

Allyson looked at me. "We'll see."

I got up and put on my coat. Allyson was

just a few feet from me and it was against all of my instincts not to touch her. I didn't. "I'll see you in the morning."

"Good night."

Under the circumstances it had been a good night. Allyson was distant, but I'd expected that. I returned to my hotel. The room was different to me now. With Carson in my room, it had seemed warm and alive. Now it seemed as cold as a cemetery. I quickly wrote in my diary then crawled into bed, pulling the covers around me. I looked at the clock. I had eleven days.

Chapter 55

SATURDAY, DECEMBER 21.
ELEVEN DAYS UNTIL NEW YEAR'S.

The next morning I arrived at the house before anyone was up. I let myself in and went straight for the kitchen. I brought out the ingredients for omelets. I mixed the eggs in a bowl then started cooking bacon in a frying pan. I was cutting vegetables when I noticed the smoke billowing from the bacon. I had turned the heat on too high, and before I could remove the pan from the burner, the smoke set off the kitchen's fire alarm. I opened the back door and was fanning out the smoke with a newspaper when Allyson ran in wearing only her underwear.

She stopped when she saw me. "What's going on?" she asked breathlessly.

"I burned the bacon."

"I thought there was a fire." Allyson surveyed my mess. "What are you doing here?"

"I'm sorry about the alarm. I thought I'd surprise you by making breakfast. My world-famous Denver omelet and scrambled eggs."

I had forgotten how cute she looked in the morning with her hair tousled.

"Don't worry," I said. "I'll clean up after myself. Why don't you go back to bed and I'll bring breakfast in like I was planning before I set off the alarm."

She looked at me dubiously then turned and walked off. Fifteen minutes later I brought the omelet into her bedroom. She was lying beneath the covers but awake. "Where would you like me to put your breakfast?"

"The nightstand."

I laid the tray down. Then I opened the shutters behind the bed letting in streaks of the morning sun. "You were out of orange juice, so I made some cranberry-apple."

I sat down at the foot of the bed, mindful

not to touch her. "So about today. I have nothing scheduled, so I'm at your disposal. You can either make a shopping list and I'll pick up some things for you, or I can take Carson with me while you go shopping."

"What's up, Rob?"

"What do you mean?"

"You go four weeks without speaking to me and now you're playing the überspouse. I deserve to know what's going on in your head."

I had been waiting for this question. "I'd tell you if I knew." She looked unsatisfied. "I have an idea. How about we take a break from reality until after the holidays."

She thought about it for a moment. "All right. We'll live in denial until Christmas."

"Until New Year's."

She slowly shook her head. "All right, New Year's." She picked at the omelet.

After several bites I asked, "How is it?"

"It's good. About today. How long can I be gone?"

"As long as you want."

"Okay," she said. She took another bite of her omelet. "This is a pleasant fiction."

*   *   *

Carson woke while Allyson was showering. She walked into the kitchen rubbing her eyes. When she saw me, she screamed with joy. I fed her scrambled eggs with ketchup, and then we sat down together and watched cartoons. She clung to me the entire time. It was about forty-five minutes later that Allyson came out completely dressed, her purse slung over her shoulder. "I'm ready."

"Where are you going, Mommy?"

"Shopping."

"I'm going to play with Daddy today."

"What time should I expect you?" I asked.

"I'll be home by seven."

"That's fine."

"There's bologna in the fridge for lunch," she said. "You'll have to thaw the bread. Did it snow last night?"

"A little. I already shoveled the drive."

She looked at me. "Thanks."

Shortly after Allyson left the house, I called Nancy. "Hi, Nancy, this is Robert."

"Robert?"

I knew that she knew who I was. ". . . Harlan . . ."

"Oh, the author. To what do we owe the pleasure?"

"Just back for the holidays."

"I've got my eye on you, mister. So where in the world are you?"

"I'm at the house."

"Really? Where's Ally?"

"She went shopping. I have Carson for the day. Listen, I wanted to see if you could watch Carson tonight so I could spend some time alone with Allyson."

"Ally agreed to that?"

"Not exactly."

There was a long pause as she considered my request. " 'Course. I'm always up for Carson. What time?"

"Allyson will be home around seven. I'll have Carson ready for bed."

"I'll see you then."

It was ten minutes before seven that Allyson returned. I met her in the foyer. "Where's Carson?"

"She's playing a computer game in the family room. You have packages?"

"They're in the trunk. But I'll wait until she's in bed. What did you guys do today?"

"A little of everything. I took her to that

candy factory in Alpine. Then we did a little shopping."

Carson ran into the room. "Mommy, me and Daddy went shopping for you."

"Really?" She glanced over at me. "Did you have dinner?"

"Not yet. I was waiting for you. I thought maybe we could go out."

"Carson was up too late last night. She needs to go to bed early tonight."

"I meant just the two of us."

"Nancy's going to watch me," Carson said.

Allyson glared. "You called Nancy?"

"Yes, I, well we haven't talked since I came back. I thought . . ."

Anger grew in her countenance. "Carson, go get ready for your bath."

"I don't want to."

"Go now."

Carson stomped out of the room. Allyson looked at me angrily. "What makes you think I want to be alone with you?"

Before I could answer, there was a quick rap on the door and Nancy stepped in. "Hi, guys. Sorry I'm late."

Allyson abruptly walked out. Nancy

looked at me with a slightly amused smile. "So I take it she didn't like the idea."

"Allyson," I shouted.

Allyson walked back in, her arms crossed at her chest. "I can't believe you put me on the spot like this."

I raised my hands in surrender. "I'm sorry. Stupid mistake. New plan. You two go out for dinner and I'll finish out the day with Carson. There's a Jazz game on tonight anyway."

"Sounds good to me," Nancy said.

Allyson didn't say anything.

"I'll see you later," I said. "Carson's waiting for her bath. It's good seeing you again, Nancy. Sorry about this."

"It's okay."

I walked out of the room. A minute later I heard the front door slam.

Chapter 56

I read Carson several books and she fell asleep before nine. I went into the living room to read. I was asleep with a book in my lap when Allyson finally came home. She lightly shook me. "Rob."

I woke disoriented. I rubbed my eyes and yawned.

"Sorry it's so late."

"What time is it?"

"Almost one."

I stood unsteadily.

"Are you okay to drive home?"

"I'm fine. The cold air will wake me." Then I staggered toward the back door, pulling on my coat as I walked. Allyson followed me. "How was she tonight?"

"Good. As always." I stopped to look at her. Though the foyer lights were off the glow from the moon shone through the transom window, silhouetting Allyson in a bluish halo. She looked at me gently.

"Robert, I'm sorry about what I said. Or at least the way I said it. It wasn't very nice."

"No, it's my fault. You were very clear on the rules at the outset. I shouldn't have assumed."

"Well, I could have been a little nicer."

"Don't worry about it."

I put my hands in my front pockets. "If it's okay with you, I'd like to go to church with you tomorrow. The three of us."

"Carson would like that."

"I'll be here, what, a half hour before."

"Better make it forty-five minutes. Being Christmas service."

"Right." There was an awkward moment. I knew that kissing her wasn't an option, but even good habits die hard. She looked at me, her expression somewhere between fearful and hopeful. "Good night, Ally."

"Good night, Rob."

She shut then locked the door behind me as I walked out to my car. By the time I finished scraping my car's windows, I was wide awake. The car clock turned one as I headed back to my hotel. These days I noticed such things.

Chapter 57

I slept in Sunday morning. I ordered room service granola with strawberries for breakfast then made the trek to the house. I figured that Allyson would be frantically getting herself and Carson ready, so I let myself in. I found Allyson in the bathroom brushing Carson's hair. They wore matching Christmas dresses. Carson saw me first.

"Daddy!"

Allyson looked up. "I didn't hear you come in."

"You both look beautiful."

"Thanks. We're just finishing up."

*   *   *

The church parking lot was completely full, and I ended up letting them off near the front of the church and parking the car a couple blocks down the street. They waited for me at the door. As I caught up with them, Carson took my hand and Allyson took her other hand. We looked like a family again. In the words of Anne, my Alabama escort, it felt *just wonderful*.

Pastor Tim's sermon was about Christmas, of course, but focused on the angels of Christmas: the angel Gabriel of the Annunciation, bringing word to Mary of the Holy infant. The angels who appeared to the shepherds bringing *tidings of great joy*.

I had always thought of angels as mystical beings. Kind of like unicorns. My encounters with Michael had changed all that. I could envision the angels gathered together before the shepherds—a small mob of people just like us. No wonder the shepherds were afraid.

On the drive home Allyson said, "Pastor Tim always gives a nice advent sermon. I had never thought of angels quite that way."

Carson asked, "Daddy, have you ever seen an angel?"

I looked over. "Your mother."

"Mommy's not an angel."

"That's for sure," Allyson said.

"Don't be too sure," I said. "The thing is angels don't have wings. They look like us. That's how they walk among us."

"They walk around us?" Carson asked.

"They're closer than you think."

Allyson turned quiet on the ride home. After Carson ran into the house, she turned to me. "Are you staying for dinner?"

"I'd like to. But I have a flight back to New York tonight. *Good Morning America* has a special last-minute Christmas shopping show. They're featuring my book."

"Do you realize that's the first time you've mentioned your book since you've been back?"

"I guess I figured that you had had enough of it. Or maybe I have."

She looked solemn. "So is this good-bye?"

"Not if you'll let me back. This is just an in-and-out thing. I fly back to Utah tomorrow night. I'll be here Tuesday morning, if that's all right. Christmas Eve."

"It's all right," she said softly.

"If it's okay with you, I'd like to plan the day."

"That will be nice. Carson will be disappointed that you're leaving," she said. From the tone of her voice I wondered if perhaps she spoke of herself as well.

"I'll say goodbye to her before I go."

"What time are you on TV? I'm sure Carson would like to watch."

"I don't know. I'll be there by six, but I probably won't be on until nine or so. You know how these things go."

"Yes, I do."

"I'll see you Tuesday."

She looked at me kindly. "Bye, honey."

It was clearly a slip, but I was glad for it. "See you, Al."

I went off to say goodbye to Carson. Another barrier had fallen.

Chapter 58

Nancy called Allyson around eight-thirty the next morning. "Hey, they just said Rob's going to be on after the next commercial break. Utah man strikes publishing gold," she said, mimicking the anchor.

"We know. We're watching."

Both Allyson and Carson were sitting on the bed looking at the television. Just then the program's lead-in music started and Carson shouted, "There's Daddy! He's on TV!"

"You heard that," Allyson said. "I'll call you back."

In New York I was seated across from Diane Sawyer. As the camera pushed in, she began to speak.

"A year ago Robert Mason Harlan was installing sprinklers. But in his spare time he began writing a book about his wife's last days with her dying father. Today that novel, titled *A Perfect Day,* is the best-selling book in America. Welcome to the show, Robert."

"Thank you."

"I'm intrigued by the title of your book. There was a Roger Whittaker song back in the early sixties called 'A Perfect Day.' Is there any connection?"

"No. I didn't know of that song until one of my readers sent me a CD of it. Actually, my wife is responsible for the title. Like you said, the story is based on her and her father. While she was away for college, he brought her home for just one last perfect day. At the end of the day he told her that he was dying."

Sawyer nodded. "A friend of mine read your book. She said it was a five-hankie read. How does your wife feel about it?"

"Allyson was the first to read it. She liked the book. But she doesn't care much for the public life or how this has affected our family."

"I imagine that your sudden success has been a little overwhelming."

I hesitated. "It has. In ways I wasn't ready for. Frankly, if I had it to do over again . . . I wouldn't."

Sawyer looked surprised. "There are probably several thousand aspiring authors watching us right now who would give anything to be in your shoes."

"I'm sure there are. And I don't mean to sound ungrateful. My readers have been great, so have my publisher and agent. But success can be a trap. Maybe someone else could have handled success better. But I lost sight of the big picture. My book is a best-seller for a little while, at least until the next big thing bumps me off, but I will always be a husband. And I will always be a father. If I give up those things for a temporary seat in the musical chairs of fame, then I'm a fool."

Sawyer said, "I almost hate to ask you this, but are you working on another book?"

"I'm under contract for another book," I answered vaguely.

Sawyer turned back toward the camera.

"The book is *A Perfect Day* and it's the number one book in America. It's a GMA Christmas pick, so pick up a copy. Thank you, Robert, for being on our show."

"It's my pleasure."

Back in Salt Lake City Allyson began to cry.

Chapter 59

I left the ABC studio on Columbus and took a cab downtown to Tiffany's. The store was impossibly crowded with last-minute Christmas shoppers, and I waited nearly a half hour just to pay for my selections. I purchased two gifts: one for Allyson, the other for Camille.

Leaving the store, I hailed a cab and directed it to Camille's condominium in Tribeca. I didn't know if she'd be there. But I had to try.

I had never been to her home. It was a nondescript ten-story building with a dark brown tile facade. I found her name on the building directory then dialed her number on the voice box. She answered.

"Hello."

"Hi, Camille. It's Rob." No response. "Robert Harlan," I added.

"Sorry, Rob. I didn't recognize your voice. I'm on the seventh floor. 7F." There was a sharp buzz and the front door unlocked. I went inside and took the elevator up. Camille's loft was at the end of a long corridor. She was standing outside her door waiting for me.

"Your interview this morning was a little surprising." Her mouth rose in a half smile. "I'm sure I'll hear from Sandra before the day's out."

"Sorry about that." I reached into my bag and brought out a small box wrapped in blue paper. "I brought you something."

"What's this?"

"An early Christmas present. Or a late Hanukkah present. You decide."

"Thank you. I was just making lunch. Would you like something to eat?"

"Thanks. But I've got a few more errands to run. I'm flying back to Utah this afternoon." I looked down for a moment. "I just wanted to tell you how sorry I am about everything. I'm not proud of how I've handled things."

She looked at me, her expression a blend of sympathy and surprise. "Things happen."

"Some things shouldn't," I replied.

She looked down at the box. "Should I open this now?"

"Sure."

She peeled back the paper then lifted out a black velvet jewelry box. She opened it. Inside was a pair of pink sapphire earrings with platinum stems. She gasped.

"They're beautiful, Rob. I love pink sapphires."

"I know. You told me once." She looked at them again and smiled.

"You didn't need to do this."

"Yes, I did." I smiled sadly. "I suppose it's a moot point, but I never signed with Darren."

She looked up at me. "What do you mean it's a moot point?"

For the first time I considered telling someone else my secret. But I didn't. There was no point in it. She'd find out soon enough anyway. "I'll explain it to you later," I said. "On New Year's." I leaned forward and kissed her cheek. "Take care of yourself, Camille. Merry Christmas." I started to turn then stopped. "You don't know where there's a stationery shop around here, do you?"

"There's one in Soho. Just a few blocks north. What do you need?"

"Just a little Christmas present I forgot." My eyes watered as I realized it would be the last time I'd see her. "Thanks for everything."

She stepped forward and hugged me. "Welcome back, Rob. Merry Christmas and a happy New Year."

"Ditto," I replied and walked to the elevator.

Chapter 60

I arrived back in Salt Lake City a little after five P.M. The airport was crowded with last-minute travelers headed home for Christmas. On my walk through the terminal I witnessed at least a dozen reunions—lovers reunited, students coming home to their families, things like that. It simultaneously warmed and pained me.

More than a few people recognized me from my *Good Morning America* appearance. Some just stared at me or pointed, while others actually said something. I thanked them for watching and wished them a merry Christmas.

I picked up my luggage, one suitcase and

two boxes of my book that I had requested from Heather. I carted them out to my car.

Tonight I only wanted to be with Allyson and Carson. But I had other errands to run. I knew it would probably be my last chance to try to set things right. My first stop was Chuck's.

It was dark as I arrived, the sky fading from amethyst to the aubergine of late twilight. It had been nearly three years since I'd been to the house. It looked smaller than I remembered. Smaller and older. But even in the growing shadows I could see that the yard was pristine and orderly, as if even the shrubbery bent to Chuck's arduous will. *Everything in its place,* he always said. The house was dark as a mausoleum. It looked like no one was home, but I knew Chuck was. Chuck didn't go places at night.

I took a copy of my book from the car then walked up to the darkened porch. I pushed the doorbell. There was no response, so I knocked on the glass pane of the outer door. After a moment there were footsteps. Then the front porch light came on, followed by the sliding and clicking of locks. The door opened. Chuck stood in the threshold.

My memory of Chuck had not cheated him of years. He looked as old as I remembered. Maybe older. He wore a light blue cardigan and slacks. He'd do his yard work in slacks. And black socks. Every pair he owned was black.

For a minute he just stared at me, his dark eyes leveled on me like a gun turret. Then he said, "Look what the cat drug up."

"May I come in?"

He glanced down at the book I held in my hand. "Your life," he drawled. He unlocked the screen door and turned away from me. I stepped in behind him. The entryway was covered in avocado-hued shag carpet. The inside of the house hadn't changed much except to grow older. There was a peculiar new smell—like a nursing home. Chuck turned his back on me and shuffled to the ancient rust-colored couch in the family room. I followed him in.

"I came to wish you a merry Christmas," I said.

He slid between the couch and the oak coffee table that paralleled it. An amused scowl crossed his face as he fell back into the sofa, his thin legs spread apart. He put his hands on his knees. "So the spirit of the season's gotten into you? Thought you'd pay your old man a visit."

"Something like that."

"Whole thing's a sham. You know what the spirit of Christmas is? It's guilt."

"Maybe," I said beneath my breath.

"What?"

"I said *maybe*."

Silence.

He picked up a newspaper from the table and looked at it. He spoke without looking up. "I heard you and Stan were working together."

"We were for a while."

"Didn't work out, huh?"

"It worked out fine. I just got involved with something else." I looked around. The sink was filled with dishes, and an ironing board was out, lined with empty hangers. There were newspapers everywhere. Stacks of them. "So what have you been up to?" I asked.

He put down the paper. "Now, why would you ask that? We both know you don't give a hill of beans."

I took a deep breath, my eyes locked on his. "I know this is difficult. So I'll speak my piece and go."

"You do that, sonny."

"I've been doing a lot of thinking lately. About us. We've never got along. My entire life I've blamed you for Mom leaving. I felt like you ran her off with your . . . *rigidity*. And, I suspect, some part of you blames me for Irene dying. We couldn't have gotten off to a worse start in life."

My father just looked at me from beneath the shadow of his caterpillar brows.

"I suppose I've always thought of you as just a mean, old man. So when I was old enough to have my own family, I swore that I would never be like you."

His eyes narrowed. "Glad to get this off your chest, boy?"

I raised my hand. "Bear with me." A lump suddenly rose in my throat. "But what I've learned is that I should have been more like you. The difference between you and me is that you never left your post. I don't know why you had children. Duty, maybe. Maybe it was only because Irene wanted them. Then life just dumped us all in your lap. But no matter, you didn't leave . . ." I looked down. ". . . Unlike me. When things got good, I moved on. I left the woman I love and my daughter high and dry." I smiled darkly. "And I thought *you* were bad."

Chuck just stared at me, anemic and tight-lipped.

"I know it wasn't easy for you. I just wanted to say thanks for doing what you had to." I stepped forward and offered him my book. "Here, I brought this for you. I wrote a book."

He didn't reach out to take it from me, so I set it on the coffee table in front of him. "Merry Christmas." Then I started walking to the door.

"Robby."

I turned around. "Yes, sir."

"I've already read it."

I just looked at him.

He nodded. "I read your book. And I know why you wrote it. I wished that I could have been that kind of father you wrote about. But I wasn't."

I glanced down, and when I looked back up, my father's eyes were wet. It was the first time in my life I had seen my father's eyes wet.

"You did well, son."

My eyes moistened. "Thank you, sir."

"And at least you figured out what was

important before you were an old broken-down jalopy like me. That family of yours is lucky to have you."

Somehow he looked different to me. Frailer perhaps. Vulnerable. More human. Like when the curtain was pulled back on the Wizard of Oz. I looked at him for a moment then said, "Do you want to come for Christmas breakfast with us?"

To my surprise he considered the invitation. "No. Better stay here."

After another moment I said, "Well, I'll be going then. Good night, Dad."

"Good night, son."

I stepped out into the cold winter air and made my way back to my car.

Chapter 61

I had one more stop for the evening. I drove through the wet, slushy streets up the east bench of Salt Lake. As I climbed the foothills, the homes grew in size and opulence. I had been to this house every Christmas season for the last seven years. Every Christmas, Sterling Call opened his home to the advertisers of KBOX. In times past it had been an extravagant, black tie affair and was the one time of the year that Allyson could dress up in an evening gown.

The party had started two hours earlier, and there were cars parked in the driveway and lining the street in front of the house. I recognized most of them as belonging to my former colleagues at the station. I parked my car then took a box filled with my books from my trunk and carried it up the sloped drive to the doorway. I set the box on its side then pounded the door's large brass knocker. Music streamed from the house as Sterling's butler opened the door.

"Merry Christmas, Eric," I said.

"Merry Christmas. Please come in, Mr. Harlan."

I reached down and lifted the box then stepped inside the spacious, marble-floored foyer.

"Everyone is gathered in the living room. You know the way."

"Do you mind if I leave this box here? It's for later."

"Not at all, sir."

As I stepped into the sunken living room, almost everyone turned to look. Sterling set down his drink. Stuart was standing on the other side of the room and looked over, his eyes wide with surprise.

"Mr. Harlan, we're pleased to see you," Sterling said above the music. "We weren't expecting you."

I looked at Stuart. "I think Stuart wanted to surprise everyone. I told him that I'd move heaven and earth to be here."

Stuart crossed the room. "That's not what Stuart told me," Sterling said.

"Well, I was supposed to be in New York. But you know how Stuart is," I said. "He's a hard man to turn down. Anyway, Stu, I brought the books. I can sit here and sign them for everyone or set up a table somewhere. However you want to do this."

Stuart tried not to appear too surprised. "We'll get a table."

Sterling smiled. "Now, I know that he didn't tell us that he arranged to have a private signing. You've gone above and beyond, Stuart. I'm impressed."

"Thank you."

"Stu, the books are in the foyer. And I have another box in my car." I fished the keys from my pocket. "You know my car."

"You bet."

Just then Mark Platt appeared in the room. He was holding his wife Becca's hand. His face lit when he saw me. "Robman, the Rob-meister, the dream catcher. I can't believe you came."

We hugged. "Of course I did. It's tradition, man."

"You remember Becca?"

"Of course I remember Becca." I hugged

her. "You look beautiful as always. Much too beautiful for this bum."

She smiled. "I keep telling him that."

Mark said, "Man, do I have someone who wants to meet you. Just a minute." He stepped across the room to a rotund, moon-faced woman. "Mrs. Gifford, your favorite author has come."

Her jaw literally dropped when she saw me. She crossed the room. "It really is you. I am so excited to meet you. Your book has made my entire Christmas season. I wish I had it with me so you could sign it."

"I brought one for you."

She clapped. "How exciting."

Stuart set up a table, and I signed a copy of my book for each of the advertisers and KBOX employees. Sterling lorded over my signing, basking in his apparent clout. I hung around with the salespeople for the next few hours sharing old KBOX war stories. I stayed for more than two and a half hours. I hadn't expected to stay that long, but I was having a good time. It was good seeing everyone again. Only Stacey, who I learned had been relieved of the sales management position, seemed uncomfortable around me. But it wasn't mutual. I felt remarkably liberated from the past. Forgiveness has that effect.

It was around nine when I thanked Sterling for the invitation and took my leave. Stuart and Mark walked me to the door. Mark put his arm across my shoulder. "Hey, it's good seeing you, man."

"It was good seeing you again. Let's catch a flick sometime."

"Love to. My number's the same." We hugged; then Mark went back to his clients, leaving Stuart and me alone on the porch.

"Were there any books left?" Stuart asked.

"No. I think Sterling snatched up the last of them."

"Thanks for bringing them. How much do I owe you?"

"Nothing. It's my gift."

"I don't know how to thank you, Rob. You really made Sterling's night. You know how he loves brushing shoulders with celebrity."

I nodded. "He's always been that way. It's a sickness."

"I haven't seen him that happy for years." His countenance suddenly turned serious. "So why'd you do it, Rob? I betrayed you."

I just looked at him, my heart full of

sympathy. "I understand how that can happen, Stu. Better than you know. I hope tonight helped."

"More than you'll ever know. Thank you."

"Don't mention it. Merry Christmas."

"Yeah. You too."

We embraced. I returned to the hotel a new man. I turned on my computer and wrote in my diary. Then I wrote a letter. A long letter to Allyson. There was one more thing I had to do. Tomorrow wouldn't be easy.

Chapter 62

The snow started falling about the time I got up. I quickly dressed and drove home to my family. I had the letter I had written the night before in my coat pocket. I had decided that I needed to tell Allyson the truth. I wondered when the opportunity would present itself. I wondered how she would take it, or even if she'd believe me. It's not like the pronouncement had come from a doctor.

I arrived at the house with my arms full of packages. With some effort I rang the doorbell then let myself in. The home was a flood to the senses. The healing sound of the old

Christmas music echoed down the hallway from the kitchen stereo. The smell of the home was just as powerful, the sweet fragrance of cinnamon-scented candles and cookies baking.

Carson came running to the door, shouting, "I'll get it!" When she saw me, she shouted, "Daddy!"

"Hi, sister."

"Guess what? Mommy's making sugar cookies." She looked at the packages in my arms. "Are those for me?"

"Some of them."

Her grin widened still more. Allyson walked into the room. She smiled at me and it was pleasant. It was the first time since I had come back that she had greeted me with a smile. "Welcome back."

"Thanks. It's good to be back," I said.

"You brought gifts?"

"A few." I looked back down at Carson. "And one for Carson to open now."

She turned back to look at Allyson. "Can I?"

"If Daddy says that you can."

"Come on, sister, we need to open this at the kitchen table," I said. "Do we have time, Al?"

"All the time you want," she replied. Then, in a softer voice, she added, "She's been under my feet all morning." As we walked back, Allyson asked, "How was your trip?"

"Busy."

"We liked your television interview."

"You watched that?"

"We all watched. So what's in the package?"

I smiled at her. "You'll have to wait and see."

I set all the packages under the tree except one. Allyson went back to making cookies. She was making three different kinds—sugar, oatmeal and pepperkaker—and the sound of the mixer competed with Bing Crosby crooning "White Christmas." Somehow it seemed to fit. When Carson and I were at the table, I set down a large paper bag. "This one's for you."

"What's in it?" she asked.

"There's only one way to find out."

She reached in and took from the bag a package of markers, a roll of tape and a bottle of glue.

Allyson glanced over but said nothing. Then I helped Carson remove the wrapped package still inside. She immediately tore the paper from it. Her eyes widened at the sight of the large, leather notebook. "Wow."

"This is a very special book I bought just for you."

She turned back the cover, and her face fell with disappointment. "There's nothing inside."

"Nothing inside *yet*. That's because we're making this book ourselves. This is a life book just like Mommy's."

Carson smiled. "Wow."

I did not look over at Allyson, but out of the corner of my eye I could tell that her gaze was fixed on us.

"This book is all about you," I said, touching her nose. I turned to Allyson. "Are the photographs still in the hall closet?"

She nodded. "Yes."

I went to the closet and brought down two photo albums and four shoeboxes filled with photographs. The first box held pictures of Allyson and me before Carson was born. I smiled at the sight of myself; my hair was long and I looked remarkably thin. We selected a photograph of Allyson eight months pregnant—a side view, Allyson posing to show the full extent of her stomach— and pasted it to a page then drew a large arrow pointing to her stomach with the words *Carson on board* in alternating pink and blue marker.

On another page we pasted her birth announcement and an invitation to a baby shower. As happy as the project left Carson, I hadn't fully counted on the impact that it would have on me. It was like seeing my life flash before my eyes one page at a time. I guess it was a preview.

Allyson brought some cookies over and watched us for a minute, but she mostly kept her distance, busying herself in her cooking and cleaning. After she pulled the last sheet of cookies from the oven, she asked if I would mind if she went to the grocery store to pick up a few things she'd forgotten. I didn't mind, of course, though I doubted her motives. I think she wanted Carson to have this time with me alone. She instinctively knew that something profound was happening.

The irony of the experience was not lost on me. Allyson received her life book on the day she learned her life would change—that a big part of her life would soon be gone. The thought that the greater part of Carson's book would be finished in my absence moistened my eyes several times, though I always chased the thought from my mind. It wouldn't do to have me start blubbering.

Carson and I went as far as we could on her life book, or at least as far as we had the energy for, and after a few hours we put the markers away and I held her while we watched a videotape of her favorite animated Christmas special, a stop-motion feature with Rudolph and an abominable snow beast. When Allyson pulled into the garage, Carson jumped from my arms, excited to show Allyson her life book. It was nearly quarter of one.

I got up from the couch as Allyson entered. "Ready for phase two?" I said.

Allyson laughed. "You make it sound like Operation Christmas Eve," she said. "Is phase two a surprise?"

I shook my head. "Only in that I haven't told you yet. First, I thought that we'd go get some lunch at Gardner Village."

Allyson smiled. It was her favorite little restaurant, a quaint eatery and furniture and knickknack shop built around a turn-of-the-century grain mill.

"You're sure they're open?"

"I made reservations."

She was clearly pleased. ". . . And maybe a little shopping while we're there?" she asked.

"Of course. It would be like waving a cookie under Carson's nose and telling her that she can't have it."

"Yes, it would be cruel," Allyson agreed.

"Then we're going downtown for a horse-drawn carriage ride to see the lights at Temple Square."

Allyson clapped. "I've always wanted to do that."

"Then we better get going. We're burning daylight."

"Carson, get your big coat and mittens, girlie."

Lunch was fabulous. Allyson and I ordered the same thing, turkey potpies with thick white gravy and large chunks of white meat. Carson just ate fries, which was pretty much all she ever ate when we went out. Afterward Allyson walked around the shop but purchased nothing.

It was snowing hard by the time we reached downtown. On our way we drove past Hotel Monaco. Carson recognized it.

"That's where Daddy lives for book tour," she said.

We parked in Crossroads Mall and walked across South Temple to where the horses were queued. A man wearing a knee-length Western coat and cowboy hat greeted us. He tipped his hat so the snow fell off; then he helped us inside the carriage.

Allyson said, "Carson, you sit between us and we'll keep you warm."

There was a thick blanket on the opposite seat. I lifted the blanket over all three of us. Evening fell as steadily as the snow while our horse clopped slowly through the twilit streets. We rode up South Temple then north into Memory Grove. The streets were still busy and decked in their holiday attire. We returned and circled Temple Square. The lights in the square were spectacular as usual, and the sound of the Mormon Tabernacle Choir could be heard even outside the tall granite walls. I put my arm around Allyson and she didn't seem to mind.

The horse stopped at the curb, and the driver pulled the brake and walked around to us. He placed a step on the ground then took Allyson's hand and helped her down. I was the last one out of the carriage. As I paid the driver, he said to me, "I'm giving my wife a copy of your book for Christmas. I wish I had it here. Would you mind signing the back of my business card?"

"Not at all," I said. I signed it and we walked away. It still surprised me that people recognized me.

We walked through Temple Square and looked at the lights. The falling snow created a dreamlike solitude around us, the colored lights of the square reflecting off our faces. We both held Carson's hand as we walked. The snow continued to fall harder, and after forty minutes Carson said she was cold, so we made our way back to the parking terrace. We stopped on the way home for a doughnut and hot chocolate.

It was late when we got home—a couple hours past Carson's usual bedtime. I helped Carson with her coat then turned to help Allyson, but she had already removed it.

"It's time for bed, girlie," Allyson said. "Give us a kiss."

She kissed both of us then ran down the hall to her room.

"I'll put her to bed," I said.

When I walked into her room, Carson had

already undressed to her underwear and was lost in the nightgown she was trying to pull over her head. I pulled it down over her head. "There you are. I lost you for a minute."

"I was right here."

"So you were." I peeled back the covers on her bed. "Hop in, Pumpkin."

"Can't."

"And why not?"

"We didn't pray."

"I'm sorry." We knelt down by the side of the bed. Carson said, "I'll say it," and immediately started into it. "Dear Heavenly Father. Thank you for bringing Daddy home and for all the fun things we got to do today. Please tell Santa to drive safe and don't be hit by an airplane when he is in the sky. Bless Daddy won't have to go to work again and Mommy won't cry anymore. Amen."

"Amen."

She looked in my face. "How come you're crying?"

"I'm not really crying," I said. "Sometimes my eyes just leak." She looked at me, her face showing her bewilderment. "I really hate it," I said, rubbing my hand over them. "I'll have to get them fixed."

She crawled into bed and I pulled the covers up to her chin. She stared intently into my eyes.

"I'm glad you're home, Daddy."

"Me too, Pumpkin. Now, you go to bed so Santa can come."

"Don't forget to leave a carrot for Rudolph."

"I won't forget."

"Daddy, will the other reindeers be sad that I like Rudolph the most?"

"Only if they find out." I switched off the lamp next to her bed. "I'll put out a whole bunch of carrots. They'll never know." I kissed her forehead. "Now, go to sleep."

"Daddy, today was a perfect day."

The words pierced me. "Yeah, it was. Good night, sweetheart."

Her eyes shut and she nestled into her pillow. I quietly walked out of the bedroom, shutting the door behind me. I realized that I had not even considered how my death would affect Carson. How could I have been so selfish? Suddenly it occurred to me that it had been wrong for me to come back. That this time together would only make their loss more difficult. In spite of what I might have told myself, the truth was

I had come back for me, not them. The thought of it exasperated me. Even when I was trying to do the right thing, I failed miserably. A wave of intense sadness swept through me. I needed to leave. For their sake I needed to leave.

Just then Allyson stepped out of the kitchen, silently waving me toward her. I walked to her.

"Is she asleep?"

"I think. She was pretty tired."

"It's been a busy day," she said, her voice pleasant and soft in remembrance. "Do you want to help me put out her presents?"

"Sure."

Together we descended the stairs to the storage room, where a locked armoire was filled with toys. Inside was an American Girls doll with an old-fashioned desk; three doll outfits; a CD of children's music and a nail painting kit.

Allyson brought out the gifts. "Would you mind getting the wrapping paper?"

"Where is it?"

"In the storage room. On the top shelf by the door. Santa uses the red paper. We use the green paper."

"She notices?"

"Remember last year when she asked why Santa had the same wrapping paper as us?"

I nodded in remembrance. "I forgot. She doesn't miss a thing, does she?"

"Just you." She looked up at me. "I'm sorry. It just kind of came out."

"I'll get the paper," I said.

"There should be some scissors and Scotch tape next to it."

I fetched the paper. We finished wrapping the gifts then laid them beneath the tree. Then Allyson turned off the lights, and we sat back on the couch in front of the tree, the room illuminated only by its lights, flashing in colorful, syncopated strands. There was gentleness to the night. A calm, alluring peace.

"Want some eggnog?" Allyson asked.

"You have eggnog?"

"I do."

I looked at her suspiciously. "You hate eggnog."

"I know, but you like it."

I smiled. "Tomorrow. Tomorrow we'll drink eggnog."

"Tomorrow, *you'll* drink eggnog."

"I'll drink eggnog," I said.

Suddenly she leaned into me. I put my arm around her, and again all was quiet except the sound of the fireplace. Earlier in the day I had imagined that this might be the right time to tell her everything. But I now realized that there would never be a right time.

"Remember our first Christmas after we were married?" she asked.

"I got you that silk shirt."

"Which you washed two weeks later. It shrunk to the size of a Barbie outfit."

I chuckled. "I was just trying to be helpful. And you got me that leather bomber jacket. I couldn't believe you had saved that much money."

"I saved all year for it. That was a lot of money back then."

"Those days weren't easy."

"No. But they were simple. We didn't have much, but we had all we needed." She looked at me. "I have nothing but fond memories of our Christmases together."

I let her words fade into silence. Finally I looked to the window then said, "It's still snowing. What time do you think it is?"

She leaned back, looking for the clock on

the microwave oven. "Oh, my. It's past mid-night."

I sighed. "I better go. She'll be up around six, won't she?"

"If we're lucky. Last year she got up at five." Then Allyson said, "Why don't you just sleep here tonight?"

I must have looked surprised, because she quickly added, "In the guest room."

"Of course," I said. "Thank you."

Then, without thought, I leaned forward and kissed her. At first Allyson started to re-coil, but she stopped and instead let me cover her lips with mine. It was a long, deep kiss. We parted and we looked into each other's eyes. She looked beautiful and vul-nerable. She took a deep breath, her lips still slightly parted. "Good night, Allyson."

"Good night."

I stood, stifling a yawn. "Is the video camera charged?"

She laughed slightly. "Yes. You know, that's the first time you've remembered that on your own?"

"Old dogs can learn. Some of us are just slower than others." I smiled. "Be sure to wake me up when she wakes."

Allyson turned off the lights then went to

her bedroom alone. I walked downstairs to the guest room. I folded my trousers and shirt across the foot of the bed. I turned off the lights then slid under the covers. My mind reeled with my dilemma. Things had become more difficult not easier. When would I tell her? Or should I? I remembered the letter I'd written. I'd let the letter do it. I closed my eyes and fell off into sleep.

Somewhere in the night I jolted awake from a sound sleep. I sensed the presence of someone in the room. As my eyes adjusted to the darkness, I could see a form standing at the foot of my bed. It filled me with terror. I pushed myself up on my elbows, waiting for the form to do something. It just stood there. "It's not my time," I said. "Not yet."

"No, it's not," Allyson replied.

I exhaled in relief. I rubbed my hand across my eyes. "Sorry, you startled me. What time is it?"

"It's only three." She stood, almost motionless, as if afraid to step forward.

"How long have you been standing there?"

"A few minutes."

"Are you okay?"

"Not really." She walked to the side of my bed and sat down. I rolled over to my side, trying to read her face through the shadow.

She sniffed. "I am so tired of sleeping alone every night, wishing that you were next to me. I know this is really stupid and I'm going to hate myself in the morning, but would you hold me tonight?"

"Yes."

I peeled back the comforter and she slid under the covers. Then I put my arms around her and pulled her into my chest. The smell and feel of her filled me as her body pressed against mine. For the first time since our trip to New York I felt whole.

Chapter 63

CHRISTMAS DAY.
SEVEN DAYS UNTIL NEW YEAR'S.

Carson first ran to our bedroom then, finding it vacant, ran downstairs to the guest room, leaving the lights on behind her. "He came!" she shouted. "Santa came!"

Allyson raised herself from my chest. "So early?"

I yawned then looked at my watch. "It's almost seven."

"He really did," Carson said. "I saw some toys!"

"Okay, hold on," I said. "Let me get the camera. Al, will you hand me my pants?"

She reached over and handed me my

trousers. I slid them on under the covers then climbed out from the sheets. Allyson said, "Wait, the Bible."

It was our tradition. Every Christmas, before we went to the tree, we always read the Christmas story in second Luke. It was our way of keeping the season in perspective. She left, returning a few minutes later cradling the family Bible in her arm.

"Do you want to read?" she asked.

"Sure." I took the book. Even though we had done this every year of our marriage, I don't think the words have ever quite looked the same. Facing one's own mortality brings life to such script. As I read of the angels, I thought of Michael. It had never occurred to me that these beings had names. Or frequented Starbucks.

When we finished, I took Carson's hand and the three of us ascended the stairway. Carson darted off toward the tree and homed in on the most visible of her presents with the intensity of a heat-seeking missile. "Look, Daddy! An American Girl doll!"

"You must have been a very good girl," I said.

Carson hunted down her presents until

they were gathered in one big pile; then she sat cross-legged on the floor and unwrapped them. There were still a few packages under the tree. I assumed that they were for Nancy.

"What about yours?" Allyson asked.

"You have a present for me?"

"Of course."

She got up and walked over to a large, flat package and brought it back to me. I slowly tore back the paper. It was a framed family picture that we had taken last spring up in the canyons. I looked at it silently.

"It was actually a family present," Allyson said. "I had it made before . . ." She didn't finish.

"It's perfect," I said.

Nancy arrived at the house around noon. As usual she just walked in, and we all knew the moment she did. Nancy makes the noisiest entrances of anyone I know. "Merry Christmas, merry Christmas, all," she shouted and jumped up and down, ringing the Christmas bell that hung around her neck.

At the sound of Nancy's entrance, Carson bolted from the floor. "Nancy, Santa came."

Nancy's arms were full of packages, and Carson was hugging her waist as she came into the kitchen. I was sitting cross-legged on the family room floor dressing a doll I think was named Molly. "Merry Christmas, Nance," I said.

"Nice doll," she said. "Hey, I caught you on *Good Morning America*. Not bad for a radio salesman."

"Thanks."

"Where's Al?"

"She's in the shower."

She set down her packages. "Do you mind bringing in some things from my car?"

"Not at all."

I put on my shoes and went outside. The snow was still coming down, and I had patches of snow on my shoulders and head when I came back in. I carried a box of food into the kitchen. Every Christmas morning since Carson was born, Nancy came over and made breakfast for us. I set the box on the counter and Nancy walked over and began removing its contents.

"Here's the menu. Blueberry pancakes. Thick maple-pepper bacon. Italian sausage from Cosimo's. Eggs any way you want them. Cheesy hash browns and Stephen's gourmet mint truffle cocoa.

"Way too much," I said. "As usual. How can I help?"

"You can cook the sausage and bacon."

"Got it."

A few minutes later Allyson came out of her room showered and dressed. She looked pretty. She wore a Christmas sweater, and her hair was pulled back with an elastic. She put on some Christmas music, the Carpenters' *Christmas Collection*; then she brought out her new Christmas stoneware, setting the red plates around the table.

Nancy picked up one of the dishes. "Are these new?"

"Brand spankin' new," Allyson replied.

"Cool."

Breakfast was a feast, and at least half the food was untouched. After breakfast Carson dragged Nancy downstairs to see her life book, leaving Allyson and me alone at the table. "What are your plans for today?" she asked.

"Just hanging out. How about you?"

"The same. Nancy wants to take Carson to her place for a while."

"Is she trying to leave us alone?"

Allyson nodded. "She's always scheming."

"I'm okay with that," I said. "If you are."

"I'm okay."

"How about we clean up this place?" I said. While we did the dishes, Nancy came back upstairs. "Hey, I was thinking I'd kind of like to take Carson back to my place."

"It's okay," Allyson said. "He knows."

I smiled at her. "Fine with me."

"Then we'll be on our way. Come on, Carse, let's get your stuff."

"I want to bring my life book. And Molly."

"You bring whatever you like," Nancy said.

"Bye, Mommy. Bye, Daddy."

"You behave," Allyson said.

"I don't know why you always say that," Nancy said.

"She was talking to you," I said. I walked over and hugged Carson. "I love you, honey."

It was all I could do to let her go.

Chapter 64

While Allyson finished wiping off the counters, I went to the living room and started a fire, which took little more than throwing a match on the gas log. The room was decorated for the season. Across the fireplace mantel was the porcelain nativity set Allyson and I had purchased our first year of marriage. Mother Mary and the baby Jesus were missing. I smiled at this. They always disappeared from the crèche a week or two before Christmas. Carson liked to play with them.

On top of the piano was something new, and I walked over and looked at it. Carson had glued macaroni to a glass candle jar; then someone, I assume her schoolteacher, had spray painted it gold. The candle was nestled in a pink swirl of angel hair.

Allyson came in and sat next to me on the couch in front of the fireplace. "How is it that you always know exactly what Carson wants?" I asked.

"I'm hardly psychic. She tells me every day for three months before Christmas." Her countenance softened. She said sadly, "I was just thinking that Aunt Denise would be calling any minute now."

"I'm sorry," I said.

"It's ironic. The older I get the more I realize that all that matters is family. And it's about the time that we start losing them." She took my hand and gently stroked it. "I can't bear the thought of losing anyone else in my life."

My chest felt like concrete. The moment fell into silence. "I have something for you," I said. I went to my coat and brought out the package from Tiffany's. It was a beautifully wrapped box, bigger than the one I had given Camille, with matte gold paper and a red silk bow.

"I didn't get you anything."

"Yes, you did. You gave me the picture."

"Well, that was really for all of us."

She held the box aloft. "Did you wrap this yourself?"

"Does it look like I wrapped it?"

"No."

"But I picked out the wrapping."

She pulled one end of a ribbon and the bow disappeared. Then she unwrapped the thick paper to find a box inside, a robin's-egg blue box from Tiffany.

"It's from Tiffany's, isn't it?" she asked.

I nodded. "Open it." Inside the blue box was a burgundy velvet box. She glanced up at me then back at her gift. She slowly pulled back its lid. Inside was a diamond and emerald necklace. She just stared at it.

"Do you like it?"

Her eyes began to moisten. "It's beautiful. It's so . . ." She looked into my eyes. "Big." She lifted it from the box.

"Here, I'll help you," I said. I walked up behind her and draped it around her neck. It lay beautifully against her throat.

"I don't want to know how much it cost," she said.

"Good, because I wasn't going to tell you. You'd never wear it if you knew."

"I want to see this in the mirror." She walked out to the hall tree, delicately touching the necklace as she admired it. "I can't wait to show Nancy."

"Far cry from your first diamond."

She laughed. "You mean my cubic zirconium engagement ring?"

"Remember how afraid I was that your dad would find out that I couldn't afford a real diamond?"

She walked back and sat down next to me. "I told him, you know."

"You told him?"

"He didn't care. My dad only had fifteen dollars when he asked my mama to marry him. He knew you'd always take care of me."

"What different worlds we came from. When I told my father that I was planning to ask you to marry me, he said 'In what world could you conceivably take care of another human?' "

"You never told me that."

"I wasn't real proud of it."

"My father knew that you'd land on your feet someday. He trusted me to make a good decision."

I frowned. "I guess I proved him wrong."

She looked at me somberly. "No, you didn't."

I glanced at her hand and noticed that her ring was still there. "I thought of getting you a new diamond for your ring. A real rock."

"I wouldn't want it. I love the simplicity of this little ring. Sometimes less is more."

"Sometimes."

She went quiet and looked down as the question rose from the pit of her stomach, ascending as if she were unable to stop it. "Are you going to stay?"

I didn't answer for a full minute. With all my being I wanted to say yes. But it would have been another lie. For once I wanted to do the right thing

I looked toward the fireplace. "When I was little, Chuck used to take my brothers fishing every summer. I was always too young. Stan used to torment me about it. He'd say, Someone's gotta stay home with the womenfolk. Then one weekend, around the time I turned eight, my father told me that I could go fishing with them. But if I wanted to be with the men, I'd have to act like one. I'd have to get up on my own and be ready to go. My father would always leave at some ungodly hour, like four-thirty or five. I was so excited to be going that I couldn't sleep. Of course, by the time I got up the next morning, they were already gone.

"I threw a tantrum any eight-year-old boy would be proud of. But my mother just said, 'Robby, you've no one to blame but yourself, little man. You should have woken earlier.' "

I turned back to Allyson. Her beautiful eyes reflected the light from the fire. "I should have remembered those words."

My heart filled with the pain of the moment, and the tears came no matter how much I fought them. I took her hand in mine and wiped my eyes with the back of my other hand. "I'm so sorry for all the time I've wasted complaining that I didn't have the life I wanted when all I really needed was right here. I'm sorry that I left you. But most of all I'm just sorry that I didn't wake earlier."

Allyson also began to cry. "It's not too late."

"I wish it wasn't. I'd give up everything to make it different. But sometimes it is too late."

"Rob, whatever you've done, I'll forgive you. I don't care about the past. We'll start again. We'll just move on like nothing happened. We can even move into that new house."

"I wish I could. But it's out of my hands now." It took tremendous strength to release her hand, but I knew that I needed to go while I still could. "I have a letter for you." I reached into my pocket and brought out the sealed envelope.

She took it fearfully. "Should I read it now?"

"No. You'll know when."

I kissed her cheek; then I walked to the door. Loneliness gripped my heart. "I love you, Allyson. I always have. I always will. Give Carson my love. Someday she'll understand. So will you."

Without looking back, I walked out the door. The sky was still dumping snow, and there was a blanket of powder on my car. I started the car, then found a scraper and brushed off the snow. As I pulled out of the driveway, I saw Allyson looking out the window between the curtains. I saw her wipe her eyes. My heart was broken. For the first time since I'd met Michael, New Year's was too far away. I wished that it could just all be over.

Chapter 65

Visibility was poor, though nearly as much from my own emotion as from the storm. The minimal traffic on the freeway—those of us foolish enough to be out in a blizzard—moved at a crawl and I passed a few cars that had slid off the road. It took me forty-five minutes to reach the hotel.

I left my keys with the valet and walked into the Monaco. Christmas music played inside the lobby, which was deserted except for the clerk at the registration desk and a group of skiers who looked like they had just returned from the slopes. They were still dressed in sweaters and snow pants and they sat in front of the lobby fireplace laughing and drinking.

I quickly passed through the lobby. I didn't want to hear laughter. I took the elevator to my room on the seventh floor. Once inside, I unbuttoned my shirt and kicked off my shoes then lay back on top of the bed. I fell asleep almost immediately.

I don't know how long I slept, but I woke disoriented. The room was dark. It was evening and the room's lights were off. Still the curtains glowed from the blizzard outside. I could hear the wind beat against the glass panes, and I walked to the window and drew back the curtains and watched. I stayed at the window for ten, maybe fifteen minutes, just looking. I watched the bellboy shovel snow. I followed the path of a car as it precariously made its way up Main Street nearly as much sideways as forward. *You'd have to be crazy or desperate to be out in this weather,* I thought, as if forgetting I had recently been out there myself. I went back to my bed.

I was lonely for Allyson. I wished that I could just talk to her and tell her everything. She had always been my confidant. This was the greatest part of my pain, that I had no one to share it with. I even wished that

Michael was around. I called out his name, but he didn't come.

Weary of the quiet, I turned on the television and began surfing the channels. *It's a Wonderful Life* was showing on PBS. It always played at Christmas. Allyson and I had watched the movie every holiday since our marriage. It was one of our most enduring traditions. Every year I'd say, *That Donna Reed is easy on the eyes* and Allyson would playfully hit me. That too was part of our tradition. I think by now she'd remind me to say it if I forgot. I set aside the remote and lay back in bed to watch.

Suddenly there was a knock on my door. Even before I was up, the door swung open to a bellman. He appeared startled to see me. "Excuse me, Mr. Hemingway. We didn't know . . ."

It was a surreal moment. "What's up?" I asked.

He stumbled over his words. "I'm sorry, there's a woman here who says she's your wife. She said it was an emergency."

Just then Allyson appeared in the doorway.

"Ally?"

She ran past the bellman, throwing her

arms around me. "Oh, Rob. I was afraid I was too late."

I looked up at the bellman, who looked just as bewildered as before. "It's okay," I said.

"If you need anything . . ." Without finishing his sentence, he stepped back out into the hall, shutting the door behind him. Allyson just held to me, sobbing.

I ran my hand over the back of her head. "It's okay, honey. What were you afraid of?"

"When I read the note, I was sure that you were going to do something awful." She leaned back to look into my face. "Your letter read like a suicide note."

I hadn't considered that. Of course it did. But then I hadn't expected her to read the note until after I was gone.

"I wasn't going to do anything," I said. I led her over to the bed and we sat together at the foot of it.

For a minute she just sat there wiping her eyes. Then she said, "Rob, I know why you wrote the note."

I brushed her hair back from her face. "No, you don't, honey."

She looked into my eyes. "You think you're dying . . ."

I froze. "How did you know that?"

". . . but you're not."

I looked at her in bewilderment. "Ally, what's going on?"

"Can you log on to the Internet from here?"

"Yes." I went over and switched on my computer. For a moment the room's only sound was that of the modem connecting. While we were waiting, I asked, "How did you find me? I checked in under an alias."

"I called Camille. She told me some of your aliases."

"I've never used Hemingway before."

"I know. I asked for a dozen author's names. The woman at the counter was helpful. She said the only dead author staying here was Ernest Hemingway."

I looked back at my computer. "Okay, we're up."

Allyson walked over to the desk. I stepped away from it and she typed on the keyboard. Suddenly a website pulled up. The name M. Stanford Hillenbrand came up first. There was a large graphic on the site that was taking time to load.

"This modem is slow," I said.

"Do you know him?" Allyson asked. "Stanford Hillenbrand?"

"Isn't he one of Camille's authors? The one who lives in Park City?"

She nodded. "The mortician."

Suddenly the graphic appeared. I couldn't believe what I was seeing. "You've got to be kidding . . . ," I said. Stanford Hillenbrand was Michael.

Allyson was watching for my reaction. "You recognize him?"

"Indeed."

I stepped up to the computer and scrolled down. There was a list of books, all of which seemed to deal with death: *Deathbed Repentance: Twelve Stories of the Dead and Dying*; *Death, Taxes and Other Necessities*; *Last Rites*; *The Shadow Beyond*; *Angel of Death*. His most recent work was titled *Conversations with the Reaper*. There was a short biography beneath the book graphics.

M. Stanford Hillenbrand graduated from Marquette University with a dual major in philosophy and theology. He is currently employed as a mortician in Park City, Utah, where he lives with his wife and two children. In 1992 he was a finalist for the National Book Award for his first work, Death, Taxes and Other Necessities. *He has been published in* Harper's, The New Yorker *and the* Atlanta Journal. *He is the author of six books. He is currently working on his first novel.*

I stepped back from the computer. "How did you know about this?"

Allyson walked over to the window, and she was silent, as if considering whether or not to reveal her source. She finally said, "Camille."

"Camille?"

She turned around. "You were set up."

The room was quiet as the reality set in. "How long have you known about this?"

"About an hour."

For a moment neither of us knew what to say. Then Allyson took a deep breath. "That's the real reason that you came home, isn't it? You thought you were dying."

I ran my hand back through my hair. As ashamed as I was of it, it was the truth. After a moment she said, "I better get back. Nancy will be back soon."

"You shouldn't drive in this."

"I'll be okay. The plows are out. I-15 was clear."

My mind reeled with a thousand thoughts, but I was incapable of selecting just one of them. She said to me, "Will you see me out?"

She waited while I put on my shoes; then I followed her down to the hotel lobby. The valet had left her car at the curb, under the protection of the awning. Allyson handed him her claim ticket and a five-dollar bill and he surrendered her keys.

I walked around the car with her and she climbed into the driver's seat. She rolled down the window.

"If I had known anything about this, I would have stopped it," she said. "It wasn't right. But I'm not sorry that you came back. It was a nice Christmas. Even if it was only because you thought you were dying." She turned away, not wanting me to see the tears welling up in her eyes. She lifted a hand to her cheek.

I touched her arm. "Ally."

She shook her head. "I'm okay. I can do this."

"I don't think you should drive home like this. This storm . . ."

"The weather is the easy part of this." She turned back to me for just a moment, and there was finality to her gaze even greater than when I had left her earlier. "Bye, Rob." Then she slowly drove away. I wondered how many times a heart could be broken.

Chapter 66

I called Camille the moment I got back to my room. I didn't check the hour. I didn't care if I woke her. I did. She answered, "Whoever this is, it better be important."

"It's Robert."

She was suddenly lucid. "Mr. Harlan, you had us worried. I take it you've been debriefed."

Anger welled up inside of me. "What did you get from this, Camille? Is this your idea of revenge?"

"That's not the way it is, Rob."

"Yeah, I believe that. How could you have been so vindictive? What gives you the right to play games with my life?"

"What gives *me* the right? You're the one

playing games with people's lives. The question is, what gives *you* the right? Everything that has come to you was a gift from someone else. Everything. Your book is your wife's story, not yours. You just put your name on it. And she let you take that sacred part of her life because she loves you. She even went back to work so you could take your shot. And how do you thank her for it? You leave her. But you've gotten good at that, haven't you? Nothing personal. *Just business.*"

My own words made potent weapons.

"Let me tell you something about *business*, Rob. Every year thousands of books are written and not published. Many of them are good books. Some of them are even great. I know because they come across my desk. If I hadn't believed in you, you'd still be in the business of screwing on sprinkler heads. You made it because I decided to take a chance on you. And that makes me a party to creating this Robert Mason Harlan monster. The least I could do was to put that monster back in its cage before it hurt anyone else." Camille's voice fell to a softer, more despondent tone. "Aside from your broken family, do you know what the saddest part of this whole affair is? I used to really like you."

I was quiet for a long time as I considered her words. Then I replied softly, "I know. So did I."

Now Camille was silent. I was the first to speak. "So the chest pains really were just reflux," I said. "Hillenbrand said his name was Michael."

"It is. His full name is M. Stanford Hillenbrand. The M is for Michael. He goes by Stan. Like your brother."

"Whose idea was it?"

"Stan has talked about doing something like this for years. But it was my idea to try it on you. The theme of most of his books is how society lives in denial of their own mortality and that it's a mistake. He believes that we're only fully alive when we're faced with death.

"In one of his books there's a case history of a man who got the wrong test back from a hospital lab. His doctor told him that he was dying from a rare disease. This man was a well-known business executive who had fallen off the moral deep end. He was cheating on his wife. He had a college-aged son whom he hadn't seen for years. And he was embezzling from his company's pension fund. When he found out that he was dying, he went through a complete reformation as he set about putting his life in order. He went back to his wife and asked for her forgiveness. He went to his son and developed a relationship with him. He paid back the pension fund with interest, and as his final penance he turned himself in to the company officers. Eight months later, when the lab discovered their mistake, the story made the papers. A reporter asked this man if he planned on suing the hospital. His response was classic. He said 'Why? They did what they're supposed to do. They saved my life.' "

I understood how this man felt. "How did Michael do it? He knew things no one could have known."

"Some of the things he got from me. You told me many of your secrets. Probably more than you remember. I provided him with all the background information. But most of the information he got from you."

"What do you mean?"

"Stan's a first-class computer geek. He hacked into your computer, hoping to read your emails. But he hit gold. Apparently you keep your diary on your computer. He would read it every night. That's how he knew everything that was going on in your life, how you were feeling, who you were corresponding with, even what you were praying about."

I didn't even consider the laws he must have violated. In light of the day's events they seemed trivial. Then Camille said, "I can understand why you're angry at me. I'd be angry too. But remember this was never about me. It was about Allyson and Carson. I was only trying to keep you from making a big mistake. So you tell me. Did I do the right thing?"

Chapter 67

The snow had started to slow as Allyson pulled into the garage. She turned on the hall light as she walked in and hung up her coat. Nancy was in the family room, sitting next to the Christmas tree. The house was quiet.

"I just put Carson to bed," Nancy said. "What happened to you guys?" Then she saw the sadness in Allyson's face. "Where's Rob?"

"He's gone."

Nancy crossed the room and put her arms around her, pulling Allyson's head onto her shoulder. "Oh, dear. What happened?"

"I can't explain tonight. I can't think about it anymore. It's too complex."

Nancy gently rubbed her back. "You don't need to talk."

"Is Carson still awake?"

"I think so."

"I need to see her." Allyson leaned back. She wiped a tear from her cheek.

"Oh, Ally." She kissed Allyson's cheek. "If you don't mind, I'm going to sleep in the guest room tonight. If you need anything, just call."

"Thank you."

"Good night, sweetie."

She hugged her again. Then Allyson walked down the hallway to Carson's room. She slowly opened the door, splitting the room with a faint, vertical beam of light. Carson was awake and shifted quickly in her sheets. "Hi, Mommy."

"Hi, sweetheart." She went to the side of her bed and knelt down, putting her face next to Carson's. "Did you have a good day?"

"Uh-huh. Nancy got a new puppy. It's so cute. Its name is Chazzy. Can I have a puppy?"

"Maybe sometime. But I think for now Nancy needs you to help her with her puppy."

"Where's Daddy?"

Allyson groaned within herself. "Well, sweetheart, Daddy's gone back to work."

"To book tour?"

There would be time to explain later. "Yes. To book tour."

"When is he coming back?"

"I don't know."

She paused before her next question. "Is he going to come home again?"

"I don't know."

"Weren't we good?"

Allyson ran her hand across Carson's cheek. "You were very good, sweetheart. You are a very good girl."

"Then how come he went back to book tour?"

"I don't know. Sometimes, when you get older, things get hard to understand."

"I think they're hard now."

Allyson pulled Carson in close. Then she climbed into her bed and held Carson against her, and they fell asleep in each other's arms.

Chapter 68

Sometime in the night the blizzard died. I was awake for its passing. It was around two-thirty in the morning when the winds had calmed and I looked out the hotel window into the darkness. In the light of the street lamps I could see what was left of the dwindling storm—latecomer snowflakes falling to the white below, disappearing like rain on the ocean.

I fell asleep around that time but woke only a couple of hours later with the dawn. My room was bright. The sky shone exceptionally blue, as if in recompense for yesterday's absence.

I didn't shower. I just quickly ran some water through my hair then followed it with a comb. I changed my shirt and put on my parka. Then, with my things still in the room, I left the hotel. I didn't have time to pack. I needed to see Allyson. I needed to go home.

In the early hours of morning the snowplows had caught up with the storm and the main roads were clear and salted, with snow piled on the roadside in tall banks. A half hour later I pulled into the driveway of my home. Everything was crystalline, and the elms in our front yard sparkled in the morning sun as if they had been dipped in sugar.

I sat a moment in the car preparing myself. Then I climbed out. The air braced me. It was even colder in the southern end of the valley than it was downtown. I knocked on the front door of my own house. I could have let myself in, I had all week, but this time it didn't feel right. I felt like I needed to be invited in. It was only a moment before Allyson opened the door. She was wearing one of my T-shirts and it draped over her like a nightshirt.

"Hi," I said. My breath froze in the air.

"Hi."

I pushed my hands deep into my coat pockets. "Can we talk?"

She nodded. "Come in, it's cold."

As I stepped in, I noticed that she was wearing the necklace I had given her for Christmas. I followed her into the living room. The room was warm from the fire as its yellow and orange flames licked futilely at the fake log. Allyson sat down in an armchair in front of the hearth while I sat on the couch opposite her. For a moment we just looked at each other.

"Carson still sleeping?"

"Yeah. She had a hard night." She brushed her hair back from her face. "Nancy slept over last night."

"I saw her car," I said. "She's downstairs?"

Allyson nodded.

"Thanks for coming down to the hotel last night. You were crazy to drive in that storm. But thanks."

"I was worried."

"I know. I was worried about you driving home." My words trailed off in silence. I could hear the tick of the grandmother's clock in the foyer. I laced my fingers together in my lap and leaned slightly forward as I searched for the right words.

"Last night was bizarre beyond words," I said. "When you told me how I'd been set up, my mind was going a thousand miles a second. At first I was mostly just angry with Camille and her friend for making me believe that I was going to die. That's pretty much where I was emotionally when you left." I looked into her face for some reaction, but there was none. I continued. "Then it hit me that *I really wasn't going to die*. You can't believe the exhilaration I felt. It was like being pardoned at the gallows after they'd already put the rope around my neck. What an amazing thing to be given a second chance at life."

I took a deep breath. "I spent all night thinking about what I really wanted from this second chance. I realized that if I could spend my next life with anybody, it would be you." I looked into her eyes. "It doesn't matter where we live or what the world thinks of me or even if I ever sell another book, just as long as I'm with you. I want to grow old with you. And when the day comes that this life really is over for me, I want to leave this world with you by my side." I looked down while I gathered the courage to proceed. "If you let me come back, I promise you that you will never again doubt that you are the most important person or thing in my life. I know I'm asking a lot after hurting you. But I'm asking. Do you think . . ." I paused from emotion. Then I looked back up, my eyes looking into hers. "Is there any way that you could let me back in your heart?"

There's always that moment whenever a proposal is made—the climatic, excruciating instant when time seems to stand still while the name is pulled from an envelope or the jury files in with their verdict. For me no moment has ever seemed so long. Allyson just looked down; then she walked over and sat next to me on the couch. She looked into my eyes. "You never left it."

Postscript

A YEAR LATER.

It's hard to believe that it's been a whole year since I went home to my family. It's been a good year. I've been true to the promise I made to Allyson. I've been true to myself. I like myself again.

I've been back to see my father. On most of those visits I took Carson and Allyson with me. Our visits were awkward at first—especially for my father—but they're getting easier. He's no longer Chuck to me, but Dad. Even this took some getting used to. In our visits I have seen glimpses of a man I never knew. He's old, and I don't suppose there's much time left for us, certainly not enough to fill in the pages of a lost story, but I've left the past to its own demons. There isn't time for regret. There never is.

The other day, while reading the paper, I came across a bookstore's advertisement for author M. Stanford Hillenbrand. I stared at the picture of him for a long time. He has a new book out, his first novel. It's called *The Reaper's Wife*, or something like that. He had a signing at a bookstore not far from my home. I considered paying him a visit. I even drove to the store, but I never made it inside. I suppose a part of me still wants to believe that he is an angel. Who's to say that he's not? God works in mysterious ways. Or maybe He's just pragmatic. Why send a burning bush when an email will do?

My next book is scheduled to come out sometime this fall. Allyson's very excited about it. It's the story of a man who believes he has just a few months left to live. I'm just pleased that it has a happy ending.

I'm back with Camille. Things are good between us. I can laugh about everything now, which is certain proof that time is the greatest of all comedians.

Darren stopped calling sometime in January. His last message was a terse rebuke predicting for me a life of obscurity. I found his prediction vaguely amusing. It was like predicting nightfall. In the end obscurity is everyone's destination. On the bright side I did get one more joke out of him. It goes like this: "What did Hemingway say when he was asked, 'Why did the chicken cross the road?' Answer: 'To die. In the rain. Alone.' "

A month ago I had a peculiar dream. I dreamt of my own funeral. As the mourners filed past to pay their respects, I stood next to my body, unseen, watching them. Though I spoke to everyone, I was unable to make them hear me. Except for Allyson. Somehow Allyson knew my thoughts as if they were her own—as if we were bound by some force that transcends death itself.

It has made me wonder if perhaps there is more to our relationships than mortality portends. If perhaps some things are forever in another realm, where clocks stop and nothing remains but the bonds we have forged through love. That and the lessons we've learned.

Perhaps. The lessons do remain. I learned much last year. I learned that the measure of life is revealed in the quality of our relationships: with God, our families, our fellow men.

I've learned that the greatest threat to love is not circumstance but the absence of attention. For we do not neglect others because we have ceased to love; rather we cease to love others because we have neglected them.

I've learned that each day is a miracle unearned.

I've learned that while life is ephemeral—a vapor—love is not. In short, I have learned what matters and what does not.

I don't know what my future holds or even in whose hands it lies, but I know where I am and what I have, and it's enough. I've lived twice and loved once, and that's more than any man should ask for. And through it all, the woman I love is still by my side.

It's been a good year indeed.

About the Author

Richard Paul Evans is the number one *New York Times* best-selling author of *The Christmas Box*. His best-selling novels have been translated into more than seventeen languages, and some have been adapted into award-winning television movies. He lives with his family in Salt Lake City, Utah. *A Perfect Day* is his eighth novel.